The Ultimatum

by

Jonas Saul

PUBLISHED BY:

Imagine Press Inc.
Ebook ISBN: 978-1-927404-57-7
Paperback ISBN: 978-1-998047-62-8
Hardcover ISBN: 978-1-998047-63-5

The Sarah Roberts Series

Dark Visions (One)
The Warning (Two)
The Crypt (Three)
The Hostage (Four)
The Victim (Five)
The Enigma (Six)
The Vigilante (Seven)
The Rogue (Eight)
Killing Sarah (Nine)
The Antagonist (Ten)
The Redeemed (Eleven)
The Haunted (Twelve)
The Unlucky (Thirteen)
The Abandoned (Fourteen)
The Cartel (Fifteen)
Losing Sarah (Sixteen)
The Pact (Seventeen)
The Terror (Eighteen)
The Chase (Nineteen)
The Betrayal (Twenty)
Sarah's Return (Twenty-One)
The Hunt (Twenty-Two)
The Delivery (Twenty-Three)
The Trap (Twenty-Four)
The Ultimatum (Twenty-Five)
The Depraved (Twenty-Six)
The Condemned (Twenty-Seven)
Payback (Twenty-Eight)
The Unknown (Twenty-Nine)
Wrath (Thirty)
The Damned (Thirty-One)

The Game (Thirty-Two)
The Decoy (Thirty-Three)
The Disappearance (Thirty-Four)
The Whole Truth (Thirty-Five)
Alex (Thirty-Six)
Parkman (Thirty-Seven)
Darwin (Thirty-Eight)
Aaron (Thirty-Nine)
Remains To Be Seen (Forty)

The Jake Wood Novels

The Immortal Gene (Book One)
The Immortal Target (Book Two)

Standalone Novels

'Til Death Do Us Part
The Drowning
The Woman in the Woods
The Threat
The Specter
The Mafia Trilogy
A Murder in Time
Frequency of the Dead

Co-Authored Novels

Collision Course (Written with Gary Ponzo)
There Will Be Blood (Written with Rania Stone)
The Soulless (Written with Rania Stone)

Short Story Collections

Twisted Fate (Tales of Horror)
Twists of Fate (Tales of Hope)

Chapter 1

WOULD THEY KILL HIM fast, end it with a bullet to the brain stem? Or would they take their time, a tortuous route to the same end?

Maybe they'd just feed him to Silvio "the butcher" Mancuso.

Overworked, alone, and tired, worried for no reason, Salvatore Prezzie watched the empty street for any sign of movement. His stomach was a roiling toxic soup of nerves mixed with fear. Could he will his legs to move, to carry him, if they refused? Each moment he stared out the windshield was another moment he was breathing, so there was that.

A single light illuminated the back door to the restaurant. Sal had sent the text telling his bosses he'd arrived. Now he waited for the light to turn on and off twice—his signal to bring the money inside. Sometimes, it was seconds later, sometimes half an hour.

After long nights collecting money from the illegal

gaming rooms throughout Toronto, Sal and Frankie often took turns staring at the light, but tonight, Sal was alone, and he had no idea why.

Frankie hadn't shown up for several days now, and Sal was ordered to do the pickups alone. He'd protested, but his boss told him there was no way anyone would bother him. Sal worked for a made man in the Lorenzo Bartleson Group —a fancy title for one of the seven mafia families in Toronto —and was virtually untouchable.

So, Sal did as he was told and drove to his regular stops, changing it up nightly as he did, performing the bagman job he was hired to do several months ago.

Close to a hundred thousand dollars in unmarked cash was in the locked steel box in the car's trunk. A nightly haul for the Bartleson Group—and that was only one side of the man's family business.

Sal blinked slowly as fatigue settled in.

Where was Frankie? Did Diego, his boss, know? Was Frankie just sick, or was he moved up and given a new job?

The light flickered over the back door of the restaurant.

Sal stirred in his seat.

Was that the signal or a power surge? It didn't flicker like normal.

Wide-eyed, he leaned forward and stared at the light above the door.

It turned off, then on.

That was it, his signal to enter with the money.

A new wave of acid filled his stomach as he exited the car and moved to the trunk area. After looking around to ensure he was alone, Sal tapped the key fob and popped the trunk. Then he flicked the combination until it was set on the right digits and eased the lockbox lid upward.

The amount was heavy tonight. Or maybe it was his imagination, and weight was more figurative than literal.

How long could he continue to do this? Sure, the pay was better than his long days in the back of the kitchen chopping beef carcasses—five times better—but chopping beef wasn't illegal or super risky.

When they first approached him, he refused the job. But they insisted, and he relented. The cash was more than he could say no to, and he had his mother's illness to think about. Special drugs and special treatments, some of which her health insurance didn't cover.

He hefted the bag over his shoulder and strode the ten steps to the door. When he was about to grab the handle, the door swung open quickly, making Sal rear back in surprise.

"You got it all?" Diego asked.

The man looked harried, strung out like he was on something. Diego's eyes were bloodshot, his forehead reflected the light above, and his hair was soaked with sweat.

That didn't help Sal's nerves one bit.

"Yeah, I got it all. Why wouldn't I get it all?"

Diego checked over Sal's shoulders, clapped him on the back, and shoved him. "Get inside."

The door clanged behind him, the deadbolts slamming into place. This wasn't usual, this wasn't normal.

Frankie didn't show up for the pickups, and Diego greeted him at five in the morning to ensure he got all the money.

No, this wasn't normal by a long shot.

Something was happening, and it spooked Sal more than he wanted to admit. At that moment, he wanted to set the bag on the floor, walk out the back, and never return.

He didn't need the Lorenzo Bartleson Group, the mafia, or the criminal life. Working for minimum wage at a convenience store was less stressful. He decided a job change was in order—if he survived the night.

Diego pointed down the hallway. "Inside. They're all waiting for you."

What did that mean? Are they *all* waiting for *me*? Who was waiting?

Usually, it was just the accountant guy and two women with cash machines. Sal and Frankie would be fed some pasta or something. They'd sip wine and head home to sleep through the day, only to return at midnight for another six-hour run through the city.

So, who was waiting for *him*?

Without a choice in the matter, Sal placed one foot in front of the other and made his way along the corridor to the last door, his boss close behind.

"Faster," Diego said. "Don't make them wait."

He pushed open the door and took in the room, a faint gasp escaping his lips before he could contain it.

Diego shoved him from behind as Sal stopped in the doorframe.

"Salvatore Prezzie," Silvio Mancuso said, his voice heavy.

Sal hated the man. He'd met him twice, and the man's presence grated his nerves each time.

Silvio Mancuso was Lorenzo Bartleson's personal

security lieutenant, hitman, torturer, or whatever they called him. His unofficial name was "the butcher," but no one dared call him that to his face.

A long slash wound on Silvio's neck where a knife had damaged his trachea caused his voice to sound gravelly, like he was chewing sand while speaking. Apropos, considering the profession he was in.

"Glad you could join us." Mancuso wore a rubber, blood-soaked apron. He stood on a floor covered with long plastic sheets while wiping a footlong knife with a white towel. It struck Sal as odd that they'd choose a white towel to wipe up the blood. Why white? Why not black or dark blue?

The place smelled of fresh meat, antiseptic, and terror.

Someone died here recently, as indicated by the blood, but Sal couldn't see any bodies or body parts—thankfully.

Something smacked his shoulder, then yanked him sideways.

It was Diego, ripping the money bag forcefully off him while he stood staring at Mancuso. More like gawking, really. The man mesmerized him, and Silvio Mancuso knew it.

The knife was clean now. Mancuso placed it on a metal table beside him and removed his thick gloves, staring at Sal the entire time.

From the corner of his eye, Sal saw Diego place the money bag on a side table, open it, and remove the cash. The sound of each clump as the wrapped hundreds smacked the table was the only thing that made Silvio "the butcher" Mancuso look Diego's way.

Then his eyes were back on Sal.

"Where's Frankie?" Silvio asked.

Sal shrugged to respond quickly because using his voice wasn't something he was sure he could do yet. His body had developed a strange all-over shake that he'd never encountered before. If he didn't get it under control soon, he'd have to sit down somewhere, as he didn't want to drop onto the plastic in front of Mancuso. That just seemed wrong on so many levels, like a lamb cutting its own throat on the altar to the gods.

"Diego?"

"Yeah?"

"How long has Salvatore Prezzie worked for us?" Mancuso's eyes hadn't wavered. They bore holes into Sal's head.

"Just over two months now."

"How many nights per week?"

"Six."

Silvio moved closer to Sal, leaving only a two-foot gap between them. Sal was so close now he could smell the man's stinky breath.

"Six days per week," Silvio rasped in his low, guttural voice. "For over two months, and you don't know where your partner is?"

Sal shook his head. He opened his mouth to answer, but only some utterance escaped that didn't resemble a *no*.

Silvio held out his hand. "Give me your phone."

Sal fumbled in his pocket, retrieved his phone, and dropped it in Silvio's hand, afraid to touch the man in case whatever psychosis he had was contagious.

Silvio handed it back. "Unlock it."

Sal nodded, retook the phone, tapped his code three times before it took, and then handed it back. Silvio's hand touched him, and Sal trembled.

He was never a tough guy. Never wanted to be a fighter. Always ran from confrontation. Getting caught up with a mafia family was never in the cards for him. But they hired him on at the restaurant, liked his work ethic, and after one year, asked him to be a bagman for close to ten grand a month. Even though he refused at first, here he was, working for the mafia.

"Looks like it's all here," Diego said from the side table.

"That helps your situation, Sal."

"What?" Sal said, surprising himself he could even speak.

"Your situation," Silvio repeated. "There have been nights that it wasn't all there."

So that's what this was about. Someone was skimming money, taking their own percentage, and Silvio Mancuso was investigating with his knife.

And Frankie was missing.

Sal stumbled on his feet, catching himself, then righting himself before falling to the plastic-covered floor.

"Diego, we need a chair."

Wood scraped the floor. Then, a moment later, a chair was set behind Sal, and Diego's hands on his shoulders dragged him down onto it. He sat so hard that he slipped sideways and had to grab the edge of the chair to avoid falling over.

"Did you know that?" Silvio asked.

Sal glanced upward, completely confused.

"Did you know that money wasn't all there every time you and Frankie brought it in?"

Sal shook his head back and forth violently.

"Did you know that there's a rough estimate given of each night's take before it's dropped into the bagman's hands?"

Sal continued shaking his head, but slower now as he felt quite sick. At least if he threw up, the floor was covered in plastic.

"When the bag arrives here missing ten dollars, perhaps even one hundred, we can't guarantee it's missing." Silvio shrugged, glancing down at Sal's phone in his hand. "But if twenty- or thirty-thousand is missing," he paused, then added, "we know."

"Twenty …" Sal muttered, "thirty-thousand?" Then he whistled. It came out sounding like a creaking door.

He felt Diego close behind him, his presence like standing too near a hot oven.

Silvio scanned something on Sal's phone, then tossed it over his shoulder to Diego. The man must've caught it because Sal didn't hear it hit the floor.

"You made no calls tonight, and there's nothing from Frankie's home or cell."

Sal shook his head again. "I don't use my phone during the job."

Silvio nodded slightly, handing the phone back. Sal pocketed it.

"It didn't surprise you when your partner didn't show up for several shifts?"

"I asked"—he swallowed, then found his voice again—"I

asked Diego and was told to do the pickups alone."

"You did the right thing, Sal." Silvio stepped backward until he stood beside the metal table again, the one with his clean knife. "A lot of blood was spilled for answers I didn't get."

"Answers, that—what?" Sal wondered if he'd pass out from the stress and fear. Maybe that would be for the better. Then, he wouldn't feel whatever they planned to do to him.

"Look over there." Silvio pointed at the table with the money piled high.

Sal fixed his gaze on it.

"Do you see the man behind the table?"

Sal shook his head, fearing his answer was wrong. "No, man." He glanced back at Silvio, waiting for the knife, waiting for the end.

"Observant." Silvio raised the knife. "Our accountant claimed he wasn't skimming Mr. Bartleson's money all the way until he bled too much."

A full-body shudder traveled through Salvatore, and as embarrassing as it was, his shoulders visibly shook.

"The two women who count it for him are there and there." Silvio pointed at deep red spots on the plastic. "Oh, and here." He jabbed a finger at splatter marks on his plastic apron, then grinned wide. "They all claimed innocence, begging for their lives."

The smell was getting to him. His heart fought to keep up with the high blood pressure and the panic attack settling over him. Sal gripped the side of the chair to ground himself, hoping Silvio would end the speech soon or just jab the blade into his throat and be done with it.

But he didn't want to die. Especially not this way, on the floor of the meat-cutting room at the back of a restaurant.

He hadn't skimmed any money. Not one dollar. But telling Silvio that hadn't helped the others, which meant there was no way out.

Unless …

"Sal," Mancuso was talking again. "If everyone says they weren't skimming, then I have no choice but to remove them from our employ and hire new, trustworthy people. You understand this, right?"

He didn't understand it at all, but he nodded twice, then stopped moving his head for fear of vomiting on Mancuso.

"Don't worry, Sal. We'll speak with Frankie when we catch up with him."

He wanted to nod again but swallowed instead, trying to keep his stomach contents where they were.

"This leads me to the next phase of our meeting."

He was dead. There was no way around it. The accountant guy was dead, the girls who counted the money were dead, and Frankie was as good as dead when they found him.

"How much have you taken, Salvatore Prezzie? Just tell me the truth so we can all put this mess behind us and go home to sleep."

Silvio moved much closer, striking distance close.

Mancuso jerked his head back once, and then Diego grabbed Sal's arms, forcing them back so hard his shoulder muscles protested, forcing a grunt from his lips.

"I've asked politely," Silvio whispered, his voice devolving into a hoarse growl at that volume. "Don't anger me by making me wait for your answer."

Sal shook his head and opened his mouth to protest, but all that came out was his last meal.

He attempted to turn his head to avoid splashing his vomit on Mancuso and angering him further but wasn't able to move fast enough.

Bile-encrusted pieces of half-digested lasagna flew at the apron, bounced off it, and covered the floor to Mancuso's right. To his credit, the man sashayed to the left quickly, escaping the full brunt of the heave.

Unable to contain himself any longer, his nerves rattled beyond what they could handle, Salvatore vomited several more times onto the plastic, the smell filling his nose, the acrid taste, his mouth.

Diego had released his arms to step back, and Mancuso had moved over by the table with the money.

With no hope of ever leaving this room alive, Sal let his bladder go and pissed himself, soaking his jeans down the right leg.

Mancuso clapped, his hands coming together rhythmically.

"Bravo," he chanted several times like Sal had just won some award for projectile vomiting. "Diego, take him to the bathroom and clean him up."

"Clean him up?" Diego asked.

That was the same question on Sal's mind. Why clean him up if they were going to kill him?

"And bring a mop and bucket," Silvio added. "There are standards, certain conditions that must be met for my work. To discuss anything further with Mr. Prezzie, there can be no vomit on my shoes or my knife."

"Understood," Diego said, his voice barely audible.

Weakened now by the loss of any nutrients he may have needed, Diego had to support him to the bathroom. Once through the door, he shoved him inside. Sal stumbled and tried to stay upright but couldn't, falling in a heap below the row of sinks.

"Wipe yourself down. Take those piss-stained pants off, and come back out when you're done."

The door closed, the lock slipping into place.

What kind of murderers cleaned up *before* they executed their victims?

Who the fuck was this Silvio "the butcher" Mancuso anyway?

And why kill innocents who *weren't* skimming?

Or was this like in grade school when the teacher couldn't tell who threw the paper airplane, and no one ratted them out, so the whole class got detention?

Detention was a far stretch from murdering all your employees.

Sal grabbed the edge of a sink, tightened his grip, and pulled himself to his feet. He was pale and sickly looking in the mirror.

After several gulps of water to wash out his mouth, he devised a plan.

His mother needed him. He hadn't been skimming shit. So, dying for someone else's theft was not only ridiculous; it was utterly abhorrent.

And if he was dead anyway, he might as well go down swinging.

He splashed water on his face, then shook his limbs to wake everything up.

After a few seconds of staring at his reflection in the mirror, he spun on his heels and entered a bathroom stall, where he removed the back of the toilet.

The heavy porcelain rectangle would serve as his baseball bat.

It was time Diego took one for the team.

In the center of his forehead.

Chapter 2

SARAH ROBERTS ENTERED THE kitchen and started the coffee before Aaron woke up. This had become routine during the first two years of their daughter's life.

Things had been calm since she'd given birth to a healthy baby girl weighing seven pounds, eleven ounces. Well, calm was a relative term because they'd had to learn to live with their daughter and her wild habits, habits they took great effort to conceal from the outside world.

Willow Roberts, now almost three years old, was strong-willed and had certain abilities that were unexplainable. Life had been easier when Willow was only six months old. Once, Sarah saw Willow's soother fall from her mouth and roll a couple of times on the carpet. Then, it lifted off the floor and floated back into Willow's mouth. It was pretty easy keeping this from onlookers as Sarah could stay home and raise Willow on her own, with Aaron's help when he returned from the dojo.

Vivian helped, too. She was back and stronger than ever, keeping them isolated from the outside world by not involving her in criminal issues anymore. Her sister told her that Willow's presence in Sarah's womb had been blocking Vivian during the pregnancy. Their daughter had unknown abilities that would have to be controlled later in life. She would need training, understanding, and, most of all, discretion.

Where all these clairvoyant gifts came from left Sarah bewildered. She'd asked Vivian but hadn't gotten an answer yet. She spoke with her mother to see if something was in the family bloodline, but it came up empty.

Maybe it was just a freak of nature that Sarah could talk to her dead sister. But if so, how the hell did Willow get all her talents?

Sarah grabbed two coffee mugs from the cupboard and remembered how worried she'd been about what this meant for their daughter. In the end, it was Parkman who had consoled her. He reminded Sarah and Aaron that Sarah had learned to cope and live in this world with her highly public abilities, so why couldn't Willow, especially if she kept a private life? And, for as long as they could, they would keep Willow hidden from the world, hidden from any form of scrutiny, until school was a must.

And now, at five in the morning, Sarah would wake each day, work out in the building's gym downstairs, come up for coffee with Aaron, then shower before he left for the dojo. The rest of the day involved her daughter and anything else she could come up with to help Willow learn to control who she was and what she could do.

Sarah poured herself a coffee, then sat at the kitchen table as Vivian hovered close.

"What brings you here so early?" she whispered.

Bad news.

Sarah sipped her coffee two-handed and then set her cup down.

"Am I going to want to hear this?"

No.

"Then don't tell me."

Vivian was silent a moment.

Sarah lifted her cup and sipped again, her stomach churning slightly. She'd told Vivian she was done. She was a mother now. There was no way she was being pulled back in. Even safe, small jobs weren't happening. They were a family now, and that was final.

Vivian understood her position and left them alone for the most part. Her visits were more like an aunt checking in on the family than her sister whispering in her ear from the other side.

But this was different. Sarah felt it through her sister's presence.

"Does it affect Willow?" Sarah asked.

Possibly. But I guarantee her safety. Let her go. She'll be fine.

She set her cup down too hard. It clattered on the table. "Don't you dare tell me that. There's no *possibly* with you. What is this, *let her go* crap?"

Vivian remained silent another moment. There was movement in the apartment. Aaron was awake.

"You going to tell me?" Sarah whispered.

This was Vivian's chance to speak without Aaron being around. She had Sarah's undivided attention.

A decision is needed.

"A decision? What kind of decision?"

You'll be given two options.

"And?" Sarah lifted her mug. Decisions were something she could handle. At least it wasn't as bad as she thought it would be. Vivian could've told her she would be fighting a serial killer or attempting to stop some kidnapping ring again.

You will be given an ultimatum. You mustn't choose either option.

"Okay, great. The decision is, don't make one. Got it."

She sipped on her coffee as the toilet flushed. Aaron was coming now.

"Anything else?"

Vivian moved closer to her, a puff of air moving several strands of her hair.

Just know that I'm watching over your family. Willow is safe and will remain so.

"My family? Willow's safe?"

She blocks me still. I know she's there, safe, but I can't see her like I see you and Aaron.

"So?"

I'm sorry, Sarah. It comes today.

"What comes today?" she asked, her voice rising.

Aaron stepped into the kitchen, rubbing his eyes. "Yeah, what comes today?"

Sarah stared at the wall like a lunatic, seeing nothing. Her heart was racing, her combat mode engaged. It would be a grave error if something were coming for her or Willow today.

"I asked you, what comes today?"

I'm sorry, Sarah. I'll be close ...

Vivian disappeared from her consciousness.

Sarah blinked, snapping herself back to the kitchen. "Fuck you, then."

Aaron stared at her, his eyes wide but heavy with sleep.

Sarah set her coffee mug in the kitchen sink so hard that it tipped sideways and broke into three pieces. "If my sister wasn't dead, I sometimes wonder if I'd kill her."

Willow called for her from the other room.

"I'll clean that up when I get back."

Then she was gone to get her daughter, to keep her close.

When Aaron leaves within the hour, she would get out her gun, load it, and wait.

Whoever was coming today was about to be taught a valuable lesson.

One that only mothers could teach.

No one would touch her child.

No one.

Chapter 3

Salvatore held the chunk of porcelain in both hands, gripping it as if his life depended on it, which, in this case, it did.

They'd allowed him to be alone in the bathroom because there were no windows, no means of escape. Diego had locked the door, securing him inside. This was a no-brainer. Mancuso was feared for his skill with the knife and his love of blood, but evidently, the man didn't work with vomit. How did he handle feces? Once people were killed, disemboweled, dismembered, or simply had their carotids cut open, didn't they shit themselves? Hadn't Mancuso seen vomit from victims in the past?

Sal had to assume that was the case. He also had to assume that every time, he had someone like Diego clean it up for him before he got back to his handiwork, which was the true love of the blade.

Footsteps approached the other side of the bathroom

door.

Already weakened from fear, his adrenaline spent, stomach roiling and empty, Sal lifted the porcelain sideways and held it like a baseball bat. He wouldn't have much time or much of a swing due to his lack of strength, but he also had no other choice. He wasn't a tough guy, a made man, or born into the family business. He was just Salvatore Prezzie, a low-educated, minimum-wage earner who found an opportunity to make serious cash to help his sick mother.

And then someone started skimming off the top.

And the mafia hitman was asking him about it.

Which meant he was dead.

The lock clicked, the handle turned, and the door eased open.

Sal swung the porcelain, mustering all the strength he could. Diego raised his arms defensively as the toilet tank lid connected with him.

The sudden stop when it hit Diego's arms and the intense vibration upon impact jolted the porcelain from Sal's hands.

It dropped to the bathroom floor and shattered into several pieces, the noise louder than he expected. A small chunk hit his shin as Diego lunged for his throat.

Remarkably, neither of Diego's arms was injured in the contact with the lid.

The man clamped onto Sal's throat so fast Sal didn't have a chance to gasp.

Eyes wide, he clawed at Diego's wrists, but to no avail. The man held an iron grip on his throat, crushing his windpipe.

This was the end. There was no way out of it. Attacking

Diego would make it look like he was guilty when all he did was lash out in fear.

As Sal dropped to his knees, he wondered if Diego would kill him before Mancuso exacted his confession—or non-confession, as it were.

Wouldn't Silvio "the butcher" Mancuso want to be the one who dealt his brand of justice with the knife?

Sal gasped for breath, his thoughts leaving him.

Both men were on their knees now.

Sal lowered to the right, and Diego followed him, pushing into his throat, jabbing with his thumbs.

Even if Diego let go, his throat had been squeezed too tight. The damage would linger.

He wouldn't see his mother again. His last image would be Diego's face before he left this wretched place. How was that fair?

Then Diego released him.

He gasped for air, but hardly any crept up his windpipe.

"You motherfucker," Diego said. "Why the fuck did you hit me?"

On his knees, both hands on the floor, he gasped with all his remaining strength to breathe. Stars swam in his eyesight, and his head spun with dizziness.

"No one disrespects a made man. No one. I'm untouchable."

Diego shuffled beside him.

Sal tried to look over, but any movement of his head was too painful.

"So, you die on the bathroom floor like the vermin you are," Diego said.

A gun materialized in his vision as Diego leaned down to show it to him.

At least the torture of trying to breathe would end.

He slipped, his hand resting on a jagged piece of the porcelain, and dropped to his shoulder.

"That's right. Lower your fuckin' head so I don't get blood and brain matter all over the bathroom."

The porcelain. Sal wrapped his hand around the piece. He pulled it closer and stared at it. The edge was sharp, cutting into his palm. It had a pointed tip that might work well to cut skin.

He could only hope.

But Diego's gun would fire at any moment, ending this nightmare.

Sal's body forced him to breathe while his brain slipped into self-preservation mode and forced him to make an effort to try once more to stay alive.

The weapon clicked beside his ear.

Diego was seconds from ending this.

In one final gasp, Sal spun sideways, raised the jagged piece of porcelain, and aimed upward for Diego's throat.

The second before impact, Diego's eyes widened in surprise.

Then, the pointed tip of the makeshift weapon split the man's skin and drove up under his jawbone.

Diego dropped the gun and clutched at the slim piece of toilet lid stuck in his neck. He moved to pull it out, appeared to debate that thought, then tugged anyway.

Blood shot outward like a broken hydrant, covering Sal's face and neck. His hands slick with it, Sal dropped to the floor and shuffled away.

Diego lay on his back and stared at the bathroom ceiling as he convulsed in the throes of death. Blood spurted from his neck, pooling around his head, the floor now covered in more ichor than Sal had ever seen in one place.

Miraculously, Salvatore's breathing tubes seemed to open a millimeter. It was enough to calm the dizzy spells, but it also brought with it the smell of copper to his tongue, and he felt he might vomit again.

But that couldn't happen.

Vomiting through his ruined throat would kill him, he was sure.

Sal clambered to his feet, leaned against the wall to get his bearings, then jostled over to the sink, where he turned on the tap. He covered his face in water and washed his hands.

That simple act woke him up enough to realize what he had done.

Killing Diego to save himself would have the opposite effect.

There was no way he would survive now. All he had done was postpone his murder. Every member of the Lorenzo Bartleson Group, whether family or paid employee, would hunt him down now.

It would be better to walk out to Mancuso and let him end it now.

But he couldn't. There was always hope, as futile as that was.

And he'd like to say goodbye to his mother one last time.

"Diego," Mancuso called from the back of the restaurant. "What's taking so long?"

Sal stared at the door a moment, then forced himself to look down at Diego.

The man was certainly dead, his eyes glazed over.

Diego's loaded weapon sat beside his body, splattered with blood.

Sal stooped to retrieve it and held it at his side, a finger resting beside the trigger guard.

His breathing was raspy, but it was getting easier by the minute. After two long intakes of air, he exhaled and opened the door.

The corridor was empty.

To the right was the back room and Mancuso. To the left was the main sitting area of the closed restaurant.

Sal moved to the left, walked by the bar area, and continued to the front, where he bumped into the locked door.

Of course, it was locked.

"Diego?" Mancuso shouted, his voice closer. The man was heading to the bathroom, where he would see what Sal had done and raise the alarm.

Sal fumbled with the thumb latch on the door, his breathing rapid intakes of short gulps. He couldn't panic at this point. He was almost free.

The latch clicked, and the door opened.

Something buzzed by the back counter.

The alarm.

A rhythmic dinging sounded, the panel waiting for someone to enter a code.

"Hey, Diego!" Mancuso shouted.

The door closed behind Sal, and he sprinted to his car.

Ten feet from his vehicle, parked around the side so he

could see the back door light flicker on and off, the restaurant's front door smashed open.

Sal glanced over his shoulder and ran as Mancuso came outside, still wearing his bloody apron.

"Salvatore," Mancuso shouted.

The sound of that man shouting his name made him stumble into the side of his car. It was a horrible sound, a guttural wail, like the call of a wounded wolf—an alpha who missed his kill.

He fumbled with the fob, opened the door, then dropped into the driver's seat. After tossing the gun onto the passenger seat, he slipped the key into the ignition and fired up the engine.

When he checked the mirrors, he gaped in horror.

The insanity of seeing Silvio "the butcher" Mancuso running up the side of the building in a bloody apron, a knife extended from his right hand, was something out of a movie like *Saw* or *Hostel.*

It was too much for Sal to take in, too much to process.

So he put the car in gear and hit the gas without checking his mirrors for over ten miles.

When he finally got the nerve to glance in the rearview mirror again, he saw the headlights of morning traffic and regular people heading into work on the side streets of downtown Toronto.

Another day in the city, the morning sun coloring the sky.

Most likely, the last day of his life.

He would have to tell his mother. What about the cops? Should he go to them?

He shook his head and glanced at the gun in the seat

beside him.

One thing at a time.

Go to his mother. Tell her everything.

They could decide together.

And when they came for him, he wouldn't hesitate. They would die, and he'd use Diego's gun to kill them.

His life was forfeit now.

Why not take out as many *made men* as he could before he died?

That thought brought a smile to his face.

The first smile he'd had in weeks.

Chapter 4

Sarah tried to talk to her sister again, but she was strangely absent. She'd called her, shouted at her, and even asked Willow if Vivian was around. But ever since she'd broken her coffee cup that morning, Vivian hadn't returned.

Aaron had left for work, and Willow was getting tired, almost ready for a nap. Sarah had enjoyed the past several years of motherhood. The change of pace from her previous decade was so dramatic at first that she didn't know what to do with herself. Within two months of giving birth, up most nights and sleeping during the baby's nap time, Sarah would spend her spare time watching the news. She'd seen muggings, murders, and mayhem on the TV screen and understood why she wasn't out there trying to stop it all, but something inside her missed it.

Grateful for Willow and her time at home with her, she focused on being a strong and supportive mother and found a rhythm that worked well for both of them. When Willow slept, Sarah often read books on child rearing and early lessons. Daytime walks to the park, evening readings together, and lots of playtime were their daily life—a welcome change from her life's chaos.

During all that time, only a few important messages came from Vivian that were acted on. Small things, like anonymous tips for the police, a few tips for cases Parkman had taken on, and three car accidents were averted—important people who weren't supposed to die yet. Aaron and Alex handled the car accident messages due to Vivian's easy instructions.

Darwin and Rosina had visited when Willow was born and returned last summer for another visit. Still, because things had calmed down in the vigilante business, they'd moved on to other ventures, turning their small group into an often-called-upon mercenary organization.

Even Bruno had returned to work for about a year now with a new name and ID. Privately, they still called him Bruno, but his ID said he was Steven Miller. Sarah wondered if she'd ever get used to him being a Steven.

"You about ready for a nap?" Sarah asked her daughter, suppressing a yawn. She could sure use one.

Willow sat on the couch, engrossed in a book, staring at the pages like she was reading them.

"What are you reading?" Sarah moved into the living room.

"Peter Rabbit story."

"I loved those as a kid. Beatrix Potter was one of my favorites. Come on, honey, it's almost one in the afternoon." Sarah held a hand over her mouth as she yawned again.

"Let's catch an hour's nap—"

Someone knocked on the apartment door hard enough to cut her off.

"Come on, Willow. Let's get you to your room."

Sarah set the book aside, placing it on the cushion to Willow's right, then gathered her into her arms.

"Mommy?" Willow whispered in Sarah's ear.

"Yeah?" She rounded the corner toward the bedrooms as the knock on the door came again, louder this time.

"Don't answer."

A chill ran through Sarah as she set Willow down on her bed.

"Why would you say that?" Sarah asked.

"Liars." Willow glanced at the floor, a dour expression on her face like she was resigned to the knowledge imparted upon her, without regard for how she just knew things in the first place.

Sarah had Vivian to whisper in her ear, speak to her consciousness. Willow just gathered knowledge from somewhere that offered awareness of a certain topic or event. Yet, Willow had limitations, too. She couldn't see the future unless it was about to happen within a short timeframe—like she was living in a permanent state of déjà vu.

"What are they lying about, Willow?"

"They aren't themselves. And clothes. All lies."

Sarah frowned. Now, she was interested in seeing who was at the door. Part of having a daughter with untold abilities was learning how they represented themselves in her world. If Willow said the people at the door were lying based on who they were and how they were dressed, she needed to see that.

"I'll be back in a moment." They knocked again. Whoever was at the door was getting impatient. "Stay in the bedroom, though, okay."

Willow nodded, her little face still downcast.

She was so cute and cuddly, Sarah couldn't imagine anyone hurting a child, yet some people did. Some people enjoyed it.

She eased Willow's bedroom door shut until it was only open an inch, then approached the door.

A shout followed another knock. "Police! Open up!"

Sarah paused her step, then continued.

The police? They're lying about who they are? And how were they lying about how they were dressed?

The peephole in the door showed two men in uniform. Were they real cops?

"Give me a sec," she called through the door, then opened the cupboard over the fridge and retrieved her weapon. After checking one was in the chamber, she placed it in the lower drawer below the coffee maker for easy access.

At the door, she unlocked it, pulled the chain back, and opened the door wide.

Two officers, both male, stood staring at her. One was tall and thick, having spent hundreds of hours lifting weights. The other man was slightly shorter but had a wiry, lithe look as if he would wiggle his way out of a fight. The kind of skinny guy you couldn't get a hold of.

"Are you Sarah Roberts?" the buff officer asked.

"What's this regarding?"

The men exchanged a glance, then looked back at her.

"We need to verify who we're speaking with, ma'am," the thin one said. "Please identify yourself as required by law."

She stuck out her hand, palm up, and waved her fingers in a give-it-to-me gesture. "ID first. I need to see that you're real cops."

They looked at each other again, that same bewildered expression. She thought she detected something like frustration or maybe anger in the bigger man's eyes.

They're lying, Willow had said. *How they're dressed—all lies.*

"Ma'am, you can't see we're in uniform?"

The skinny one was the most convincing. Without Willow, she'd completely believe they were cops, and maybe they were. After all, didn't some cops put on the uniform to be someone else, to live the lie of serving justice while bringing their own brand of justice to the street? Sure, there were more good cops—great cops, in fact—than bad ones, but Willow saw something in these guys that Sarah had to remain cautious about.

"ID or get lost." She glared at them. "Anyone can put on a uniform from a costume store. Fuck, I ask for ID from the electricity guy, the maintenance man. The uniform means shit without the ID to back it up."

Skinny shrugged and slipped a hand into his breast pocket. By the time he produced his ID and showed it to Sarah, the buff guy was doing the same.

"Okay, Officers Jack Campbell and Ron Smith, what can I do for you?"

"Are you Sarah Roberts?"

"Yes."

"ID?"

She stared at them for a long moment, then shook her head and said, "Cute."

"What's cute, ma'am?"

"You two got all dressed up in uniform to come to my apartment and knocked on my door, knowing full well who I am and what I look like. Asking for my ID is a waste of time. You're playing games, and that'll remove what patience I still have at the moment. We all know I'm Sarah. So, I'm either shutting this door and going back to my day, or you'll tell me why you're here, and then I'll shut this door and go back to my day."

"What patience do you still have?" Officer Campbell echoed, his considerable muscles making him look uncomfortable in the uniform.

Maybe these guys weren't cops, and their IDs were fake, too. Could Willow be on to something? And if so, to what end? Why do all this?

The only reason she'd let it go on as long as she had was due to Vivian's visit that morning. She spoke of a decision Sarah would have to make and that *it* was coming today.

"Have you heard of the murders in the Little Italy section of Toronto last night?" Officer Smith asked, pulling up his pants as they had been slipping.

No way these uniforms were theirs.

What the hell was going on? She wanted to slam the door in their faces and call the real cops. But she didn't. There was no actual proof they weren't *real* cops yet.

"Murders? In Little Italy?"

Campbell nodded. "It's been all over the news."

"Oh, those bodies found at that bistro. They were found in the restaurant's bathroom or something, right?"

The men looked at each other one more time.

Then the door slipped from her hands—or was yanked—and slammed shut so hard, Sarah wondered if it would break the frame.

Willow!

She spun to her right and saw Willow standing in the hallway. She'd been crying.

"Honey, you can't do that," she snapped at her under her breath. "People will see what you're capable of." She swallowed, the surprise of the door being yanked from her catching her off guard. "Let me handle this. Go back into your room. Stay out of sight."

Sarah turned away from Willow and reopened the door.

"Sorry about that." Sarah smiled at them. "The wind must've torn it from my hand."

Smith leaned up and glanced over her shoulder. "I don't see any open windows."

Campbell wore an impatient look like they were running out of time.

"You were saying," Sarah prompted them as she moved closer, placing her shoulder blades against the door so it couldn't be yanked from her hand again. "Something about some murders last night."

"Our boss asked us to come pick you up in relation to the murders."

Her stomach did a backflip. She fought the urge to step away, moving deeper into the apartment.

This couldn't be happening. Why didn't Vivian warn her about this? She was finished with crime-solving and dealing with cops. She no longer got involved.

"I was home all night. I can verify that."

"That's not what we were referring to, ma'am."

"Then what exactly are you referring to?"

Smith stepped closer. "We need you to come with us, Miss Roberts. You can discuss it with our boss at the station."

"Your boss?" She held her ground, even though she could smell Smith now. "And who is your boss."

"The new chief of police," Campbell said. "You know, the one you put in that position because the other chief was killed. Weren't you involved in that somehow a few years back?"

Something tugged Sarah's shoulders. Willow was trying to shove her back inside the apartment. The door pressed hard against her back.

There would be a long discussion about the use of telekinesis in front of others when this was over. Willow wasn't mature enough to know when and when not to use it.

"This new chief is more than welcome to come visit me for a chat, but I'm too busy to help in any way." She moved aside and held the door in a vise grip. "Thanks for stopping by."

Officer Campbell slapped a thick hand on the door. "Not so fast, Miss Roberts."

"Excuse me." Anger rose in her so quickly that it startled her. "Get your hand off my door."

"You're coming with us whether you like it or not."

"Are you charging me with a crime?"

"That can be arranged."

Decision time came faster than she expected. "Okay," she said to calm the tension. How could she fight two men with her daughter in the other room? Who would take care of Willow? Aaron was at the dojo with the boys, which was an hour's drive at least. "Were you supposed to bring me in to discuss the murders and see how I could help? Or am I a suspect in some way?"

Campbell, the large, thicker man of the two, stepped just inside the apartment, forcing Sarah backward.

She eased toward the kitchen. The loaded weapon was three feet away.

"This was supposed to be easy," he said. "Come willingly, or these cuffs go on, and I drag you to the car." He jerked his head toward the hallway, the common area of the apartment building, when he said, "You think I care who watches? We're in uniform."

"I'm not going anywhere with you two." She backed up to stand beside the drawer with the weapon. To the men in uniform, her retreat was presumably the result of the fear she was feeling, which would bolster their confidence. That would be their mistake.

Campbell yanked the cuffs off his belt and dangled them at eye level.

A thousand questions raced through Sarah's mind, all surrounding what would happen to Willow. How soon could she get someone here to look after her? What the hell was this all about?

Most of all, where the fuck was Vivian?

She placed her hand on the counter beside the drawer.

They had put her in a corner. Were these two men legitimate overzealous cops trying to do a stellar job? Or were they arresting her for something?

Should she pull the weapon and let the chips fall where they may?

Decisions, decisions.

Something Vivian told her was coming.

She also told her not to decide either option.

What the hell did that mean?

The door moved again.

"Willow," Sarah shouted. "Don't."

Without warning, the door jerked so fast that it smashed into Campbell's back and sent him sprawling toward Sarah. She slipped sideways and hopped up onto the counter as the large man lost his balance, tumbled into the counter, and fell to his knees with a low, guttural moan.

Sarah hopped back off the counter as the front door swung back open. She clutched the drawer, then withdrew her weapon, swinging it in the direction of the other cop as he jumped inside the apartment, a weapon extended in his hand.

In less than a second, Sarah and Smith both had weapons aimed at each other's faces from less than one foot away.

Smith's hand was shaking. Sarah's was steady.

"Lower it," she whispered without moving her lips.

Smith shook his head.

"I said, lower it—"

The door banged behind him, making him jump. Sarah saw the movement and leaned away from Smith's weapon in case it went off carelessly.

Then, what felt like a wall smashed into her. She was crushed against the fridge, then shoved to the floor, her gun lost from her grip as she fought off whoever had jumped her.

The man was too strong, too heavy. Officer Campbell had recovered and, after getting to his feet, tackled Sarah to the floor. He yanked her left arm behind her back, and cold steel clamped on it. She tried to fight him but could not move under his massive body weight.

Then he got a hold of her other arm and forced it back with brute strength, cuffing them together behind her.

His weight lifted off, and she inhaled a breath, having not been able to breathe the entire time he'd crushed her into the floor.

Roughly, he yanked her to her feet, straining the muscles in her shoulders.

"Take it the fuck easy," she shouted at him.

"Smith, call downstairs. Tell them to come up now."

"Tell who to come up?" Sarah asked as the other officer slipped his weapon away and pulled out a cell phone. Then he disappeared in the hallway.

"Shut the fuck up." Campbell stepped sideways into her view and wiped his mouth where spittle had slipped over his lips. "This was supposed to be easy—arrest one woman and seize her daughter. Who knew this would be so fucking tough?"

"Seize my daughter?" Sarah repeated the words, trying to spin around to face the man. "What the fuck does that mean?" Panic rose in her throat.

He clasped the cuffs, holding her from behind. "A representative from the Children's Aid Society is waiting downstairs. They're coming to take your daughter into custody until this matter can be sorted out."

"On what grounds?" Sarah felt hysterics overcome her. Even her voice had reached a falsetto she hadn't heard since puberty. Her mind raced from Aaron to Parkman, then called Darwin and sent Bruno after all of them. Someone would pay for this intrusion.

"How about we start with loaded weapon sitting accessible to the child in kitchen cupboards? How do you think they'll feel about that, huh?"

She yanked the cuffs and almost succeeded in breaking his grip. "I meant, on what fucking grounds before you knocked on my door, asshole?"

"Oh, you are a feisty one. Are you aware of the charges you just brought down on your head for drawing a weapon on two police officers, assaulting officers, resisting arrest, and a host of other things I'm sure we can write up?"

"This is bullshit, and you know it." She yanked on the cuffs again as Willow appeared around the corner. The sight of her daughter's face sobered her instantly. "It's okay, sweetie. Mommy's fine. We're all just going for a car ride, and we'll be back together again soon."

"I said, no door answer," Willow whispered.

"I know, honey. But these men are police officers, and they want to take me to their office for a little chat." Voices from the apartment hallway alerted her to the other cop returning with the CAS worker. "Someone's coming to take you with them temporarily. It'll be okay."

Campbell moved to stand beside her, his grip on her arm slightly above her elbow. Willow closed her eyes, and Sarah felt a tug on the cuffs as if someone was behind her. They loosened a notch.

"Willow?" Sarah spoke in a stern tone. Willow's eyes opened, and the cuffs stopped moving. "That's enough for today. Remember what we discussed. No one ever sees the real you."

Willow nodded, her face forlorn. Sarah never wanted her daughter to see her in handcuffs or deal with the authorities in such a way.

She figured it would come one day, but she hoped it would be when Willow was older. She imagined as Willow got older, there would be times when Vivian and Sarah would take on certain tasks and help out the good guys, but this was something else entirely.

Vivian, any chance you could've told me to have Aaron stay at home for Willow?

Officer Smith entered with a woman in her sixties. She wore gray business attire and actually looked the part.

"Sarah Roberts, my name is Gwen Pasternack." She flipped open her ID and held it long enough for Sarah to read it. It looked as legitimate as possible. One more notch in their I'm-who-I-say-I-am belt. "Are you the only adult present at this time?"

Sarah nodded. "I am."

"I understand these men have been asked to take you in regarding a murder case." At least Gwen lowered her voice on the word *murder*.

Sarah glanced at Willow. Their eyes met momentarily, and her daughter offered her a slight smile. Was her daughter reassuring *her*?

"That's what I'm led to believe," Sarah whispered.

"Due to the nature of the issue you seem to be tied up in, I've been asked to tag along and remove little Willow from the home until there can be a complete investigation."

"That won't be necessary. Willow's father, Aaron, can be called. He could be here to care for our daughter in one hour."

"Your boyfriend?"

"Think common law. We've been together almost a decade."

"I assure you, Sarah, Aaron Stevens will be called. We have to interview everyone to ensure little Willow Roberts isn't in danger."

"Why would she be in danger? What would ever lead you to think that?"

Gwen straightened and faced her. "Sarah, the details of my involvement cannot be discussed in front of the child."

"Mommy," Willow said. "She no lie."

Willow was aware and in tune with everything happening around her. How did she get so lucky with such a mature child? She debated getting Willow to break the cuffs, fighting her way out of this, but only saw it ending badly.

"I see you soon again, Mommy," Willow said.

"Then we go with them?" Sarah asked. "Is that what you're saying? Because my sister isn't here."

Willow nodded.

How did she get to be so mature so fast? A tear leaped to Sarah's eye before she could quell her emotions.

Officer Campbell pushed her toward the door. "Let's go."

"Wait, the apartment needs to be locked."

After several more moments of debate, Gwen Pasternack from the Children's Aid Society walked Willow toward the elevator while Officers Smith and Campbell locked her apartment door.

Cuffed and left with no other options but to comply, Sarah allowed herself to be led toward the elevator as well.

Whoever was behind this would have to be taught to never fuck with the Roberts family again. She had nothing to do with those murders last night, and she wasn't going to help them on any level after being forcibly removed from her home and having her child seized.

But deep down inside, Sarah knew this wasn't about any of that.

This was something else entirely.

It was about the ultimatum Vivian spoke about that morning. Some decisions were supposed to be made soon, and she had to find her own way.

Vivian's words from that morning echoed in her head. *Just know that I'm watching over your family. Willow is safe and will remain so.*

Without the guarantee that Willow would be fine, Sarah probably would've lost her shit and killed someone upstairs.

They could fuck with her, and she'd deal with it, but go after her child at their own peril.

She feared there would be more bodies scattered around the city before whatever was happening came to an end.

Chapter 5

Salvatore Prezzie fell asleep in his car for a couple of hours, started awake, and used a YMCA to have a shower. Refreshed and still feeling slightly sick from the adrenaline of the previous evening, he grabbed a McDonald's breakfast and drove out to London, Ontario, to visit his mother.

St. Joseph's Hospice for cancer patients was a lovely facility. They treated his mother well, eased her pain daily, sometimes hourly, and made sure she got proper exercise. Bound to a bed or wheelchair, on oxygen daily, his mother was still filled with life.

She fought on through six years of cancer surgeries and chemotherapy treatments until the diagnosis came that it had gone into her lungs. Inoperable lesions had formed throughout her lungs, and several treatments later, they had grown in size. Hence, the oxygen tank was needed, as her lungs weren't operating at full capacity anymore.

She was only fifty-three years old, and Salvatore had

wanted to do right by her. So he researched the kind of cancer she had, and he'd learned that chemo wasn't always the best option. He'd also learned that miracle drugs were upwards of two thousand dollars apiece, which he could never afford.

Then he discovered the Mayo Clinic in Arizona had developed breakthrough treatments for people like his mother. All he needed was ten grand to get her down there and placed on their list.

Then, another ten to twenty grand is required for the first set of treatments.

And this became the reason for taking the job as the bagman. Since that job paid him enough to send his mother to the Mayo Clinic within four to five months, why would he ever skim off the top? Who would be stupid enough to steal money from such an organization as the Lorenzo Family?

Sal pulled into the hospice and parked in the visitors' parking. He sat in the car a moment, the engine off, and glanced around. As far as he could tell, no one had followed him here.

Also, he'd only told Frankie about his mother. No one else knew he even had a mother.

Margaret Doyle, of Irish descent, had adopted him—figuratively, not literally—at the age of seventeen. She'd taken him in after his father drowned in a freak boating accident. Margaret had been their neighbor and acted like a mom since he was three years old. Sal's biological mother had died in childbirth, and at seventeen, after his father died, he was able to make his own decisions in the eyes of the law, so he moved in with Marge. She'd never had children of her own, and they'd always gotten along so well.

She'd fed him and taken care of him while he finished college. Even though she wasn't his blood mother, she'd been the closest thing to a mother he'd ever known—so he called her Mom.

No one in his life knew about her but Frankie, and Frankie was missing, presumed dead. Which meant none of Lorenzo's Bartleson Group would be coming to visit her. His mistakes wouldn't follow him to her doorstep.

He pulled Diego's gun out of the glovebox anyway and got out of the car. The weapon offered a level of comfort he wouldn't otherwise have. Once the gun was safely stored and covered at the back of his pants slightly to the left of his spine, he trudged toward the front doors where he'd sign in and go visit his mother. With an eye over his shoulder, Sal watched everyone during the short walk to the building. The odds were extremely low that anyone from the Bartleson Group would be here, but he still had to be vigilant.

The hospice was quiet today. Within ten minutes, he stood outside his mother's door, staring at the handle, so grateful he'd made it for one more visit before returning to the city.

It was either heading back to Toronto and working it all out with Lorenzo, explaining how he had no other choice, or spending the few remaining days of his life looking over his shoulder. And on what money? Since he wasn't skimming and hadn't been paid this month, there was no way he could go off the grid and hide from the Lorenzo Family for too long.

His voice was still somewhat raw, and there was massive

bruising around his neck, but the woman at the front counter politely didn't stare when he signed in. On the way up the hall, he passed three other people with his head down to avoid eye contact.

Marge would ask, but he had a story for her.

Sal knocked lightly, then pushed open her door and slipped inside.

Mom sat up in bed, watching a daytime talk show. The laughing track was on as he entered.

She glanced over, the tube in her nose trailing beside her. "Oh, I didn't expect you today," she whispered.

He shrugged. "I have a few days off work."

She studied him as he sat down in the guest chair.

"What happened to you?"

The oxygen machine whirred beside her bed. "Accident in the gym."

She clicked off the incessant laughing on the talk show, then set the TV remote on the table beside her.

"No hug today?"

He hadn't wanted to get too close on account of the injuries to his neck, but she'd already seen it. What was he thinking? Possibly one of his last visits, and he wasn't even making it special.

After pushing up off the chair, he embraced her in a strong hug. Surprisingly, he had to fight off tears. This could be their goodbye moment. It all depended on Lorenzo and if he'd let him live to work out a consequence for killing Diego —even though it was self-defense, through and through.

"Tell me about the gym accident," she said as they pulled away from each other.

Sal retook his seat. "I was on the bench press without a spotter. Stupid me. The bar dropped on my throat and stayed there for almost a minute, choking me and bruising me until someone noticed and helped me out. Affected my voice, too."

"I can hear that." Her tone was suspicious, her expression skeptical.

She didn't believe him but was willing to let it go.

After several minutes of small talk, Sal got anxious to leave. He'd checked on her and made sure she was safe. But something about being here made him question that safety. What if they had tracked his phone? What if they attached a GPS tracker to the cars of all their employees? There was a possibility that Lorenzo's people knew exactly where he was and were on their way.

"And they never change the meals," Marge was saying. "What do you think of that?"

He blinked, coming back into the room. "It's terrible," he said, getting to his feet. "Mom, I should go. Long drive back to the city." He stretched. Sleeping in the car stiffened his muscles and made him feel old.

"That's fine, you should go. You haven't been listening to a word I said."

He moved up the side of her bed and kissed her cheek. "What do you mean? I love listening to you." He took her hand and squeezed it.

"Well, tell me if that'll work for you."

"If what'll work for me?"

She snickered. "See, you weren't listening."

"Then tell me again."

"I can get cleared to fly in two weeks. I was talking about

the food at the Mayo Clinic and how the online brochure makes it look so much nicer because they never change the meals here."

Sal frowned. Having her out of the country at this time in his life was a fantastic idea, but how would they afford it?

"Mom, since when are we going to Arizona? That takes money, which I don't have enough of yet."

Now, it was her turn to frown. "That Italian came by with an envelope."

Sal's stomach dropped, and he wondered if he could handle a second full-blown panic within twelve hours.

"What Italian?" he asked, worried what she would say.

"Tony, or Paulie or something." She snapped her fingers. "Frankie, that was his name."

Sal took a step back. "What did Frankie want with you?"

They'd never met. Sal had not introduced his mother to his bagman partner. They'd talked each and every night at length. Frankie wanted out. He had found God and wanted to attend church or something. Or it was the woman of his dreams. Working nights wasn't good for him. He claimed he wasn't a gangster, a made man, or a mafia man. He was simply born into the family, which to him did not constitute employment in a criminal organization by itself.

"You're acting strange, Salvatore," Marge said, leaning back to take him in better. Her eyes roved over him. "There's nothing to be defensive about."

"Mom." Sal shrugged. "I just didn't know Frankie was coming today."

"He came yesterday."

Sal waited, and when she didn't add more, he asked,

"Well, are you going to tell me why he was here?"

"He came to give me the money for the trip and the treatment in Arizona. Said you asked him to drop by in order to help him out."

The money? For the Mayo Clinic? That had to be five thousand or more.

"Help him out?" Sal asked, his voice hesitant. "How's that?"

"I'll tell you this: for two work buddies who hang out at work all the time, you guys really don't know each other, do you?"

"Mom, just please tell me how I was helping him out."

She gasped at Sal's tone. In a stern voice, she said, "He told me he had done some bad things in his life and was making amends. He said the cash was a delivery from you, the money you earned, and I was to take it and help heal my body. How you helped him was by letting him deliver the cash unto me, as he put it. Those were his words, that *unto me* part. Like he was speaking out of a Bible. Then he talked for ten more minutes about righting wrongs or something. I was busy counting the money you sent me."

Sal stepped away from the bed and moved to the window, where he drew back the curtain.

Frankie had been skimming. People were dead because of it. That accountant guy with the two female cash counters, and now Diego—all dead. Soon, they'd find Frankie and kill him, and they'd find Sal and kill him, too.

Stealing money from the mafia never ended well—ever.

And their money was stashed in a hospice in London, where they'd never find it.

Unless they got to Frankie.

If that happened, they'd get to Sal's mother here in the hospice, and getting to Margaret Doyle would make the cancer seem mild to the pain they'd inflict before killing her.

Sal couldn't allow that. He had to get to Frankie first. There was no way around it.

He pivoted back to face her. "Where's the money now?"

"I got one of the nurses to deposit it in my account for me."

"What?" he gasped. More people knew about this supposed windfall, this amount of money her son had delivered to her. "You said you were counting it. How much money did Frankie give you?"

"Are you saying you don't know how much you sent? Or are you wondering if you could trust Frankie?"

"Mom, how much did he give you?"

She studied his face momentarily, then said in a low voice, "Twenty-two thousand or thereabouts."

Sal whistled and spun around in a circle on his heels.

"What?" she said, smiling at him. "That's good, right?"

He approached the bed. "Mom, how fast can you get out of here?"

"How fast?"

"Mom," Sal said too forcefully. "I just need to know how fast you can get a flight down to Arizona."

She pushed back into her pillow at his outburst but didn't ask why he was getting upset.

"I could leave within a couple of days. That's what I was saying earlier when you zoned out. When is a good time for you, too?"

"Never." He stopped himself. "Well, what I mean is, don't wait for me. Just buy a plane ticket and go. The sooner, the better. If you can leave today, do it. If not, tomorrow."

"What's the rush, honey?"

"Your condition. Don't let the cancer get any more of a hold on you. Just go there and get situated, and I'll join you as soon as I can."

She touched his arm. "That's so selfless of you." Her eyes watered. "What kind of a son did I raise? You deliver the money in a way that helped a man redeem his values, money you made to help me with my cancer." She wiped at her eyes. "Sometimes I wonder how I deserve you."

"I wonder that, too." Sal started for the door.

"No hug goodbye?"

He stopped, then headed back to her bed and embraced her. His voice muffled in her nightgown, he said, "I'm so happy you're going to the clinic. This will help immeasurably."

"I'm happy, too. The health insurance plan only helps so far."

They pulled away, both wiping tears.

"I have to go back to the city. Work beckons."

"Work? I thought you had a couple of days off."

He was halfway to the door. "Oh, right. Well, I'm working overtime to help with more money."

"Such a good boy," she whispered as he got to the door.

"Love you, Mom."

"Love you, too."

Outside the building, he took long strides toward his car, his mind racing on all the possible places he'd find Frankie.

Wouldn't that make it right if he found Frankie and delivered him to Lorenzo?

Sal stopped at the car door and stared into space, wondering if he could do that and deliver the man to Lorenzo. That would lead to Frankie's torturous death.

But it could also lead to his mother's death, too. Why wouldn't Frankie tell them where the money went?

Ultimately, Lorenzo would have Silvio, "the butcher," Mancuso kill them all without another thought.

He dropped into the car and started back toward Toronto.

First step first—find Frankie and talk to him.

Then, talk to Lorenzo.

And pray he lived long enough to spend quality time with his mother in Arizona.

Chapter 6

From the cramped back seat of the cruiser, her knees scrunched against the wall of Plexiglas between the front and back seats, Sarah watched the road. The emptiness she felt, the void created by not having Willow by her side, was massive.

What could she possibly have to do with the murders that took place across town when she was home with Aaron last night? Unless this had nothing to do with those murders, and these fine examples of officers of the law were being used to pick her up and nab her daughter.

But why? To what end? Who would want her picked up?

If Vivian hadn't come that morning to warn her, everything could've turned out vastly different. And without Willow's assurances, something Sarah had grown to trust, she wouldn't be sitting in the back seat of this police car, and both men up front would either be dead or en route to a local hospital.

Yet, here she was, sitting slightly sideways to relieve pressure on her cuffed hands, her knees aching with every bump in the road as they drove her to their chief for a discussion about some murders she knew nothing about—and a decision she wasn't supposed to make, according to her sister.

What the hell is going on, Vivian?

When there was no answer from her sister, she leaned forward to address the officers in the front seat. "When do I get my phone call?"

"Everything in its time," Campbell said.

"What the hell does that mean?"

Smith turned in his seat to look at her. "Don't worry about phone calls. You have a lot more to worry about than that."

"Okay, let me ask again, what the hell does *that* mean?"

Smith turned back to face the road. "Just that you'll know everything in twenty minutes or so."

"Sounds like there's a lot of shit you guys haven't told me."

"Just shut up and wait."

She leaned back in her seat, her mind on Willow. "You arrest me in front of my daughter, traumatize her by having her seized by a CAS worker, only to tell me there's more to this narrative, and you're holding out on me?"

"All in good time."

"Yeah, well, you know what else will happen, all in good time?" When they didn't respond, she added, "Several cops buried up north somewhere, unmarked plot. Imagine the press release when they announce Laurel and Hardy, the buff one and the skinny one, both missing. Maybe CNN will run with it. You guys can be famous, post-mortem."

Smith snapped around in his seat. "Are you threatening an officer of the law?"

She leaned forward until her nose touched the wire screen separating them. "You're fucking right I am. If anything happens to my daughter, you're both dead men. I guarantee that." Then she smacked the mesh with her forehead for effect. It clanged loudly, making Smith jump and Campbell check his mirrors.

"Just sit back, little bitch, and shut up," Campbell said. "This ride is almost over."

Sarah sat back, not because she was told to, but because the effort of leaning that far forward was too hard on her knees.

Her stomach was knotted at the thought that these men were up to something terrible. Even if they were real police officers, they were lying, just like Willow said.

Who they are, how they're dressed. All lies.

When Willow said *lies*, she meant *deception*, as far as Sarah could figure it. Although, Vivian hadn't warned her to avoid them—or not to go with them. And Willow said she'd be safe. Her daughter's permanent déjà vu allowed her to see someone's intent, too, like she could read minds. It was more of a perception. Willow could detect their demeanor on a spiritual level, analyzing their thoughts and their motivations. If she felt that CAS woman was on the level, then she was.

For now, Sarah was convinced Willow was safe. She knew that in her heart because Vivian also understood the rules of fucking with Sarah and Willow. If her sister didn't warn Sarah in advance that Willow would be in danger, then Vivian had another thing coming as well.

The cruiser took a hard left.

They were driving through a richer part of Toronto. The houses were separated by large green yards and thick trees. Mansions were set back from the road. In some cases, gates met the road, with winding driveways twisting behind them.

Rosedale, an area she rarely visited.

"A police station in Rosedale," she said. "How rich must you be to hire two police officers to pick me up? Hmm, tell me. How much are you being paid to deliver me?"

"Shut the fuck up," Campbell said. "Everything will be made clear to you soon enough."

"That's where you're wrong."

He met her gaze in the rearview mirror. "How's that?"

"Everything is already quite clear."

"Fuck you." Campbell glanced at Smith. "Stupid woman cuffed in the back seat has no idea what she's talking about."

"It's clear that if you are real cops, you've gone rogue. It's also clear that the chance of you two still breathing for another week would surprise me."

"What? You psychic or something?" Campbell asked.

Smith nudged him. "Don't egg her on."

"Why not?" Campbell snapped at him. "She just threatened us."

"Because that's Sarah Roberts. She just knows shit sometimes." Smith snatched a glance back at her. "Didn't you see how violently her apartment door slammed shut? When we entered her apartment, none of her windows were open. I checked."

"So?"

"She said it was wind, but it wasn't. And, she didn't shove it closed with her *hand*."

"Are you saying she did it with her mind?" Campbell sounded completely dumbfounded like he'd just been told humans lived on Mars.

"All I know is she's been around a long time working with cops and shit. She may not be some super detective, but everyone she goes after gets caught or gets dead. She's been called a *psychic* detective."

"A psychic detective," Campbell repeated, looking at Sarah in the rearview mirror. "How about that? A bullshit name for a con artist."

"Con artist?" Sarah asked. "Interesting term coming from you."

"Nothing psychic about you." Campbell laughed, a short burst, his head shaking back and forth. "You just make shit up."

Smith ran a hand through his hair. "I said, don't egg her on. It's one thing to pick her up for this meeting, but something completely different to challenge her."

"You're such an ass, Smith. If she was psychic, why didn't she know we were coming? How about knowing the reason, the *why* we came to her door? If she were psychic, why doesn't she know where we're going or what this is all about?" Campbell scoffed, then chuckled. "She's not psychic. She's full of shit and has a bad mouth. Men are usually afraid of confident women, and Sarah Roberts has learned that, so she acts tough and intimidating. That's all there is to her. A scared little girl who can be overpowered by a more confident man." Campbell smacked Smith's shoulder. "Didn't you see how I cuffed her? Just held her down and forced her. That's what women are good for. Hold them down and force them. Shuts them up real good."

Vivian, you got anything on Campbell? Sarah squirmed in the back seat in agitation. Campbell needed a lesson on how to treat women. She swore he'd get that lesson whatever happened over the coming days.

"I don't know," Smith said. "I looked her up. They say she actually knows shit. Stuff that no one else knows."

"Then why didn't she go out this morning before we came, huh? We could've knocked on an empty apartment door. If she knew where we were going and who we would see, don't you think she would've made arrangements not to be home?" Campbell shook his head. "I can't believe you fall for that shit."

"Maybe she does know." Smith glanced down at his lap as Campbell took a right at a stop sign. "And just maybe she let us take her because avoiding Mr. Bartl—"

"Don't say his name," Campbell shouted.

"All I'm saying is, avoiding him is pointless. Better to see him and be done with it."

"So you're saying she's *so* psychic that she allowed all this to play out?"

Smith shrugged. "I have no idea. Just presenting theories."

"You're so fucked up, you know that?"

Campbell slowed to enter a driveway.

Mildly entertained after listening to them debate her abilities, Sarah sat up to take in her surroundings. The lawn and trees were immaculate. As soon as they entered the laneway, several men appeared from small guard shacks on either side of the asphalt. When they saw Campbell driving, they nodded, and he proceeded forward. Every man was visibly armed.

This did nothing to calm her.

Fifty meters along the driveway, a gate opened as they approached it. Once through the gate, they drove another hundred meters until the foliage opened up to a fieldstone mansion. The place was huge, bigger than any home Sarah had ever seen. Serious money was needed to buy and maintain a place like this. She ran through a list of potential people they were taking her to see. Who the hell had this much clout?

As the car stopped, Vivian showed up, whispering several details in her inner ear.

Step back to avoid blood.

It appeared Campbell was going to be taught that lesson after all, and Sarah could do nothing to stop it.

Both men got out and met at the passenger side back door. Campbell opened it and grabbed Sarah under her arm.

"Let's go," he said, dragging her out of the car and to her feet.

She stumbled, caught herself, and pulled her arm free from Campbell.

"Don't touch me. I can walk on my own." As much as she wanted to be angry with him, now knowing his fate, she felt somewhat sorry for the man.

Campbell's face had reddened. He'd had enough of her backtalk.

She saw the hand coming and waited for the blow, eyes closed. Her head snapped sideways. Then she dropped to the soft grass onto her shoulder. It was a mild hit, nothing serious. Men inside the house were watching, Vivian said. And listening, as they had bugged Campbell's phone.

She smiled at him as Campbell hauled her to her feet.

He leaned in so close to her ear that his lips brushed them. "You should watch that mouth of yours. Could get you in trouble."

She twisted and yanked her arm, wanting to be free of the man who had put a target on his back. This time, Campbell held on so tight his hand acted like a tourniquet.

"Open your mouth again," he whispered, "and I'll put it to good use."

She waited a moment, ignoring him, then faced the house. There was a slight sting where he'd smacked her, but no blood. It wasn't hard enough to break skin or cause a lot of bruising, but definitely hard enough to redden the side of her face.

Smith had stayed out of it, hands in his pockets, standing ten feet away.

Campbell guided her across the wide driveway toward the front doors that opened as they approached. Officer Smith followed several feet behind.

Three men spilled out of the front of the house. They were all dressed in expensive suits, hair cut back and trimmed clean, and each man wore a white earpiece in their left ear.

A rich politician or a movie star owned this place. Someone who needed this sort of security was a serious player.

They also had cops on the payroll evidently, or Smith and Campbell had great costumes and great ID because they even fooled the CAS worker, who Willow assured her was real.

The tallest man of the three in suits stepped forward. "Take the cuffs off her."

Campbell stopped several feet from the men. "You sure? She's a wiry bitch."

The man nodded, his deadpan expression unchanging. If a psychopath could be labeled by their eyes alone, then this man needed heavy therapy and drugs. Those dark orbs emitted no feelings, no lightness, no soul.

Campbell stared at him a moment longer, then shrugged and stepped behind Sarah to remove the cuffs.

"She's all yours."

"Who cuffed her?" the man asked, looking from Campbell to Smith, then back to Campbell.

"Why?" Campbell grunted as he stepped back beside Sarah, arranging and fitting the cuffs into the holder attached to his belt. "That matter?"

All three men stared at him. The moment stretched to a dozen seconds of silence, then Campbell said, "She fought us, didn't want to come in."

"You're cops. You can't ask a girl to accompany you without such force?"

One of the men in the rear touched his earpiece and glanced downward as if listening to something. After a moment, his hand lowered from his ear, and he glared at Campbell.

The men flanking moved to stand beside Officer Smith.

Campbell didn't seem to notice the positioning of the men, but Smith certainly did. He stared at the men flanking him, his face white with fear.

Sarah rubbed her wrists where the cuffs had bit in, getting the blood flowing again, wondering who the hell they'd brought her to meet while repeating her sister's message in her head. *Step back to avoid blood.*

"Hey," Campbell said, his ego bruised in front of his partner. "You weren't there. She fought hard. Had to drop her on the kitchen floor and handcuff her. Don't tell me how to do my job. I don't instruct you on security measures for this place. We were told to bring her in, and we did. That's the end of it."

"And you did this in Sarah's apartment?" the man asked. "In front of her daughter?"

Campbell glanced back at Smith, a dumb smirk on his face. "Get a load of this guy." He turned back to face the man. "I'm an officer of the law. We were asked to bring her here. We provided a service." He gestured at Sarah with both his hands. "Here she is. I'm not the bad guy here."

"Slapping her on the lawn over there," the man continued his interrogation, pointing toward the cruiser, "was necessary?" He crossed his arms over his chest. "In your opinion?"

"Damn right it was," Campbell said, his voice rising. "Are we done here? Can we get on with it?"

It would appear that Officer Campbell was about to learn a lesson in civility.

The man cracked a smile, but the skin around his eyes didn't move. A smile without the eyes wasn't the genuine article, but Campbell wouldn't know that.

All the preamble to snatch Sarah and Willow from her apartment made Sarah want to interrupt this little battle of male egos, what amounted to a pissing contest, whose dick was larger shit, but she wanted to give it a few more moments to see where it was headed. Would they actually kill a police officer in front of so many people, or just hurt him badly?

The security man edged closer to Campbell, his arms uncrossing to rest lazily at his sides. His colleagues eased closer to Smith.

"The man who requested Sarah's presence today left instructions to bring her here unharmed. You have brought her here, and she's about to go into a meeting with a red mark on her cheek and red bracelets where handcuffs have chafed her wrists."

Campbell shrugged and stepped forward, closing the gap between them in a threatening manner. "And? What, you're going to hit a cop? Go for it. I did the job. I got paid. That's it. That's how this works. You don't intimidate me, and you don't tell me how to do my job. Now back off, fucker—"

The knife came out of nowhere.

The man was standing with his arms at his sides, then his right arm was swiping sideways, and Officer Campbell's neck was open, a red blotch where the slit was made.

Smith jumped behind Sarah as she stepped back several more feet to avoid being sprayed with blood.

The security man also took a step to the side as the arterial flow from Campbell's neck shot toward him.

"What the fuck, man?" Smith said, already reaching for

his weapon from its holster. He aimed it at the man with the knife.

The men beside Smith were right beside him. One smacked Smith's arm upward while the other kicked out his knees. The officer's gun flew harmlessly away to land on the grass six feet from them while Smith dropped awkwardly to the ground, both men landing on him, holding him down in expert wrestling holds.

Sarah turned back to Campbell, who was now on his back, his eyes wide as he clutched at the wound on his neck.

To his credit, Officer Smith stopped squirming, a horrified expression of grief on his face.

They stood around in silence until Campbell lurched on the grass, his life oozing out of him.

The man with the knife stared impassively, trance-like, as if watching someone make a bologna sandwich, idly wondering who would eat it.

Sarah had killed in the past and seen enough people killed to be bothered by it, but not moved in a way that made her appear weak or threatened to those standing around. Nor did she savor a death, watching it with admiration as the man with the knife was doing now.

After a moment, the besuited man with the knife blinked, like he snapped back to the here and now, then leaned down to wipe his knife on Campbell's uniform. Seconds later, the knife was slipped inside a sheath under his jacket.

He addressed Sarah, gesturing toward the entrance to the massive house.

"Shall we?"

Sarah started up the steps, the man close behind.

"Get rid of it," he told the other two men with whom he'd stepped onto the porch. In a louder voice, he added, "Smith, follow us."

The threesome untangled from the grass and got to their feet.

Vivian had told her there was no saving Campbell. That he was already earmarked for execution. She'd offered Sarah a glimpse of the way he beat his girlfriend at least once a week. How Campbell put two prostitutes in the hospital last month after they wouldn't fuck him in exchange for not writing them up on solicitation charges—one of the women was beaten, then fucked anyway. Campbell let her go without charging her.

No wonder the man could be bought. He was a dirty, asshole cop—the worst kind. And now he was a dead cop, which Vivian had stressed couldn't be avoided anyway. She may have stopped it on the front lawn today, but he'd be dead by tomorrow in a back alley. Campbell bought his own death certificate when he cuffed her back at the apartment.

Smith would live through the day, but Vivian wasn't telling her more about his overall life expectancy. Although, Sarah felt a hint that Smith would be important somehow moving forward.

What Sarah found odd as they entered the enormous foyer of the massive, gorgeous residence was why Vivian didn't tell her who she was about to meet. Yet, even without her sister's help, she was starting to put it together. The elaborate security, the purchase of the police uniform and cruiser, and the use of a legitimate CAS worker had to have some sort of pull and a lot of cash.

It was the kind of money only criminal activity and organized crime came from.

The person she was supposed to meet—man, she was sure it was a man—required something from her.

The decision Vivian had mentioned. She'd said they'd come today, and they came. And now they were treating her like a willing guest when she was essentially kidnapped from her home, and her daughter snatched, too.

A shudder ran through her, her shoulders shaking. Images of Campbell's final convulsions as he died flashed through her thoughts. Okay, sure, she'd seen a lot of shit in the past, but it had been over two years since she'd seen someone die so violently.

Fuck, get control of yourself.

The man with the expert knife usage led them along a corridor toward the back of the house. No one spoke. No sound was uttered, just the clicking and clacking of shoes.

As they approached French doors at the rear of the corridor, they began to open, a man holding them on either side.

This was an obvious preamble for something. Whoever set up this meeting, whoever went to such efforts, wanted Sarah to see he was a serious, rich, and well-protected man. His questions would come, and finally, the decisions she had to make. The man knew she would struggle with what he had to ask of her, so he wanted the best footing to debate from, the strongest placement on the mat as they began their verbal sparring. Otherwise, why go to all this trouble? Why not just call her?

Outside, in the rear gardens, a large seating area was

arranged in a courtyard lined with bushes of varying colors. Purples, oranges, and bright reds competed for the eyes' attention. Sarah had never been much of a gardening type, but she appreciated such a well-kept arrangement.

A man sat with his legs crossed in a large chair at the center of the courtyard, flanked by two more men.

What the fuck is going on? Who needs this much security?

"Mr. Bartleson," the man with the knife said as he waved a hand toward her. "Sarah Roberts."

Bartleson pushed up off his chair. The man stood an impressive six and a half feet tall. His suit had to have cost several thousand, and the bits of jewelry he wore probably cost more than the latest Cadillac out this year.

"Miss Roberts, my name is Lorenzo Bartleson. I thank you for joining us today." He bowed slightly but didn't offer his hand.

"Like I had a choice."

The man studied her, then gestured at the chair opposite his. "Please. Sit."

Sarah remained standing. "Before we start, I need to know where my daughter is."

"Of course," the man said. "Walk with me." He moved past her.

"My daughter?"

Over his shoulder, he glanced back and said, "I'm taking you to her. They arrived minutes before you did."

That got Sarah moving.

She followed him for a moment before he slowed to walk beside her. Over four security men flanked them the entire time, never farther than an arm's reach away. Each man was armed with several weapons where unnatural bulges were detected under their jackets, and she was sure they had weapons stored in other places as well, like small ankle holsters. These men were prepared for war, but with whom?

"I must apologize for the way you were handled today. That wasn't my intention."

"Oh, right. Well, next time, just call. We could go for coffee and discuss what's troubling you."

They strode through a brick passageway, then came out into a large yard.

"You don't seem to grasp the nature of security I have here. I wouldn't be meeting anyone for a cup of coffee that wasn't properly vetted, the area locked down and secured."

"Why would that be, Mr. Bartleson? I wonder what one must do for a living to require such security measures."

He glanced over at her. "The organization I run has enemies. It makes casual dalliances at a Starbucks a relic of a bygone era for me, I'm afraid."

"You're missing out then. No one does a better pumpkin-spiced latte."

He raised a finger and smiled. "I didn't say I couldn't access their menu."

They rounded a corner where another yard opened to a swing set and a teeter-totter playground area.

Willow Roberts was on the swings, being pushed lightly by the CAS worker.

Sarah quickened her pace, but two security men moved to step in front of her. She tightened her jaw and clenched her hands.

"Please, Miss Roberts, I've shown you your daughter. She remains unharmed." There was a subtle threat in his tone. "She will be waiting for you once we discuss our business."

Sarah inhaled deeply, unclenched her fists, and turned back to Bartleson.

"What is it you want to discuss?"

"Back this way, where it's more comfortable." He held up a hand, pointing toward the elegant chairs she'd found him in.

"Then we bring my daughter with us."

"I'm afraid that's not possible."

She glared at him a moment. "I'm going to walk over to those swings and ensure my daughter is okay. When I finish my brief visit, I will listen to what you've dragged me here to listen to." Heat rose to her face. She wasn't asking him. She was telling him. A part of her wanted him to deny the request. What kind of man refused a mother her moment with her daughter?

Lorenzo Bartleson blinked several times, his eyes locked on Sarah.

"Very well." He turned to the man with the knife. "Silvio, escort Sarah to her daughter, then bring her to me. Carmine," he said to another man. "Stay with me."

Silvio nodded and addressed Sarah. "After you," he said, in the same tone he spoke to Officer Campbell.

The man was a psychopath, all the way to the rubber room and back. There were no two ways about it. He sliced a cop's throat open on the front lawn of this estate not ten minutes ago and was now escorting a mother to visit her child as if they were all headed out for ice cream by the beach.

Behind her, she overheard Bartleson tell Officer Smith to walk with him and explain why they didn't follow his instructions. Was he not explicit enough?

All of that faded for her as she ran to Willow.

Willow saw her, slowed the swing, jumped off, and ran toward her.

The CAS worker stood off to the side and watched with a smile.

When she grabbed her daughter and hugged her close, she wondered if they'd fallen down the proverbial rabbit hole. Instead of finding a vast wonderland, they had dropped into a psycho playground filled with grinning childcare workers capable of taking children from their parents for a payoff, murderers with knives and special talents, and a variety of apathetic psychos, all armed for war.

Vivian, what the hell is this? she whispered internally as a tear dropped off one cheek.

No one knew where they were. Aaron was at work, and Parkman was investigating a cheating husband somewhere in Oshawa, about a forty-minute drive from Toronto.

Sarah and Willow were alone and unarmed, completely vulnerable to Bartleson's whim. She would have to listen to him, then hope they would be able to leave.

She hadn't felt this weak in a long time, a position she would strive never to be in again.

"It's okay, Mommy," Willow whispered in her ear, then pulled away to look her in the eye. "We leave soon." She nodded at Silvio, who wasn't looking their way. "He'll drive us back to the apartment within the hour."

Sarah held her daughter close, marveling at Willow's abilities. How strong was she? How deep did it go? Was she still developing, meaning she'd be even stronger in years to come? Or was someone whispering to her like Vivian spoke to Sarah?

The futility of protest in such a well-secured location, isolated from the rest of Toronto as it was, left her no option but to set her daughter back down to continue playing with the CAS worker.

That and her daughter's assurance they'd be fine.

She stepped closer to the CAS worker, out of Willow's earshot. "You will suffer for what you did today." The woman frowned like she had no idea who she was playing with. "I have no issue dying for my daughter. Hurt her, take her from me, and we'll test that theory as I come after you with everything I've got."

Sarah spun around and followed Silvio back toward Bartleson and the meeting he'd gone to great length to set up, only looking back at Willow's smiling face once more.

She didn't want to enter such a serious meeting with tears in her eyes.

Chapter 7

Salvatore returned to Toronto in the late afternoon and drove directly to Frankie's neighborhood, a few blocks off St. Clair Avenue on Prescott.

Sal drove by Frankie's house, stopped at Rockwell Avenue, then did a U-turn and drove back along Prescott until he parked five houses from Frankie's place.

He knew exactly where his bagman partner lived as he was the one who picked him up for their nightly runs. The man had confided several secrets to him, but never once had he told Sal that he was going to go off on some religious binge and spend time redeeming himself or whatever shit he told Sal's mother. That kind of shite wouldn't sit well with the Bartleson Group, especially if you predicated that religious pilgrimage with tens of thousands of their cash without their knowledge.

It was always about money or women with men, and this was about a woman—Salvatore was sure of it.

Was Frankie's house being watched?

Sal needed to find Frankie and get him to Lorenzo and Mancuso so that he could stay on this side of the ground. Bringing Frankie in was a peace offering for what happened to Diego. So, if Frankie's house was being watched, what choice did Sal have?

Although, would they see it that way? Or should he just drive away and keep driving until he ended up in Moose Jaw, Saskatchewan, or Medicine Hat, Alberta, where he could work on a farm under the table? Try to live in hiding, as far off the grid as possible.

They'd find him, though. Bartleson was too powerful. They'd find him and slit his throat—or worse—while he slept in the middle of the night. Even if he traveled to Siberia and hid in a bunker under a mountain of snow, Sal was sure they'd find him.

It would be easier to just get it over with than race around the Earth, eking out a living, counting another day, breathing as another day of success.

He cracked open his door and stepped out of the car.

This was a risk, but what wasn't with Bartleson?

They could be waiting inside Frankie's place, and it could come down to kill or be killed last night on repeat.

The only hope, the only ray of salvation in this bloody mess, was to find Frankie and deliver him unto Bartleson. That was the only answer. He could do it with a clean conscience, too, because Frankie had given Sal's mother Bartleson's money. As kind and noble as that was, giving her stolen mob money was as good as putting crosshairs on her forehead. If Bartleson knew she was Sal's mother and she'd recently come into a large amount of cash, she'd be executed. Frankie did this to him and his mother. Not to mention, Bartleson would conclude that Salvatore had stolen the money and not Frankie.

Deliver Frankie to Bartleson and explain everything, or die trying.

That was the only way.

Having talked himself into bravery, Sal grabbed Diego's gun and his cell phone, then locked the car's doors and started up the sidewalk.

He stared at everything, his senses on full alert. Every car, house, window, and even the house with a for sale sign in case the mafia had "borrowed" the house for a week to watch Frankie's place.

When nothing stood out as strange or off-putting, Sal stopped in front of Frankie's house.

Shit, he'd done this all wrong. He should have approached from the back of the house. What was he thinking? He wasn't a professional in any sense of the word. He wasn't even sure the gun he carried would work, only that Diego had it, so it probably would.

Being the amateur sleuth he was, with all measures of covert subtly gone, Sal trudged up the front walkway to the house and rang the bell. While waiting, he watched the road to make sure no one approached him from behind.

He rang the bell again and added several knocks on the door this time.

Footsteps approached the door from the inside. He reached around to the gun, slipping his fingers around the butt of the weapon.

The curtains in the windows to the right of the door moved aside.

Sal froze on the spot, then relaxed when he saw the smiling face of Frankie's landlord.

A moment later, she unlocked the door and opened it.

Sal released the weapon and pulled out his phone instead.

"Hi, Salvatore," she said. "Frankie's not home. He's gone."

Gertrude stood with her shoulders bent slightly forward, like gravity was winning the fight over her long years. Heavyset for her age, she lifted her legs with effort as she stepped out onto the porch.

"Any idea when he'll be back?" Sal asked.

She shook her head and lifted a hand to shield her eyes from the sun. "He didn't tell you?"

"Tell me what?"

"He moved out three days ago."

Sal stepped back to feign surprise. "Where'd he go?"

"Said he was moving into God's house or some shit like that."

Sal raised his eyebrows in surprise. "God's house? What the hell does that mean?"

She shrugged, her shoulders shaking the double chin framing the bottom of her plump face. "No idea. Maybe there's a church somewhere that's taking in derelicts or something. He was preaching a life of poverty and how money was some sort of sin." She raised a thick arm, a fold of skin hanging over her elbow, and added, "I told him money wasn't a sin and that he had to pay his rent." She lowered her arm. "People have to eat, you know."

Sal nodded. "Of course, Gertrude. You're right. Money's important."

"Damn straight." She leaned on the doorframe, then turned back toward the house and stepped inside. "Frankie won't be back here. I need paying tenants."

"Any idea what house of God he was heading to?"

She clutched the door like it was holding her up, her face reddened with the effort.

"Something about an angel stole his heart and how he found God—and his brother. He went on about a brother, but I tuned him out."

"An angel? A brother?"

"Maybe he meant like a monk. Don't they call them brothers or something?"

"Sometimes a priest is called a father, but I don't know enough about religion to tell you who are called brothers."

"Right, a father. That's it."

Sal frowned. "What's it?"

"He was going to his father's church. Something like that. Or *her* father's church." She made to close the door, but Sal leaned forward and stopped its forward motion.

"Gertrude, one last question. Did he leave a forwarding address?"

She scrunched up her eyebrows. "Huh, no way. He knew I'd send his final bill there and eventually the rental tribunal. The man hadn't paid rent in three months."

"Oh, I'm sorry to hear that—"

The door slammed in Sal's face, making him jolt in surprise.

What the hell was Frankie up to? Not paying rent,

possibly living in a church somewhere, and stealing Bartleson's money to pay for Sal's mother's cancer treatment in Arizona.

Sal spun around, approached the sidewalk, and turned toward his car. Now that he was done, he wanted out of the area as fast as possible. If Bartleson's men were here or on their way, it would appear they hadn't seen him yet, and he didn't want to make a target of himself unnecessarily.

When he dropped into the front seat of his car and placed the gun in the glove box, his phone rang, making him jump so badly he dropped the car keys on the floor.

Call display said it was his mother.

He grabbed the keys, fired up the car, dropped it in gear, and answered the phone on the fourth ring as the vehicle started back along Prescott toward St. Clair.

"Hi, Mom," he said. "Everything okay?"

Margaret was crying. "I don't know what happened."

Sal tapped the brake and pulled over to the side of the road. "What's going on, Mom? What happened?" A sick feeling pervaded him as he wondered what Bartleson had done to his mother.

"That nurse is gone."

"What nurse, Mom?" Sal's fingers tightened on the phone, pressing it into the side of his head to make sure he heard every word.

She coughed once, gasped in a breath, coughed again, and then breathed into the phone, her breath sounding hoarse.

"The one I gave the money to so she could deposit it for me in the bank."

Sal processed what his mother was saying. The money

Frankie stole from Bartleson that she was going to use for cancer treatment was now stolen from one of the hospice nurses.

"I was going to book the flights, and …" It sounded like she sniffled into a Kleenex. "And the money wasn't there. So, I called the head nurse and found out that two days ago, on the day I gave her the money, that nurse had disappeared early from work and hadn't returned. Phone calls to her house go unanswered. Oh, Sal, what am I going to do? The people at the Mayo Clinic are expecting me."

Holy fuck, how could this be happening?

"I'll see what I can do. Don't worry, Mom, I'll find a way to fix this."

Sal hung up without saying goodbye. He couldn't stand listening to the tears of a dying cancer patient who had lost the last hope she was clinging to, all because a nurse got greedy.

"What the hell is this world coming to?" Sal asked the empty car as he started along Prescott again.

He had no idea where Frankie was or how to find him.

And he had no idea how he would help his mother find some missing nurse who made off with her money—well, Bartleson's money—but still, hers because Frankie gave it to her.

Wait, could that nurse have a connection to Bartleson?

Was the money *re*-stolen to be given back to Lorenzo?

The odds of that happening were too high to even be considered, but he had to find out.

He picked up the phone to dial the hospice in London.

He needed the missing nurse's name to track her himself.

There had to be some way to sort out this mess.

Chapter 8

THIS WOULD END SOON. Silvio would drive her and Willow back to their apartment, just as Willow had told her.

So, for the next forty-five to sixty minutes, she was willing to listen to what Lorenzo Bartleson had to say. She had grown quite curious about what was on his mind. The man had gone to great lengths to arrange this meeting—illegal lengths—but that didn't seem to bother a man like Bartleson. He lived on the other side of the law like only the ultra-rich could.

"Can I offer you a beverage?" he asked.

"I'd rather just get on with it."

Bartleson nodded slightly, then leaned back in his chair and sized her up. "You're thinner than I imagined."

"Is that a compliment?"

"Take it however you wish."

They allowed the silence to fill the gap between them, Sarah waiting for him to state his business. The security men fell back to a comfortable distance, offering them privacy and breathing room.

"As you can imagine, Sarah, I've got a unique problem that I would like to request your assistance with."

"I'm listening."

Bartleson raised his right hand and leaned his head onto it, a finger pressing up the skin at his temple. "I have a daughter. She's twenty-one-years old now and has a mind of her own—"

"That can happen with women these days."

He straightened his head, the hand dropping back to his side. "Don't misunderstand me. The conviction upon which she lives her life and her resolve is no threat to me. I see it as an asset, and I prefer her to have these qualities, these attributes."

Weren't they just talking about confident women in the police cruiser and how men find that a threat? Of course, Bartleson was listening. That's why Campbell was dead. But Bartleson was unaware that Sarah knew he'd been listening. She settled back in her chair and waited.

"Well, as I was saying, Bianca has a mind of her own, and she's decided she doesn't want to be a part of the family."

"The family? Or the family business?"

"Both."

"And why's that?"

Bartleson shrugged and brushed at something on his thigh absentmindedly. "Lack of gratitude? Misguided intentions?" His eyes met hers. "The rebellious nature of youth?"

"I'm sure you're leading up to something other than asking me to persuade your daughter to come back into the family fold, correct?"

Bartleson nodded once. "Yes, that sort of conversation will be held with me in private."

"Then why am I here?"

A slight breeze picked up and ruffled her hair, tickling her neck. She avoided scratching at it, giving Bartleson her undivided attention. The big reveal was coming, and she needed to hear every word.

"I'll speak plainly with you, Miss Roberts." He leaned forward and placed his elbows on his thighs, staring her in the eye. "I'm a family man. Always have been, always will be."

She nodded.

"Bianca is my daughter, and I want her back."

There was a moment of silence where Sarah wondered about his choice of words. This wasn't a man who misused words—they were his tools. He knew what he was saying and how he wanted to say it. But if that was the case, what did *I want her back* mean?

"Did someone abduct her?"

He frowned and leaned back in his seat to rest a hand on the rear of the patio sofa.

"Is that what you're seeing?" he asked.

Then, it all became clear.

Bianca Bartleson had gone missing, probably after running away from her controlling father and the illegal family business. Lorenzo Bartleson wanted to hire Sarah, a renowned psychic, to locate her.

"Is this an interview?" Sarah asked.

Bartleson shook his head. "No, interviews are for *potential* employees. You've already been hired."

"Oh, have I now? To do what, exactly?"

"Find my baby girl."

"She's no longer a baby."

"Forgive a father, the adoring figure of speech I've chosen to use in reference to my daughter."

"What if she doesn't want to be found?"

"That appears to be the case. When I look for someone, I always find them. With Bianca, she knows how to stay hidden."

"What else can you tell me? Did she just walk away? Has she run away, or was she taken away?"

"As far as we can tell, she organized this herself. Although, we suspect she had help. But we don't feel this is a rival family or a kidnapping, as we haven't seen any ransom demands."

"How long has she been gone?"

"Eight days now."

Sarah considered everything he was saying, then asked, "Why me?"

"I can't go to the police with this."

"You used Smith and Campbell. Why not continue in that direction?"

"They're off duty, being paid for an event I organized at Nathan Phillips Square, downtown Toronto. The Toronto Police often offer private organizations the ability to hire off-duty police officers for private security for concerts and other events of that nature. Since I have a personal relationship with Smith and Campbell—well, only Smith now—they were tasked with bringing you here. These sorts of men couldn't run a meticulous investigation into the disappearance of my daughter with any sort of efficiency or rectitude."

Sarah glanced around the gardens, taking a moment. "I can't argue with you there."

"Will you help me?"

She faced him again. "And if I don't?"

He shrugged. "I've lost my daughter. I'd hate for others to go through the same pain I'm experiencing."

Sarah jumped to her feet so fast that the chair went flying.

Men rushed in to stand beside her. She reached for the man on her right, placing a hand on his shoulder, her thumb at the base of his neck. Then she pushed inward before he had a chance to dislodge her arm, choking off his airway. She was already spinning toward the other man when a long-barreled weapon was shoved into her face.

"Stop," Bartleson shouted.

"Are you threatening my daughter?" Sarah asked without facing him, her eyes not leaving the tip of the gun aimed at her. Other men were moving in. There was no way she could post a win here.

The man to her right coughed quietly, then moved to the side to recover. The gun lowered from her face, but the man holding it remained where he was, his eyes dead, glaring at her, the weapon tight in his hand. These men were soldiers, trained for battle, always willing, always ready—killing was just removing an obstacle for them.

"Sarah," Bartleson said, imploring her to look at him.

She inhaled deeply, then faced the man.

"What you experienced today wasn't pleasant. The removal of you and your daughter from your home can be rather traumatic. But let me ask you something. It appears that you have somewhat retired from your vigilante antics over the past two years. Why's that?"

"I'm raising a daughter." Her voice was firm, with a don't-test-me tone, as she considered her options.

"As I'm sure you can understand, I can't file a missing persons report for my daughter, and my personal team of security experts hasn't been able to locate her."

"What does this have to do with me? Why come after me in such a threatening manner?"

"I want you to use your abilities to locate my daughter and return her to me. At which point, we remain friendly."

"And if I don't, you're suggesting other parents will lose their children, namely me and my daughter?"

"As mentioned a moment ago." Bartleson paused, then nodded at the man to Sarah's left. The gun came back up and pointed at her head. "You saw how easy it was for me to get to you, to your daughter. I can take Willow from you any time I choose, on any given day. Next week, next month, or next year." He snapped his fingers, his voice hardening. "Just like that, and no one will see it coming. So, if you refuse to help me find my Bianca, then you leave me a grieving father, at which point, I'd have no choice but to do the same to you."

Sarah thought of every expletive she could come up with. She considered attacking the man to her left, relieving him of his gun, and shooting Bartleson in the face, even though she knew it was a fight she couldn't win as there had to be over twenty armed security personnel on the property, yet she yearned to do it anyway. Instead, she relaxed her hands, let her arms hang loosely, and glared at Bartleson.

"As a peace offering," he said. "I'm willing to let you leave with your daughter today."

"Gee, thanks. You're being a real sport about everything."

"You will go home, think it over, and respond by the morning."

"Spell it out for me. What are my options?"

"Finding my daughter and bringing her to me is option one. Refuse, and you will lose your daughter. We can grieve together. This is your decision to make."

"That's not a decision of any kind—it's an ultimatum. Do this, or else."

"Call it what you want. Those are your choices. I'm a man who's used to getting what I want, and right now, I want my daughter back. As a parent yourself, you understand the lengths I'm willing to go to achieve that goal."

"Now you're justifying the sick terms you've laid out."

The meeting was over, and the terms were set. The security display, the elaborate pick-up, and the CAS involvement were all for show. Bartleson wanted her to understand the stakes before the meeting. He had banked on her being rattled, willing to say yes to anything he asked. Threatening Willow was his ace card, and he played it early, probably due to her lack of initial agreement to his plea for help.

"And if Bianca doesn't want to be found?" she asked.

"That's of no concern to you. I'm asking you to find her and bring her back to me. That's where your responsibility to me ends, and we forget this meeting ever took place."

"And you will kidnap my little girl, take her from me, as punishment for not helping? You're actually capable of this?"

He regarded her momentarily, then got up and moved within a foot of her, staring downward as he was half a foot taller.

"All consequences must have meaning. When one is needed, it often must reflect the mistake, the bad choice. I want you to feel the grief I'm dealing with on a daily basis if you so choose to *not* help find Bianca when you're in a unique position to help. That is putting it in a logical realm."

"Logical? No, I think that's more like putting the *psycho* in psychological."

"Cute, but however you wish to view this, I need your help and am willing to pay for it. Find Bianca within a week, and you'll receive one hundred thousand in untraceable cash. Sooner, and there will be a bonus. At the end of one week today, if there's no progress on my daughter's location, I'll assume our business arrangement has concluded, and I'll be forced to find other means of locating her. I believe you're aware of the consequences of failure now or lack of action on your part."

"Quite."

He clapped his hands once. "Then that concludes our business for the day. Silvio, please take Sarah Roberts and her daughter back to their home. Oh, and give her a cell phone with my direct line." He turned away and started up another path. "I'll be in touch, Miss Roberts. Please call me tomorrow with your answer either way. I'll be waiting."

Lorenzo Bartleson disappeared around an alcove draped in vines, four security men trailing him.

Silvio, the man with the superior knife skills, moved in beside her.

"This way." He pointed toward the side of the house where the swing set lay beyond.

Just like Willow said, they'd be leaving with Silvio within the hour. What she didn't know was how much weight this brought down on Sarah's shoulders. She'd have to call everyone and plan some sort of response.

Bartleson hadn't met Darwin, or Bruno, or even Alex. Lorenzo's security team would have a tough time with Sarah's expert fighters.

And where was Vivian?

She followed Silvio toward her daughter on the swings, thinking about Vivian's words.

Something about a decision coming and that she wasn't supposed to choose either option.

So, don't try to find Bianca Bartleson. Was that what Vivian had meant? If that was her sister's position, then why? What would happen to Willow?

They didn't want to have to move from the city to hide from the mafia. Aaron's business, Daniel, Benjamin, and Alex were all here. Even Parkman spent so much time in Toronto that he relocated permanently last year to remain close to them all.

There was no way Bartleson was getting to Willow again, and there was no way they would allow him to run her out of town.

Then how will this play out, Vivian?

There was no response.

The thought she'd had earlier in the day came back to her: There'd be bodies scattered around the city before this all came to an end.

Preferably, the bodies would be from Bartleson's mafia family, as opposed to Sarah's family.

Only time will tell.

Chapter 9

SALVATORE PREZZIE HUNG UP the phone and smashed the steering wheel with his open hand.

"Fuck," he shouted, then smacked the steering wheel again.

The hospice wouldn't give him anything over the phone. He couldn't get the nurse's name, address, or anything, which made sense but was also extremely frustrating. The woman had stolen from his mother. Sure, it was ill-gotten gains in the first place, but still. That money represented hope—survival.

Now, he had a decision to make. Should he drive back to London to go after the nurse who stole the money from his mother or continue trying to track down Frankie?

He wasn't a detective and knew nothing about finding anyone.

Sal lowered his head and rested it on the top of the steering wheel.

"Fuck," he whispered. "What the hell am I going to do?"

The nurse absconding with the money was one thing. But if Bartleson's team sent someone to reclaim the money, then his mother might be known to them and, if so, in danger. Could Frankie have been sloppy? Did he somehow lead them to his mother, and they followed the trail to the nurse?

Sal lifted his head and stared out the windshield. So many questions without answers and nowhere to go.

"Or did Bartleson locate Frankie," he whispered to himself. "Did he get him to confess that he stole the money and where he'd taken it?"

Sal stared out the windshield, his mind going blank.

Then, an idea hit him, and he wondered why he hadn't thought of it before.

He snatched up his phone and opened Facebook. Once he found Frankie's profile, he checked the last status update. A political statement about Trump, dated five days ago. So, while on the run, Frankie was staying off social media.

After a moment, he scrolled farther past a meme, then another meme with two talking mice on it. Finally, Sal got to a picture of a meal with the caption alluding to a date Frankie had been on. *My favorite meal while out with my sweetie.*

The ribs and veggies on the plate told Sal nothing about where Frankie and his sweetie had gone for dinner. He posted about being out with a woman, but no picture of her. The plate was nondescript, the food generic in that it could come from any number of restaurants in the city. The picture was posted nine days ago.

Sal scrolled farther, but all he passed were memes and small political rants. It was useless. He thought he'd be able to learn something from social media, but evidently he wouldn't.

Before setting his phone down, he thought of checking the relationship status on Facebook.

Frankie hadn't said anything about a woman in all his time riding with Sal on their nightly money collection. Why hide a woman from him?

Unless Frankie were gay, that would explain why there was no picture. Maybe Frankie was hiding it from the world.

Sal shook his head. He was no expert on human psychology, but Frankie didn't strike him as a gay man.

He moved to Frankie's *About* page and saw the relationship status was set to single. So, he was hiding whoever he was with, or perhaps the relationship was so new that he just hadn't updated his status yet.

His thumb tapped the photos tab in case a picture of his woman—or man—was stored there, but no luck. Just more photos over the past couple of years of a variety of meals, from pasta dishes to gigantic steaks. Almost forty percent of the food images were of that ribs meal.

Frustrated, Sal scrolled to the end and was about to close the Facebook application when something caught his eye. He opened a picture and then enlarged it.

Beside one of the ribs meal photos was a menu. Zoomed in, the name of the restaurant was quite clear.

Tony's Ribs and Steakhouse.

Wasn't that the one on Dundas and Dixie in Mississauga?

He quickly brought up a current picture of Frankie and took a screenshot of it, then got the car in gear and started for the steakhouse.

Maybe someone there would remember Frankie.

Especially if the ribs were his favorite and he frequented the place. And if they remembered him, if they knew him, they might recall his meal last week when he was with someone.

Finding Frankie could potentially save Sal's life with Bartleson.

Finding the nurse could potentially save his mother's life at the Mayo Clinic.

What seemed of paramount interest to him was saving his own life first. That way, he could work on new options for his mother.

Providing she was still alive when all of this was over.

Every breath he took was a blessing, a gift. He was supposed to die under Mancuso's blade last night. The thought sent a shiver through him.

At least there was a consolation if he didn't find Frankie and couldn't save himself. He could use Diego's gun and kill Silvio Mancuso before leaving this wretched place.

There was no way he wanted to die without at least easing the world's suffering somewhat by taking out Silvio and sending him to Hell. It would probably be a blessing.

Like a get-out-of-jail-free card, a pass into Heaven.

He could only hope ...

Chapter 10

Sarah got Willow settled in for a nap, then stared at her daughter as Willow's tiny eyes slowly closed with fatigue. Sarah marveled at how well Willow had coped with her tumultuous morning. The mafia abducted them, a cop was murdered and then delivered back to their apartment like nothing more than a Sunday drive took place.

On the ride back to Mississauga, Silvio rarely spoke, and when he did, he used soft, caring tones, like the man had a heart. He explained the cell phone was a burner with only two numbers in it. One was Silvio's if she needed help with anything, and the other was Lorenzo's direct line. That call wouldn't be vetted—Lorenzo would pick it up himself.

If and when Sarah found Bianca, she was to call Lorenzo first, then he would delegate resources to pick up his child.

Sarah mumbled her compliance to get out of the car with Willow safely. Then she'd make a plan.

Lorenzo gave her until the morning to make a decision—

which she'd already made. By then, her daughter would be in a safe place.

Sarah left the bedroom door ajar as she slipped into the living room, grabbed her phone, dialed Aaron, and stepped out onto the balcony to avoid waking Willow. She stared back at the coffee table where Lorenzo's cell phone sat and closed the glass doors to cut off all noise from the apartment.

Aaron answered on the first ring. "Sarah?"

"Aaron—" Emotion cut off her voice. She covered her mouth with a hand. The morning's events hit her all at once.

"Sarah, are you okay?" His office chair squeaked as she imagined him sitting up.

Did having a child and being a mother make a woman *even* more emotional? She'd been through so much worse than this morning, yet on some level, she still couldn't believe what had just happened, not to mention the ultimatum Lorenzo gave her.

"Aaron," she said, finding her voice. "We all have to talk."

"What happened?"

She stared out over the busy traffic of Mississauga. "It's a long story. How fast can we gather everyone?"

"Everyone? As in me and the teachers?"

"Everyone we know. Parkman, the teachers, you, Bruno, Disco, or anyone else."

"Shit, you need an army or something?"

"It's looking that way."

A fast squeak of his office chair signaled Aaron had gotten up to pace. A door closed. "You want to tell me what's going on?"

Sarah placed her free hand over her eyes, then recited her morning adventure with Bartleson.

After calming Aaron down on the details regarding Willow, she reminded him that Willow was having her nap and everything was still fine—for today.

"Now I see why you want everybody." His tone had darkened, gone colder. "Who is this fucking guy, anyway? Who goes around threatening mothers with the loss of their children?"

"Psychopaths. It meant nothing to him. No expression on his face. No wonder his daughter got out of there."

"What are you going to do, Sarah?"

"That's why we all need to meet. I need assurances Willow will be safe. Then I'll refuse his demand, and we'll find another way to deal with this man and his organization. I won't live on the run or looking over my shoulder, nor will I do what some rich mobster demands of me."

"Our options are limited. None of them sound good."

"Would you rather have me locate his daughter, Bianca Bartleson?"

"That's not a bad idea—"

"Aaron!"

"No, listen. Find Bianca, make a hundred grand, and our lives go back to normal. Then, privately meet with Bianca and help her escape for real this time. Fake her death or something."

"No."

"No what?"

"No, I won't do it. On principle. Men like Lorenzo need to understand they don't *always* get their own way."

"Okay, you're right. Just throwing out options."

"I don't need options, Aaron. I need assurances Willow will be safe. When can we all meet?"

He paused a moment. "Let me make some calls. I think Bruno is in Toronto, but only Darwin knows where he is."

"Italy's seven hours ahead, so Darwin will have finished dinner by now."

"I'll call him and get back to you."

"Thanks, honey." She choked off a sob.

"Don't worry, Sarah. No one's getting to Willow."

"I knew that. They'd all die by my hand first. I just don't like any of this. And to not know who is real and who isn't. Those cops were real cops. How do you *not* go with them? The CAS worker was real. Lorenzo is powerful, with a massive reach."

"And you still want to do it your way?"

She raised her gaze to the clouds, having no real idea what she wanted to do but knowing that the best plan was always to do the hard thing first. That, and never compromise her principles. She would never work for a man like Lorenzo, and if his twenty-one-year-old daughter took off for whatever reason, then that was her business. Everything Sarah knew and understood told her to go how she'd planned.

The only reservation was Lorenzo's ability to retaliate against her and her child. Due to his massive power and influence and his threat to take Willow from her, she had to hit back just as hard, with or without Vivian.

A plan was already forming.

"Sarah?"

"Yeah?"

"You still want to do it your way?"

"There's no other way. Gather everyone. Meeting tonight at the dojo for six. Then we go after Lorenzo with everything we've got."

Aaron didn't respond for a moment, then he finally said, "I'm in. Fuck him. Let's take him down."

"Everything we've got."

"Everything, baby."

She clicked off the phone and started researching the man.

It was important to learn about your enemy.

A man who would be dead or in jail by the end of the week.

Chapter 11

Salvatore found a spot to park near the back door of the steakhouse in case there was a need to leave quickly. There shouldn't be, but one could never be too cautious.

When he opened the car door, the smell of the steaks and ribs cooking from the kitchen hit him, twisting his stomach in hunger. Before driving out to London that morning, he hadn't eaten since the McDonald's breakfast. Too bad he didn't have time to sit and have a full meal. He could sure use it.

Inside the front entrance, he slowed to stare at a wall of pictures depicting happy families and children celebrating some event in the restaurant. This was another world to him, an unfamiliar world. He had his mother, and he had issues. Having lost his mother early and then being taken in by Margaret, he'd struggled with relationships, not having a girlfriend longer than two or three months. Getting married and having kids wasn't in Sal's future, and he knew that and had learned to accept it. Seeing entire families laughing and carrying on always mystified him, though. How easy it all looked for them.

"Table for one?" a woman asked.

He jolted and spun toward her.

"Oh, sorry, I didn't mean to scare you," she said, a smile hidden by professionalism. She was trying so hard not to laugh at his surprise.

"It's okay," he said. "I'm not here to eat. In fact"—he withdrew his cell phone and opened the picture of Frankie— "I was wondering if you knew this man."

Sal leaned closer so the brunette could catch a good look at the photo on his phone. She wore the drab brown uniform well, tight-fitting around her waist and breasts. Although she was too young for him—in the eighteen-year-old range—she was easy on the eyes. Her nametag said Steph.

"What's this about?" she asked, skepticism in her voice.

"That's Frankie. He's a friend of mine who's gone missing. Didn't show up for work the past few days, and now the boss is looking for him. I said I'd check around his usual haunts." Her eyes told him she knew something, but she was waiting to be convinced he wasn't *after* him instead of genuinely looking for him.

"Are you a cop?"

Sal shook his head and offered her a warm smile. "Nothing like that." He slipped his phone away. "Just a dear friend. So worried about him."

She nodded.

"Have you ever seen him? Based on his Facebook updates, he comes here often and enjoys the ribs and—"

"—veggies," she finished for him.

Sal's eyes widened. "So you know him?"

"Everyone here does. He's a huge tipper."

"When was the last time he was here?"

"About a week ago, I guess."

"Was he with anyone?"

She shrugged. "Can't really recall. I think so, though. A pretty lady."

Okay, so not gay. Makes sense.

"You didn't serve his table?"

She shook her head and returned the menu with the pile on a side counter. "I was dealing with a twenty-group birthday party that day." She moved beside Sal and pointed at the pictures on the wall he'd stopped at when he walked in. "That one."

Sal took in the photos tacked to the board, studying one after another. Kids were caught mid-laugh, cake and foodstuff smeared on their faces, candles lit on the cake, and presents piled haphazardly in front of the birthday boy.

"Frankie's table was one over from this group, and he gave the birthday boy a hundred-dollar bill. Such a generous man."

Sal thought about the money Frankie gave his mother. "Indeed, the man's generous to a fault."

"Oh, there," Steph said curtly, pointing at a specific picture. "That's him right there. Our staff took these pics. If we studied them long enough, I knew he'd probably be in one of them."

Salvatore leaned in closer to examine the photo she pointed at and saw the back of Frankie's head, the edge of a slight profile. What was quite clear, though, was the face of the smiling woman Frankie was sitting with. Frankie's new girlfriend, the one he hadn't told his bagman partner about, was having the time of her life, her face lit up by the fascination she had watching the kids' party.

Salvatore would know that woman's face anywhere.

And now he knew why Frankie had disappeared.

Because his new girlfriend was Bianca Bartleson, the daughter of a powerful mob boss named Lorenzo Bartleson. Rumor had it she disappeared a week ago under suspicious circumstances, and Bartleson was looking for her.

"I'm going to need this picture," he said, his tone firm.

Steph frowned and stepped back. "I'm sorry, we can't let you have a photo from that wall. The restaurant owns them. It's against our policy."

"This man is missing." He jabbed a finger at the photo. "This woman, too."

"Well," Steph said, her voice taking on an indignant tone. "When the police come looking for them, I'm sure we can give them the photo."

Sal crossed his arms and spread his legs. "I'll need you to go get your manager. I want a word with him."

"Her."

Sal frowned. "What?"

"The manager is a her."

He released his arms and gestured toward the back. "Then go get *her*."

Steph rushed away, obviously upset now.

"Her? Him?" he whispered to himself. "Who the fuck cared?"

Salvatore snatched the photo off the corkboard, slipped it

into his jacket pocket, then quickly exited and ran to his car. Frankie was either dead, his body at the bottom of a river, or Bartleson's people were still looking for him.

No wonder Silvio was ordered to kill all the people involved in the bagman job. The accountant guy, the women who counted the money, all dead.

Bartleson wasn't looking for a skimmer and executing everyone until he found him.

He was looking for his daughter.

And a man like Bartleson would stop at nothing to find his baby girl, his blood.

He'd murder everyone in his path, even if they had nothing to do with it.

And Salvatore was still on that list, a list he endeavored to get his name off as soon as possible.

Chapter 12

Willow woke up over two hours later, and after eating a light lunch, Sarah took her in a taxi to the dojo, where Aaron had called everyone to join them. As it turned out, Bruno—going by the name Steven Miller now—was in Toronto on a surveillance job of some sort for Darwin and could easily put that job on hold for a few days to help them out.

Parkman drove in from Oshawa in the late afternoon, and the three teachers, Benjamin, Daniel, and Alex, were already there.

Aaron closed the dojo early and canceled the evening classes. A note on the door said it was due to a family emergency.

The phone rang several times in the other room, then got cut off and went to a prerecorded message that they'd be open again in a few days.

Sarah started talking, filling everyone in on what had happened with Willow present as she'd endured the abduction, too. When she was ready to tell them about Lorenzo's threats, Benjamin took Willow out to the main part of the gym and played a game of catch with her on the blue mats.

"And that's about it," Sarah said. "Lorenzo is expecting my answer by tomorrow morning."

Parkman placed his hands behind his head, a toothpick fidgeting back and forth in his mouth. "Have you decided on a play here?"

Sarah nodded. "Yes."

He leaned forward and placed his hands on the table. "What is it?"

"Bruno," she said, turning to the large man. "I need you to take our daughter and keep her safe. Can you do that?"

Bruno nodded, his entire massive bulk jolting with the enthusiasm of that one nod. "I'm honored. I'll keep her safe and protect her with my life. Nothing will happen to that little girl as long as she's with me."

"I know that, but you can't tell a soul where she is. No one in this room can know, and that includes me and Aaron."

"Understood." He nodded once more.

"We'll be in touch through Darwin when it's over."

Parkman was nodding. Then Daniel was. Only Aaron didn't seem to like it, but she would deal with him.

"Next step is to hit Lorenzo where it hurts."

Bruno raised a hand like he was in school.

She nodded at him. "Speak freely."

"I don't want to hear this part. If my job has been assigned, I'd prefer to take Willow and go into hiding until I hear from you through Darwin."

Sarah scanned the faces in the room. "Anyone have any issues with that?" Normally, she just went with what she'd decided. But something told her to include Aaron as often as possible—Willow was his daughter, too.

No one spoke up.

She nodded at Bruno. "Give me a moment with her. Then take her."

Bruno pushed his bulk up from the table and started for the door. "I'll be at the back of the building when you're ready." At the door, he stopped and stared at Aaron, his eyes wide and determined. "I swear to you, Aaron, as Willow's father, your daughter means more to me than life. I thank you and Sarah for this honor and will swear upon my life that she'll be safe. That, and I don't ever want Darwin coming after me."

Aaron stood and nodded at him. "Go with God, my friend. Keep her close."

"I will do as you say." The giant of a man slipped through the door, bending slightly to avoid hitting his head, then was gone.

"Fuck," Sarah said. "Where does he come from? Reminded me of a *Game of Thrones* episode or something."

"He's from another era for sure, but just what we need right now."

"Of this, I have no doubt. Actually, we always need Bruno."

Sarah left the room and found Willow playing on the mats with a few rubber balls, Benjamin watching over her.

"Hey, honey." Sarah lowered to her knees. "We need you to visit our friend Bruno for a few days."

Willow set down the balls and then glanced up at her mother.

"I know." She smiled and got to her feet. "Ice cream first, Buno thinking. Then Netflix for the rest of the day in a building under the floor." She hugged Sarah. "Don't worry, Mommy. Buno feels safe under the floor. I'm safe there."

Sarah held her daughter an extra few moments, then pulled her back and stared into her eyes, knowing Bruno's underground bunker/basement was what Willow was referring to.

"How far ahead can you see?" she asked.

"Up to thirty minutes. Less sometimes."

"Then how do you know you'll be okay there? Is someone telling you that? You know, like how my sister talks to me?"

She shook her head, her pretty hair lifting upward.

"Because you're sad, silly. Want you happy. And I …" She glanced over Sarah's shoulder. "I always safe with Mr. Buno. He's big man, a bear." She made a claw with her tiny hand and a short roar, swiping the air with her delicate fingers.

Sarah hugged her once more, then took her daughter's hand and walked to the back door, where she handed her off to Bruno, cursing the name Lorenzo Bartleson under her breath. Losing one day with Willow was already too much. The thought of not seeing her for several days, maybe even a week, made her crazy with worry and anger. They had to attack Lorenzo and his people hard and fast and get this done so Willow could come home.

"When this is over, we'll contact Darwin," Sarah said,

her throat almost closing with emotion. "Darwin will reach out to you. Then bring her back to us. And stay online."

Bruno nodded, then slipped out the back, Willow in tow. The door closed hard, making Sarah jump even though she watched it close.

After taking a moment to collect herself, she rejoined everyone in the kitchen, ensuring her tears had been wiped dry.

Benjamin had reclaimed his seat at the table.

"Next phase is going after Lorenzo Bartleson with everything we've got," Aaron was saying.

"Any ideas?" Parkman asked, glancing around the table at everyone.

Sarah cleared her throat, then leaned on the back of her empty chair. "Hit him in the pocketbook. Make him come to us. When he does, we end this. I remove the threat, the target he placed on our backs."

"Okay," Daniel said. "How do we go after his pocketbook?"

"The Lorenzo Bartleson Group is involved in construction and strip clubs, and he owns several restaurants. Undoubtedly, he's got his hands in unions, forcing tenders to go his way and underpaying his employees at construction sites. The strip clubs are a cash business. He probably launders most of his money through them, and the restaurants are also a way to launder cash, although less so."

Parkman whistled, his toothpick shooting from his mouth. He tried to catch it but missed. It hit the table and slipped off the other side.

"How the hell do you know so much about this guy

already?" He asked. "That Vivian in your ear?"

Sarah shook her head. "Google. When Willow napped this afternoon, I researched the man's name and company. Read newspaper articles on him, arrests that never stuck, everything I could on the guy to see who we were dealing with."

"So," Alex said. Everyone turned his way. "What are we hitting first?"

"Not so fast." Benjamin raised a hand. "Guys, we're talking about a mobster, a powerful man here. Going after him could cause untold damage to us, where we live, this business. We can't predict how he'll retaliate." By his tone, it was evident he didn't want any part in attacking a man as powerful as Bartleson.

"One thing we can predict," Sarah said, her tone gentle, "is what Bartleson will do if we don't hit back. He'll try to take Willow."

"What about helping the man find his daughter?" Benjamin asked.

For some reason, that being the easiest solution, the least antagonistic, no one had asked Sarah why they weren't going to help the man. Aaron had, but not in front of the others.

"No," Alex said. "Not after giving Sarah an ultimatum. Fuck him."

"I agree," Parkman added. "You want help, you ask nicely. Threatening to abduct Willow to teach Sarah a lesson is not only wrong, it requires a response—something painful."

The tension in the room elevated, but no one attempted to quell it.

"My point is," Benjamin continued as if he hadn't heard what the others had said. "Going after someone like this might end up causing a war. This could bring other parties to our doorstep."

"A war?" Alex echoed. "Then we keep fighting. No one touches Willow." He glanced at Sarah. "Or you."

She smiled at him, then offered a soft nod of gratitude.

Benjamin made a sound of derision. "I'm not suggesting —"

"We know," Sarah said, tapping his shoulder. "Going after Lorenzo might be the earthquake that causes a tsunami, we might not walk away from. I figured all you were saying was, don't bite off more than we can chew, and make sure we're aware that some of what we're about to do might have far-reaching consequences."

"Yeah. That." Benjamin leaned back, rubbing his thighs like he was nervous.

The man had changed over the years, wanting less to do with their exploits. And who could blame him? He'd been shot more than any of them and always seemed to be struggling to keep up with whatever fight they were involved with. The past two years off had been a blessing for Benjamin. He'd even gained a little weight and was settling into the evening classes at the dojo, giving the others more time off and Aaron more time at home with her and Willow.

"And what *I'm* saying is," Alex spoke up. "We don't have a choice. We hit, and we hit hard. And we keep hitting until all threats evaporate."

Parkman nodded. "With men like Lorenzo, there's no other way. Or you give in and do what you're told. The problem with giving in is they own you. The only way out after that is death." He held up a hand, index finger raised. "But going after Lorenzo until the threat evaporates means only one thing."

"Death or imprisonment for Bartleson," Sarah suggested.

Parkman nodded. "Jumping off this bridge means you fall to the water or the concrete. One could hurt upon impact. The other could kill you. There are no half-measures, no pullback. As of tonight or tomorrow, it's a war, and the other side has to be decimated to win." He glanced at Sarah, then Alex, and finally Aaron. "We could take losses."

Alex nodded. "I'm all in. This is the only way. We're survivors, and our business and vehicles are insured. Have at 'em."

It was so good to see Alex playing a key role in these discussions. He'd been lost for almost a year after getting trapped in an attempted murder plot. Lost in the sense of being depressed, quiet, and withdrawn. But they fought for him, though. Kept involving him, pushing him from his self-imposed internal prison. There were times she wondered if the old Alex was still in there, but over the past six to eight months, he'd opened back up. Willow helped. Hanging out with Willow made him smile, something none of them had seen in years.

"Parkman's right," Sarah said. "We can't give in, even if we wanted to. If I could just say no, that would be the end of it. But I can't. Bartleson made that abundantly clear." Aaron touched her forearm. She leaned into his comforting touch and continued. "He threatened to take Willow. That can't go unchecked. Not only does no one get the right to do that to a mother, but no one does that to me and my daughter. Now, Willow's safe with Bruno, so we have to hit him hard, set up a meeting, take him out, or have him arrested or something. We have to end this and have two days to do it."

"Two days?" Benjamin gasped.

Alex was already getting to his feet. He paused, then sat back down, his knees bouncing with anticipation.

"We hit him tonight and tomorrow morning. Then I call him and set up a meeting. This is done in twenty-four to forty-eight hours. I'm not living with this threat over my head any longer than I have to. And I want my baby girl back."

Aaron squeezed her arm, then let his hand drop. "I totally agree. Let's get some food and start discussing the businesses we'll hit, how we'll hit them, and what would make a dent in how he does his business."

"Burn them," Alex whispered. "Burn them all." Alex got to his feet again. "To the fucking ground."

Parkman frowned. "Tell us more. What are you thinking?"

Alex glanced over at him. "Burn them all. Arson. The construction sites go down. Burn the strip clubs at four in the morning when they're empty. I say we take out his businesses tonight. See how he feels in the morning."

"Not bad." Aaron nodded. "But I can't think on an empty stomach. Food, then more talk."

Sarah nodded, and everyone pushed back their chairs to get up from the table.

Aaron stepped out of the kitchen while Parkman held Sarah back to hug her. He whispered in her ear that they'd fix this and get Willow back. She hugged him tight, suppressing the tears that sprang to her eyes.

"Hey," Aaron shouted from the front room. "What the fuck?"

Sarah and Parkman pushed apart and ran out of the kitchen, Sarah in front.

Five men in suits stood outside the dojo, three cupping their hands on the glass to look inside. One of the men shook the locked door.

"Could be Bartleson's men," Sarah said. "More intimidation."

"We're closed," Aaron shouted.

The man knocked, then waved at another guy dressed in combat gear. He held a small device in his hand.

"Hey, what are they doing?" Aaron started toward the door, but a loud thump stopped him ten feet from it.

The deadbolt shot from the door, and then it popped open several inches.

The men in suits filed inside, spreading out to stand shoulder to shoulder.

A whirl of wind slipped past Sarah, and without thinking, she lashed out, grabbing Alex's arm just in time to stop him.

"Wait," she whispered into his ear.

Alex stared back at her with a fierce glare of violence.

"Don't," she said under her breath. "Let's ask questions first."

The tension in his forearm eased, and she let him go. He remained standing beside her.

"Sarah Roberts," one of the men said, his voice loud, commanding. He was the same one who'd tried the door and ordered it opened by the man in combat gear.

"Who wants to know?" she shouted back at him.

The man slipped a hand inside his jacket and then produced a leather wallet.

Alex sidestepped in front of Sarah when the man's hand disappeared in his jacket. Even though Aaron, Parkman, and Daniel would all die for her, Alex had always been her self-appointed security officer, putting himself bodily in front of her.

"Alex," Sarah said, caution in her voice. "Remain calm."

She felt his urge to move toward the group of men and had to assuage his temptation to violence.

"Call your dogs off, Sarah," the man said, flipping open his wallet. He'd seen Aaron and Parkman moving closer and Alex pulling on Sarah's restraining grasp. "Wouldn't want everyone in jail while you're trying to deal with Bartleson on your own."

Shadows moved across the windows on the street behind the wall of men. Sarah counted at least seven fully armed men on the sidewalk.

"I've got half a dozen men at the back of the building, too. No one leaves until we talk, Sarah. Just listen to what I have to say." He stepped forward. Alex lowered his center of gravity. "Stay calm." The man moved once more. "I'm Special Agent Max Hartman with the FBI, and I'm here to discuss Lorenzo Bartleson with Sarah." He showed his ID in a semi-circle, waving it for everyone to see. "There may be a way to deal with this man that'll make all of us happy."

Chapter 13

What Salvatore Prezzie had found out about Frankie and Bianca must be enough to get his life back. Information was valuable and came with a price in Bartleson's world. What if the price of telling him that his daughter was with Frankie was enough to save Sal's life?

Sal had nothing else, no other play. He couldn't investigate shit on his own. How the hell would he find Frankie and Bianca when Bartleson had unlimited funds and resources?

It was time to reach out to Bartleson.

But how?

Salvatore mulled that over and then came up with a plan. He drove downtown to Queen Street, parked and slipped several coins into a meter, then rummaged in the glove box for a roll of tape. When he couldn't find one, he shoved Diego's gun in the back of his pants and started up the street to a small hardware store. Inside, he bought a roll of silver duct tape, then strode back up the street to Johnny's Bar and Grill, one of Bartleson's restaurants. He would tell the waiter who he was and that he had to speak with Bartleson. Someone would call Bartleson to set up a meeting. Then, he'd have dinner while he waited for the calls to take place.

Once inside the restaurant, they seated him and brought him a menu. He browsed it, his stomach in knots. He could never go through with this in another world, in another place. A week ago, there was no way he could imagine this working. Even going through with it was on another level for him.

And as much as Sal's life was forfeit to these people, he now possessed valuable information. Sharing it might just save his life.

He set down the menu and looked around the quiet, dimly lit restaurant. There was no other way, was there? He didn't want to die, but he also couldn't spend his life on the run.

The waiter came over, took his order, then relieved him of the menu.

Sal inhaled a couple of deep breaths, steeled himself for what he had to do, then pushed back his chair, got up from the table, and went to the men's room.

Once inside, he secured the door and dropped to his knees. He'd recalled that this bathroom had cabinet doors under the sink. Neither of them were locked. Inside, he found the usual supplies for the cleaning staff. Brushing aside the Windex and paper towels, he leaned down to look up under the sink.

Just as he suspected, there was a cavity at the base of the

sink bowl where a hidden gun would remain hidden—until he wanted it back.

Someone knocked as soon as he yanked a strip from the duct tape.

"Almost done," he said, cutting the tape with his teeth.

After reeling out three strips, he placed Diego's weapon up under the counter, set it as high as it would go against the belly of the sink on the right side, then leaned in with his other hand and pushed the duct tape onto it, pressing down on either end of the tape to secure the weapon to the underside of the sink.

Once all three pieces of tape were affixed to the weapon, he tugged on the barrel. It was locked firmly in place. It wouldn't move until he peeled back the tape.

To double-check it was high enough and out of sight, he closed and reopened the cupboard doors under the sink, staring in at the cleaning products. Then he replaced the Windex and the paper towels.

Someone knocked again, startling him.

"I'll be right out," he said, his tone harsh.

He leaned down until he was level with the sink but still couldn't see the edge of the tape as the weapon was secured into the cavity between the sink's side and the cabinet's outer wall.

They knocked again, this time much harder. Obviously, someone had to go.

"Holy fuck," he whispered to himself.

He was about to flush the toilet to make it sound like he'd been busy doing what he was supposed to do when he heard a key sliding into the door on the other side.

"Hey," he shouted, lunging for the door handle as it turned.

The door opened so fast that his hand smacked it, cracking several of his knuckles.

"What the fuck, man," Salvatore shouted, his voice raised in alarm.

A man pushed his way in, shoving Sal to the floor. Another man entered. Before he understood what was happening, one of the men wrapped his arm behind his back, and another wrapped around his neck.

Sal fought and tried to protest, but his airways were restricted, and all that came out was a whiny rasp. His hands grasped the thick forearm, cutting off his airflow, but it was useless. The man's arm was robot-strong.

The final struggle in Sal was to breathe. He thrashed out, thought about the weapon he'd just stashed, and wished he'd still had it. Things would be vastly different if he did.

One of the men moved in front of him as the bathroom door closed. The man lowered his center of gravity and drove a fist into Sal's gut.

Any air he still had shot out of his nostrils. Luckily, the arm around his throat relaxed enough that he could draw in more oxygen because the room around him had darkened at the edges and was wavering.

"Calm down," the man behind him said. "Stop squirming so much."

In his panic to breathe, Sal had fought hard. He had no idea who these guys were or why they barged in and attacked him. All he wanted to do was curl up on the floor and breathe as his stomach ached from the blow.

"Someone wants to talk with you," the man who'd punched him said, moving in close enough that Sal could smell the man's last meal with each gasp of air he snatched.

"Check him for weapons," the man said.

Hands roamed over Sal's pants, crotch, and ankles. After a moment, the search over, the man nodded at the others, and the arm around his neck eased more until it slipped away.

Sal almost dropped to the floor. If it weren't for the man in front of him, he would've dropped, his legs too wobbly to hold him.

Who the hell would send three thugs into a bathroom to rough him up and tell him they wanted to talk with him? It had to be Silvio "the butcher" Mancuso. Or maybe it was Bartleson himself. If so, how had they found him? Were they tracking him all this time, following him?

"Prezzie," the man said.

He grabbed the side of Sal's face and jerked his head around to stare at him.

Holding Sal's ears, the man said, "We're going to head back into the restaurant. There's a table at the back. It's the only table with people. You good with that? You understand what I've told you?"

Sal's ability to breathe had greatly improved. He tried to say *yes*, but only a small grunt escaped his lips.

"Nod if you agree."

Sal nodded.

"Good," the man said, using his right hand to straighten Sal's hair. "See, we're getting along."

When the man released Sal, he was happy to be able to remain on his feet.

"There's one more thing we'd like to clear up, Salvatore Prezzie," the man said.

Sal moved to the side to lean on the wall. He caught a glimpse of himself in the mirror and didn't like what he saw —a white ghost of a man, eyes rimmed in red.

He nodded for the man to continue.

"We didn't hear a toilet flush." The man smiled like he was in on the secret. "Tell me, what have you been doing in here for so long?"

In a panic, Sal remembered the duct tape roll. Where the hell did he set the roll after using it? He couldn't glance down at the sink in case they followed his gaze, saw the roll, and asked what he had been taping.

Sal blinked, willing his eyes to stay on the man's face. When he tried to speak, he coughed. Then he tried again.

"I felt sick."

"Oh, right." The man laughed. The two men behind Sal laughed with him. "Like last night when you killed Diego? Sick like that night?"

They were going to kill him.

He was sure of it now. He'd made a fatal error somewhere. Bartleson's men were here. They'd followed him, or he happened to choose the one restaurant in all of Toronto where Silvio Mancuso was out for an evening meal with his cronies, pals from murder-by-knife school, where all hitmen are taught the tools of the trade.

"I was able to hold it in," Sal said when the laughter calmed somewhat.

The man slapped his shoulder. "Stop," he said. "You're killing me."

There was a short pause as the three men snapped their heads upward to look at each other, and then they all burst into a ruckus of laughter.

"'Killing me,'" one of the men repeated behind him.

Sal entertained the idea of falling to the floor, opening the cabinet door under the sink, and snatching the gun back. He was dead anyway and didn't think they'd let him get the gun and fire three times before stopping him, but at least he could try.

After several minutes, they calmed down enough to stand straight and adjust their jackets.

"Okay, Prezzie, we're going to be civilized now." He held back another short burst of laughter. One of the men behind him sounded like he hiccupped a laugh. "And we're going back out into the restaurant, where I'll guide you to a table. Do you understand?"

Sal nodded.

The man shook his head, a wide smile on his face. For some reason, that one comment had these guys in stitches. If Sal got the chance, he would be *killing them*. Then they'd see who had the last laugh.

"I need to hear it."

"Hear what?" Sal asked, his voice still raspy but better.

"That you understand what I said."

"Yes." Sal nodded. "I do."

"Great." He slapped him on the shoulder again. "Then let's go out and have our little chat."

The man opened the door and shoved Sal out in front of him. From over his shoulder, he heard one man whisper, *killing me*, to the other guys. Like school boys, they giggled up the hallway until they stepped back into the main restaurant.

Most of the tables had been cleared—even the table Sal had been sitting at. Near the rear exit sign, five men sat sipping beers.

One of the men shoved him from behind. "Keep walking. Last table at the back."

Johnny's Bar and Grill was a decent-looking establishment, with dark wooden tables and comfortable chairs. Today, it looked foreboding, dark, and scary. On the way through the tables, meandering left and right toward the back table where Lorenzo Bartleson and his number one hitman, Silvio Mancuso, waited, Sal wondered if this was where he would die.

How could life go this way and that way, up and down, lessons learned, mistakes made, and ultimately lead him to a restaurant on Queen Street where he would die at the hands of a mobster, a criminal? How was that fair?

Silvio gestured at an empty chair opposite Bartleson.

Sal moved to it, hesitated, then sat.

"So," Bartleson said, staring him down. "You got away with it."

Sal opened his mouth to protest, but nothing came out, so he closed it. He wondered if he'd piss himself, shit himself, or just vomit on all of them as they tortured and killed him.

"We know it wasn't you who stole from me," Bartleson said. "We know you weren't skimming."

Sal inhaled shallow breaths. Was that a good thing? Was he going to live through this?

Hope was so fickle. You grasp at it even in the most

hopeless of times, begging for more of it, even though, rationally, you know there's no hope.

"But we also know you killed Diego." Bartleson leaned forward, his expression hardening, his eyes aflame with hatred and anger. "For Diego's death, you'll pay."

In his muddled brain, a ray of hope came to him, a glimmer of a chance.

Salvatore Prezzie knew what to do. The plan that would get him back to the bathroom, back to the gun.

It could work. He wondered how many he'd kill before they got him.

Chapter 14

SARAH STARED AT THE intruders as Agent Hartman put away his ID. At first, she figured they were just more hired thugs on Bartleson's payroll, but there were so many of them. How could that be? And for what reason? He'd already made his point and was giving her until the morning to consider his ultimatum.

"Sarah?" Hartman said. "We should talk."

He stepped forward, and then Alex moved.

Aaron shouted at Alex to cease and desist, but it was almost too late.

In a blur, Alex slid around Daniel and stopped less than one foot from Agent Hartman as the man stepped backward. Other agents behind Hartman raised their weapons.

"Easy," Hartman said, his hands raised. "We didn't come here to fight. We came to talk."

"ID," Alex said. "I need to examine it."

"I showed you the ID—"

"Show it again," Parkman said from behind Sarah. "Or get the fuck out." He moved closer to her.

They had all been so protective of her over the years, but now that she was a mother, she felt their protection of her had multiplied a hundred times. Like she wasn't allowed to fight or even argue with anyone anymore. There was something about it that felt comforting while denying her a voice.

"Show the fucking ID to Alex," Sarah said, stepping forward. "Unless you're afraid of any sort of close scrutiny. In which case, fuck off the way you came in."

Hartman released a nervous chuckle while easing out the ID. He handed it to Alex, who examined it closely, then after a moment, he handed it to Parkman, who also examined it closely. Parkman nodded at Sarah, Alex nodded, then the ID was back in Hartman's hands, and Alex moved off to the side, keeping a wary eye on the men with weapons as they lowered them again.

"Sarah, is there somewhere private we can talk?"

"Right here works. But first, tell us what the FBI's doing in Canada. How is it that you're even carrying a weapon on Canadian soil? Convince us that you're not working for Bartleson."

Hartman let out another short chuckle. It seemed that was his response to everything.

"Working for Bartleson?" He repeated her words in a higher pitch. "Clearly, you're joking."

Sarah glared at him, hands on her hips. Only Alex moved, but it was hardly noticeable. The little fucker was always getting into some position or another, analyzing an attack strategy he created in his head. Sarah was convinced he could disarm all of the men at the front of the dojo single-handedly and hospitalize at least half of them in the process.

"It's quite obvious to us, Mr. Agent Man," Sarah said, "that you aren't here to talk. So, get out of our place of business. You're not welcome."

Hartman glanced around the dojo. "Sarah, what I've come to discuss with you must be done privately."

"This is as private as you're going to get. Start talking, or leave."

Hartman's face grew serious. He stopped staring at everyone else and zeroed in on Sarah. "You met with Lorenzo Bartleson earlier."

"So? Why do you care?"

"I care because a cop—"

"—was murdered on Bartleson's front lawn," a woman finished for him.

A dark-haired woman stepped in behind the men in combat gear. She strode up to Hartman, nodded slightly, then stepped by him, moving up to Aaron, who tensed. Even Daniel moved closer to Aaron as Alex was still sizing up the armed men by the front windows.

They knew about Officer Campbell's death already?

"Aaron Stevens," the woman said. "So good to finally meet you."

The woman turned and took in Parkman. It was obvious to Sarah that this woman was in charge. She suspected Hartman was supposed to break the ice, offer a deal, or get them into a dialog of some sort. Then, she would arrive and seal everything up. But Hartman wasn't getting anywhere, so she entered early.

After a moment, her gaze left Parkman, moved to Daniel, and then over to Alex on the other side of the room. Alex regarded her with a wary eye before refocusing on his targets in case a fight of any sort broke out.

Finally, the woman stared at Sarah, her eyes moving up and down until she met Sarah's gaze.

"Sarah Roberts."

"What a lovely show you're putting on." Sarah moved several steps toward her. "Grand entrance, but who the hell are you?"

The woman went for her ID, and Parkman and Daniel formed a wall in front of Sarah.

"My ID," the woman said, her hand stopping inside her jacket. "I'm just reaching for my ID. We actually are the FBI. We've created a task force, working with several local agencies to stop the Bartleson Group. We're here with special permission from the Canadian government." Her hand came out of her jacket with a small wallet, which she flipped open. Her FBI ID was plainly evident from where Sarah stood.

Parkman and Daniel moved back to where they had been the moment before.

"I'm Hartman's partner, Special Agent Tracie DeOcampo." She offered Sarah a warm smile. "I'm here to be your handler."

Sarah gestured at Daniel and Parkman, pointed at Aaron, and then nodded toward Alex. "As you can see, I'm fine. Don't need a handler. Thanks anyway. I'm sure you know where the door is."

"Bartleson has been involved in every crime imaginable, from drug dealing to murder and everything in between."

"How does that have anything to do with us?"

"You were taken from your home today, along with your daughter, and you saw a Toronto Police officer be killed. What was his crime? How serious would it have to be to be murdered on Bartleson's front steps?"

They knew a lot more about what happened today than Sarah thought they could, leaving her without a response as she was speechless for the moment.

"You're uniquely positioned to help us finally stop Lorenzo Bartleson, Sarah. We came here to offer you a deal."

"A deal?" How many deals was she going to get in one day? "What sort of deal?"

"Help us take down Bartleson. We want you to wear a wire, meet with him, get him to talk about Campbell's murder, what happened with his daughter, anything that'll help, and we'll bring in the troops, arrest the lot of them, and be done with it."

"Not interested."

DeOcampo's expression soured so briefly that Sarah almost missed it. Now, she looked amused.

"So, you've decided to help him find Bianca? Is that it? Find the daughter, collect the payment, and be done with it?"

"We don't work for Bartleson." Sarah turned to walk away, then stopped. "The man is welcome to find his own daughter on his own terms. I'm sure he has the resources. We want nothing to do with it." She moved toward the kitchen. "Shut the door on your way out and send a cheque to fix the door you broke or leave cash on the mats."

"Sarah, wait. Didn't he take your daughter this morning as well?"

Sarah stopped, then glanced over her shoulder at the FBI agents standing around the dojo. After a moment, she turned back to face DeOcampo.

"Perhaps I'm not making myself clear. I don't work for or work with the authorities—"

"You have in the past," Hartman cut in. "Los Angeles Police Department, to name one. The priest killer case."

She cleared her throat. "I'm not working with the FBI in any capacity. I'll say it once more in the nicest possible way. Get the fuck out of our place of business."

"Sarah," DeOcampo shouted. "We will be back with charges filed against you then."

"For what?" Threatening her wouldn't solve a thing. It would only serve to anger her, and she'd end up working against them for sure. "Come on, tell me what I'll be arrested for."

"We know Bartleson wants your help. If you refuse to help him, there will be consequences. You leave us no choice but to arrest you for murder."

The mood in the room changed from a tense social situation to an intensely hostile one.

Sarah stormed across the mats to stand in front of DeOcampo. Her men moved in, as did Sarah's.

"Who did I supposedly murder? Huh?"

Alex was on his feet at the window, and Parkman, Daniel, and Benjamin were all in position beside Sarah.

"Officer Campbell and Officer Smith picked you up today. Campbell was murdered. We're still working out the details, but in the meantime, arresting you and detaining you as a flight risk might save your life when Bartleson calls."

"How's that?"

"Also, you wouldn't have to do what Bartleson is asking of you."

From the corner of her eye, Parkman's brow lowered in a frown.

"Twisted logic," Parkman said. "Help us, wear a wire, or we'll arrest you for murder to save you."

"What the fuck is that?" Aaron asked.

"It's an ultimatum," Sarah said. "Second one today."

"Is that what Bartleson gave you? An ultimatum? Tell us about it, Sarah. We can help."

"You can help by leaving."

"Don't do that, Sarah." DeOcampo sounded like she was pleading now. "Work with us. It'll be a mistake otherwise."

"What will be?"

"Whatever it is you're planning."

"Somehow, we don't think so." Sarah pointed at the door. "Get out, or we'll call the real police."

Now, it was DeOcampo's turn to frown. She withdrew a card from her pocket, set it on a table several feet to her left, then started toward the front door.

"Call me in the morning if you change your mind. Otherwise, we'll be back with an arrest warrant." DeOcampo stopped at the door and looked back as her agents all filed outside. "Oh, and Sarah, don't test me. You'll lose."

DeOcampo moved into the sunshine and then out of view as the front door closed.

"Fuck 'em," Sarah said. "Let's go back to planning the hits on Bartleson's companies."

"Sounds good to me," Parkman said.

"Still hungry, though," Aaron added. "Ordering food first."

"Doesn't anyone want to discuss what the fuck just happened?" Benjamin said, his voice cracking twice. "I mean, shouldn't we consider their offer and let them do the heavy lifting?"

"Benjamin," Alex said from the front door. He had moved there to watch the agents retreating along the sidewalk. "There's nothing to discuss. Everything that needed to be said was said."

Sarah placed an arm around Benjamin's shoulders. "You have to lighten up. Everything will be fine. We hit Bartleson. He comes to us. We don't do what criminal organizations order us to do, and we don't take kindly to threats to our welfare. We got this. I mean, look at Darwin. He's the perfect example. The entire Italian mafia and the bratva, the Russian mafia, were after him, and he still lives a wonderful life in the hills of Italy, traveling where he wants, when he wants."

"Yeah, that's because he killed most of them until the survivors *wanted* to forget his name."

"Well, there's that. But the point is, we've always done it our way, and nothing's changing that."

Sarah had some doubts, though. And was starting to wonder why her talkative sister wasn't around today. Over the past few years, ever since Willow was born, Vivian had dropped in daily, and so far today, Sarah had barely felt her presence.

"Pizza?" Aaron yelled for everyone's benefit.

"Pizza," Parkman and Alex shouted back.

"Buy five," Sarah said. "We may want leftovers after

burning down strip clubs and construction sites tonight."

Chapter 15

"BEFORE WE DO ANY damage, you won't walk away from killing Diego," Bartleson said. "Tell us why you did it."

"He was going to kill me." At that moment, surrounded by a group of thugs and hitmen, Sal hated his weak voice. He felt like a ten-year-old among men.

"Wrong," Mancuso said. "I was going to kill you."

But vomiting stopped Mancuso because he couldn't stand bile. Blood is one thing. Bile is something entirely different. All Sal had to do was just pretend he was about to hurl. Then they'd take him back to the bathroom. If there were a way he could actually make himself throw up, he would do it. Whatever happened next, he needed to return to that bathroom to get Diego's weapon.

"I've got information," Sal squeaked out.

Bartleson tilted his head sideways, regarding him with a pensive stare. "What sort of information?"

"It's regarding your daughter."

The pensive look disappeared, replaced by something far more insidious. It took Bartleson a moment to compose himself and respond.

"Go on."

Sal wanted to say, *what's it worth to you?* But didn't know how that would sound. How would someone bargain with a man like Bartleson for information about his daughter?

"Before I say anything, I'd like to think you'd show mercy on me—"

Bartleson smashed the table with his open palm so hard it sounded like a hammer punching through a wall. All the dishes and cutlery on the table rattled, and two beer bottles toppled over, spilling their contents onto the carpeted floor in soft chugs as if starved for the air rushing inside their small nozzles.

No one moved to right anything as all eyes were locked on Sal.

He had jumped so hard in his chair, his heart racing double time, it felt like a defibrillator had hit him.

"This is the last sentence that mouth will utter before you die," Bartleson said. "Make it good. Persuade me to hear another sentence. That's the only mercy I'll afford you."

Beside Bartleson, Mancuso had already pulled out his knife.

Sal's hands wouldn't stop shaking as he watched Silvio use the tip of his knife—the same tip that entered the flesh of his victims—on his teeth in place of a toothpick. The man was unquestionably dead on the inside. No human being with any sort of emotion could take that much pleasure in murder, torture, and pain. Or love a knife as much as Mancuso did. The man took it everywhere, even to bed with him, it was rumored.

"Frankie didn't say a word to me," Sal started. "I swear, I had no idea."

Bartleson didn't move or acknowledge Sal's words. The man barely blinked as he stared at Sal, waiting for more.

"I think Frankie and your daughter are together."

Silvio's knife tip flicked off his molars, then he laid the knife on the table, his hand covering the hilt.

Bartleson waved one finger, and the knife came off the table and back into Silvio's teeth.

"What brought you to that conclusion?" Bartleson asked.

The men from the bathroom who had cracked themselves up with the *killing me* comment shifted behind him. They were waiting for their cue to grab his arms, hold him down, and do whatever mobster hitmen did to victims.

Sal had never felt what it was like to be on the edge of a cliff, death at the bottom of the fall, but at that moment, sitting in Johnny's Bar and Grill, he saw death, and it wasn't pretty. He wanted no part in it.

Sal placed a hand over his stomach. "I think I'm going to be sick."

The tension broke slightly as the men glanced around and took a breath, a few of them stepping back. Even Mancuso leaned back in his seat.

Only Bartleson remained fixed on Sal's face, staring him down.

"Be sick. Throw up on the table, the floor, I don't care. But pray and hope you're telling me what I want to hear as you spew, or your stomach contents will be the least of your worries."

Sal nodded. "Can I reach in my jacket?"

Men moved, edging closer. Mancuso placed the knife on the table again, his white knuckles telling Sal how tight he held it.

"Ease off," Bartleson said. "He isn't packing. Carmine?" Bartleson glanced over Sal's head. "He was frisked?"

The man who punched Sal in the stomach, the one who said the *killing me* comment, stepped into view beside Sal.

"Yes, sir. He's clean."

Bartleson nodded at Sal, who then eased a hand into his jacket and withdrew the picture. He set it on the table, face up, then slid it across toward Bartleson, missing the spilled beer on the left side of the table.

The man stared down at it.

"After going to Frankie's last known residence, I scrolled through Frankie's Facebook profile. His most recent photo was a dinner he had several days ago. I couldn't tell the restaurant from the photo, so I went to all of his photos in the app, detected similar dishes he had posted, and saw the menu in one of the photos. There was a kid's birthday party when I went to the restaurant. Photos were taken and displayed on the wall by the staff. I found this photo on that display, taken within the past week." He stopped to catch a breath.

Bartleson touched the picture, examining it from different angles. Then he lifted it closer to his face. After a moment, he set it down in front of Silvio.

"That's Frankie's profile?"

Mancuso leaned in close, then righted himself. "It is."

Bartleson regarded Sal with a faint glimmer of what he thought might be respect, but there was something else in his expression. Repugnance or contempt, perhaps.

"Why would Frankie steal from me and give that money to your mother?"

That question startled Sal. How could they know? And if they did know, did they do something to that nurse? Did Bartleson already have his money back?

He decided to answer without missing a beat. "Frankie told my mother he was turning over a new leaf. Making wrongs right, something like repentance for all the wrong he'd done."

Bartleson leaned to his left and whispered something into Mancuso's ear, then straightened and met Sal's gaze again.

"You've done well." Bartleson inhaled deeply, then sighed. "Where will we find Frankie?"

"I don't know. I'm still trying to locate him." He swallowed, wondering again if he'd leave here alive. "Find Frankie. You find your daughter."

Bartleson's eyes narrowed. "I'm aware of that." He picked up one of the beers that hadn't been knocked over and drank from it. "You worked with him for a few months. You must've learned something about his likes and dislikes and places he enjoyed visiting."

"We focused on staying away from anything too personal due to the nature of the job. I mean, I knew he liked rap music. Grew up with Beastie Boys and Ice T, then moved on to Eminem. I recall his favorite drink was rum, but other than that, we kept it professional. When he stopped showing up for work, I called Diego and was told to do the runs alone, so

I did."

Bartleson's demeanor seemed to change, softening. He glanced down at the picture on the table, then back to Sal.

"Frankie has caused us a lot of trouble. You worked with him. Understand how that must look."

Sal nodded. "I do."

"You've won a reprieve."

"A reprieve?"

Bartleson leaned forward, his elbows on the table, his right resting in spilled beer.

"I'm rather impressed with your amateur sleuthing. You've produced more in the past twelve hours than any of my men. So, you've won a reprieve. You won't die today. Find me, my daughter, locate Frankie, and you'll get your life back. I'll even give back the money your mother needs for her cancer treatment as payment for your efforts." Bartleson stopped talking to wipe his wet arm with a napkin.

That explained a lot. They got to the nurse, but at least they knew he didn't steal the money. Did that mean his mother was safe from them?

Sal felt like he could breathe again. What had Bartleson whispered in Silvio's ear, though? Don't kill him? I've changed my mind?

Bartleson set the napkin down on the table hard enough to make the table vibrate.

"Although, there's one thing you still have to pay for."

Sal nodded, afraid to speak, one hand still resting on his stomach, the other on the table.

Mancuso moved so fast it was a blur. He barely saw the movement before he felt something bump into his hand.

When he looked over, his left hand was impaled to the table, Mancuso's trusty knife sticking out of it. There was no pain and no blood initially. It was just stuck there, like the plastic hand used in a Halloween trick. Then the pain started, and it rolled in fast, like a crashing wave on the concrete bluff of a pier, yet the waves increased in size, causing a low moan in Sal's throat.

When he turned his attention back to Bartleson, the man rose from his seat.

"Your debts are paid—for now. Find me Frankie and my daughter. You can have your job back." He patted Sal on the shoulder. "No hard feelings, eh."

Mancuso leaned over the table and yanked out the knife.

Sal screamed as blood spurted upward when the knife exited his flesh. Pain raged through him, making it feel like his hand was on fire.

"Better get that looked at," Mancuso whispered in Sal's ear. "Then find Frankie or my knife will take out your eyes next time."

Silvio Mancuso laughed, the sound fading as the man strode away from the table at the back of Johnny's Bar and Grill.

Sal blinked several times, trying to get his bearings. The table was empty around him. He'd survived but wondered if it was worth it.

This was like death row, and the governor had just granted him a stay of several days. Who cared? Just get on with it. He'd be dead anyway.

Without thinking much, working on automaton, he took a large black napkin and tied it around his left wrist using his right hand and his teeth.

He stumbled with his phone, dropped it on the carpet, leaned to pick it up, and had a dizzy spell that made him pause a moment, holding tight to the edge of the table.

Consciousness wavered for precious seconds, and he wondered what would happen to him if he passed out. Would he die of blood loss? A major artery wasn't hit. That had to be good, right?

After several short breaths, he tapped 911 into his phone, then hit the speaker button.

When they answered, he told them where he was and that he'd stabbed himself, then hung up.

He would go to the hospital, get bandaged up, then think about Frankie again. What might Frankie have said in their final week together? Were there any clues? Could Frankie have said something mundane that, knowing what he knew now, Sal would see it as important?

The stumbling out to the front of the restaurant took sheer willpower. Someone watched him from behind the bar, but he was too focused on the door to pay attention to who it was.

On the sidewalk, the sun had set already. Sal dropped to the concrete, his hand above his heart, and waited.

He closed his eyes and wondered if his death would be painful. Mancuso would make it so, but it didn't have to be painful.

And what about the gun he'd left in the restaurant's bathroom? He'd have to come back and get it. Lucky for him, he had done that. They would've taken it from him when they checked to see if he was armed.

The pain continued to intensify in waves, but something about sleep lulled him, his head lowering.

A siren called out in the distance like a wailing alarm clock.

But he didn't want to wake up. It felt too good to rest.

Sal lost consciousness, and his hand dropped to his lap.

Chapter 16

"I'M STUFFED," SARAH SAID. "Ate way too much. Now entering a food coma."

"You probably should sleep," Aaron said. "It's going to be a long night."

Sarah shook her head and got up from her chair at the table.

"I'll make coffee. Who wants some?"

Everyone chimed in.

"I'll make a full pot then." She ran the water in the small sink and set up the coffee maker. "So, everyone clear on what they're doing tonight?" She glanced over her shoulder as several of them nodded. "We leave at two in the morning. Each team hit their respective locations in the order we assigned and agreed to."

"I have a question," Benjamin said, raising a hand in the air.

"Shoot."

"This is illegal."

Sarah stopped what she was doing and turned to him. "That's a question?"

"My question is, since this is illegal, and we're about to break the law, why are we doing it?"

"What? Why?"

Benjamin nodded. "What if we get caught? The cops won't understand our reasons. To them, we're arsonists, plain and simple."

"Okay," Parkman said. "I'll play devil's advocate while we wait for the coffee."

Sarah turned back to the coffee maker, wondering if Benjamin had softened too much over the years of inactivity.

"If we scrap the entire plan, what would you propose?" Parkman's voice was friendly, gentle, non-threatening.

She glanced over her shoulder as she pushed the ON button in time to see Benjamin shrug.

"I don't know." He glanced at the table. "I would say work with the FBI."

"They gave us an ultimatum, too," Aaron said. "Work with them or arrest Sarah. Since when have we ever been *ordered* to work with anyone?"

"True, but at least we aren't breaking the law with them."

"You know as well as everyone else," Parkman said, "that wearing a wire isn't all they would need. They'll tell Sarah they didn't hear enough to make a case, then get her to do something extra risky. They don't care about us or Sarah. Eventually, she'll be in a meeting with Bartleson, his people will detect the wire somehow, and we have our friend, Sarah, new mother to Willow, at risk. The FBI will even try to reassure her that they'll protect her, but that won't happen in time. Working with them is a mistake." After his long diatribe, Parkman inhaled, then said, "What's the next idea?"

"How about finding Bianca?" Benjamin chanced a look at Sarah, then turned back to Parkman. "Why couldn't Vivian tell us where Bianca is?"

"Maybe," Sarah said, "because Bianca left for good reasons and doesn't want to be found."

"Look, I don't have all the answers." Benjamin threw up his arms. He studied everyone's faces. "Arson is against the law. People could get hurt. I think there's another way to go about this. I'm not comfortable with breaking the law."

Daniel scoffed. "Dude, how many times have we broken the law? How many people have we killed over the years to protect ourselves and our family?"

"All in self-defense. And any laws we broke were to stay alive."

"How is this any different?" Sarah asked. "I mean, think about it. Bartleson made it abundantly clear that Willow was in danger if I didn't do what he said or follow orders like a good little girl. When one of us is threatened, all of us are."

Benjamin was nodding now. "I get all that, and deep down inside, I feel this is the right thing to do." He scanned the faces, all looking back at him while the coffee maker burped and sputtered brown liquid into the pot. "I just thought we were past this."

"See, that I can understand," Sarah said. "Because I thought the same thing since Willow was born." She clapped her hands to wake everyone up. Most of them jumped, but Alex. He just regarded her with interest. "But it is what it is.

A mafia, money-laundering motherfucker abducted me and Willow, then threatened to take her from me, and I'm going to retaliate with everything in my power. They will understand their mistake through the loss of money, which communicates something valuable to men like Bartleson." She moved around the room behind their chairs like she was giving a motivational speech. "These things we are about to do aren't criminal. We're ending illegal enterprises, stopping the flow of drugs and cash, and releasing women from dancing half-naked on stages and in VIP rooms, some no doubt trapped there or victims of trafficking. I see what we're about to do as righteous."

"Hear, hear," Daniel said, lightly punching Benjamin in the arm. "See, we're doing a good thing."

"Hey, Benjamin," Aaron said. "Just because you were part of the action years ago, you don't have to be now. You can sit this one out if you want. This shit we're about to do tonight is always voluntary."

After a few moments, Benjamin shook his head. "Wouldn't miss it," he muttered. "Just wanted to make sure we were doing the right thing. Something doesn't feel right. Like, where's Vivian on all this?"

Sarah frowned. "Been asking myself that all day."

"So," Parkman jumped in. "We have our marching orders. Aaron, Alex, and Benjamin will go to the Peaches 'N Cream Gentlemen's Club at around three in the morning, and once you've accessed the building to make sure it's empty, you'll torch the place. Then move on to the next one." He cleared his throat as he looked at the piece of paper with buildings and addresses written on it. "I'm heading to the construction site on the 400 North with Sarah and Daniel. Then we'll hit the one near Kleinburg." He looked up to stare at everyone. "If there's time left before the sun rises, Sarah and I will go to the restaurants on Queen Street and see if we can damage them somehow and cause a little mischief before we head home to bed."

"Where's Aaron going when you two hit the restaurants?" Benjamin asked.

"Aaron will be heading to bed by four in the morning so he can open the dojo on time—"

"Not on time," Aaron cut in. "About ten or so. A little late."

Parkman nodded. "The FBI's watching. We want everything to look as normal as possible. We all clear?"

Heads nodded around the room, even Benjamin's.

"Still think we're missing something here." Benjamin glanced down at his hands.

"We are," Sarah said. Everyone stared at her. "A reminder that tonight should involve no fighting and no deaths. Got it? Limit personal risk to us."

Several of them nodded.

"Seriously, I don't want murder investigations haunting us. That would be worse than Bartleson. So, I'll repeat: no one kills anyone. Let me hear it."

"No one kills anyone," they all said in unison.

"Great, and now"—Sarah reached for the coffee cups—"who wants coffee again?"

Chapter 17

Aaron sat behind the wheel, staring at the Peaches 'N Cream Gentlemen's Club's back door. No one had come or gone in the past hour.

"Think it's empty?" he asked Alex, who sat beside him.

Benjamin had fallen asleep in the back seat, even though he'd drank more coffee than the others.

"We've been here at least forty-five minutes. No one has come or gone in that time." Alex moved slightly in his seat. "Parking lot is empty."

He glanced down at his phone. The brightness on the screen turned low. "Nothing from Sarah and Parkman yet. Hope Daniel was able to stay awake." He glanced over the seat and stared at Benjamin. "Should we leave him here?"

"No. We're all in this together. He came along. He does the job, too."

"You're right. Just didn't want to wake him, and you know, with his reservations and all …"

"But he's here. And once this is done, and Bartleson has been taken care of, Benjamin won't be able to feel any sense of success personally if he didn't at least carry a gas can."

Aaron stared at the back of the strip club. "Well, I say we go now."

Alex pulled on the door handle in response. He stepped from the car and then closed the door slowly.

They were all dressed in black, and it was a warm, moonless night. Aaron had parked on a side street under a large tree where they could watch the strip club parking lot and the back entrance.

The conditions couldn't be better.

He reached over the seat and shook Benjamin. "Wake up, buddy. Time to go burn down a building."

Benjamin moaned something, then rolled over in the seat, curling his hands up under his chin.

"Dude," Aaron said louder. "Time to go—"

The back door opened, and Alex leaned in over Benjamin. He squeezed the man's nose closed, holding it that way until Benjamin jerked away from Alex.

"Wakey, wakey," Alex said before Benjamin could protest.

He set two red gas cans on the concrete beside the open back door. "You're carrying these. Let's go."

Aaron got out and closed his door, the whole time listening to Benjamin's mumbling about being woken up at four in the morning.

Once they collected all of the supplies, they raised their hoodies to cover their features and trotted along the back fence line, staying in the darkest sections under large trees.

Sarah and Aaron had chosen this club to hit first mainly because of its location. On the outskirts of Woodbridge, an area north of Toronto, it was surrounded by fields and several industrial buildings. The prying eyes of the public would be at a minimum. Also, none of the surrounding buildings would be affected if the fire got out of control before the fire department arrived.

All three of them made it to the back door without much noise other than the scuffle of their shoes on gravel.

Aaron pulled out the oscillating hand tool with the metal-cutting blade and set to work on the door's hinges while Alex moved along the building, watching the street, leaving Benjamin to watch Aaron's back. Within a minute, all three hinges had been seared clean off.

Then, he used a screwdriver to pry the door out of its frame at the top and another screwdriver at the base.

Alex returned from scouting out the building, and all three men placed their fingers on the edge of the door, pulling outward.

It popped off, still only attached at the deadbolt. But there was enough room to slip inside where the hinges had once secured the door to the frame.

Benjamin went first, followed by Aaron and then Alex, who pulled the door closed as far as he could so if someone drove by in the ten minutes it took them to prepare the burn, it wouldn't look like the door was ajar at a wrong angle.

"Okay," Aaron whispered. "So far so good. The alarm must be a silent one. Besides, who would hear it out here?"

"Why are we whispering?" Benjamin asked. "If no one's here, can't we talk at normal volumes?"

"Habit," Aaron said. "Take these." He handed Benjamin the gas cans. "Hit the bar area and around the back room."

"What about the stage?"

"If they kill this fire fast, a stage is a quick fix. I want the bar, the booze, and the back room or change rooms ruined. We must ensure Lorenzo can't launder money through this place anymore, or at least not for the foreseeable future."

Benjamin nodded. "Got it." Then he stumbled away, both hands laden down with gas, skirting tables and chairs while making his way toward the bar area.

Alex was already gone, moving through the empty club with stealth and silence to make sure the building was, in fact, empty. They had no idea when a cleaning crew worked in the club, and as Sarah said, no one dies tonight.

Aaron glanced around the door, looking for an alarm panel, but couldn't find one. He jogged toward the other side of the building, headed for the front. There had to be another door, another entrance. Maybe that was where the employees came and went, where the alarm panel would be.

He checked his watch. They were set to leave in a few minutes. This project was done, but he hadn't heard gasoline sloshing yet.

After a twenty-second search for the alarm panel, he gave up and ran out into the main area.

No one was around.

The emergency lighting—night lights—offered enough illumination for him to see the entire bar area. A Budweiser neon sign lit the back of the bar a bright red.

There was no sign of Benjamin or Alex.

Aaron frowned, a spike of worry shooting through his

gut.

What the hell happened to them?

Something shuffled behind the bar. A door cracked open, and a light came on.

"Guys," he said. "What are you doing?"

Another light flickered to life behind the bar.

"Aaron?" Benjamin said, his voice cracking.

That wasn't good. Something had gone wrong.

"What?"

"Can you come here?"

He took in his surroundings, then lowered the hood to give him better peripheral vision. There was enough light to see most of the interior now. Nothing moved.

"You almost done with the gas?" Aaron asked without moving.

"I found something," Benjamin said. "Behind the bar."

This time, Aaron was sure it was fear in Benjamin's voice. What could he have found, a dead body?

"Coming," he said.

Aaron started forward as cautiously as he could, his hands out at his sides, ready for anything.

Something moved on the far right side of the stage, making Aaron duck down. When he saw nothing over there, he continued toward the bar area.

When he saw the top of Benjamin's head, he slowed.

"What did you find, buddy?"

"Me," a man said, standing up from behind the bar, a gun aimed at Benjamin's head. "Don't move, Aaron Stevens. We'll wait here like good little boys until my associate brings Alex to join us. They're over in the change rooms."

That was the noise Aaron had heard on the other side of the stage, the one that made him duck down.

"Empty your pockets and drop all your weapons on the counter," the man ordered. "Or I fire a bullet into Ben's brain."

Aaron raised his hands and noticed they were already shaking. "Okay, take it easy. No one needs to get hurt here."

The man smiled. "You three should have thought about that before trying to burn down Bartleson's strip club." He whistled. "Boy, won't he be disappointed when he hears this? I guess we have Sarah's answer." The man cocked the weapon as if he was preparing to fire. "Now, weapons on the counter, fuck face."

Benjamin's features were drawn downward in terror and disappointment. He was a fighter, a martial artist like the rest of them. Somehow, he got sloppy and let this man get the drop on them. Was he still sleepy, or perhaps it was just a fluke? Maybe they were waiting inside in case someone came to vandalize the place. But that didn't make sense. Why would Lorenzo spend manpower on that chance?

Aaron pulled out his pants pockets, setting the car keys and little change he had on him on the top of the bar.

"Weapons, too."

"I don't have any weapons."

"Oh right, you came here to burn the place down. Why carry guns and knives, eh?"

Something banged from the other side of the stage again.

"Hey, Silvio," the man called. "You okay in there?"

When there was no answer, the man's jaw tightened—a crack in his cocky-I'm-a-big-man visage.

"Come around here and sit down," he said.

Aaron moved slowly, doing as he was told. Benjamin was seated in a padded chair, the gas cans on either side of him. Another padded chair was set up four feet from Benjamin. Aaron lowered onto it, keeping his hands on his thighs.

"Man, you're both so lucky Silvio enjoys torture so much." The man shook his head, his eyes lit up as if someone had said something astounding.

"How does that make us lucky?" Benjamin asked, his voice cracking again. "Torture isn't luck."

In that tone, Aaron heard the despair, the regret, and the reason he had protested about this job so much earlier. If something happened to him, Aaron would feel personally responsible. There was a reason the two teams were divided the way they were. Alex and Aaron would take care of Benjamin if he lagged behind in any way.

They weren't doing such a good job of it.

"If Silvio didn't enjoy using his knife so much, I would've shot you both in the head by now. We don't take prisoners, and we don't need hostages. So, you're lucky because, at this moment, you're still breathing. Although, as much fun as this'll be, I can't wait for tomorrow, or should I say later today."

Aaron watched the man expectantly, waiting for more.

"Once we've taken care of you three, and Lorenzo hears what happened here, we'll go pick up that bitch Sarah and her kid and be done with it. Besides, Lorenzo is already working another angle on his daughter. As it turns out, he may not have needed Sarah's help after all. One of our own has a lead." He smiled wide, showing stained teeth.

"Working another angle?"

"Yeah, the guy his daughter took off with—Frankie. Looks like we'll find him soon." He glanced over at the stage area. "Hey, Silvio, you okay?" he shouted.

The door to the back room kicked open so hard that Aaron was sure it broke the frame.

Two men stepped out, but in the darkness of that area, he couldn't tell who was in front and who was behind.

"Silvio?" the man said, doubt in his tone.

Aaron waited, ready for anything.

The man changed gun hands, adjusting his body to keep the weapon aimed at Benjamin.

"Don't shoot anyone, Carmine," a man's voice said.

"What?" the man holding the weapon—Carmine— replied. "Why not?"

At the corner of the stage, the men came into view.

Alex held a knife to the throat of a man whose face was bruised and bleeding heavily.

"What the fuck?" Carmine whispered, then pressed the tip of the weapon into Benjamin's neck. "Let him go, or I'll fucking execute this one," Carmine shouted.

"Don't shoot him," Silvio shouted back. "Alex has a deal for us."

"I don't fucking care." Carmine was going into hysterics. "Nobody gets the drop on you, Silvio. Nobody."

They moved closer until Aaron could see Alex's face, unblemished.

"Drop the weapon," Alex said, his voice hard and controlled. "Or I'll slice this man's throat open, then come over there and kill you next."

"No fucking way," Carmine yelled. He lowered the weapon to Benjamin's leg, pressing the barrel into his thigh. "We're going to negotiate."

"No, we are not," Alex shouted back. "You've got mere seconds left to save this man's life."

"Don't do anything stupid, Carmine," Silvio said. "I'm ordering you to stand down."

"Sorry, Silvio, but I have the upper hand this time. I have the gun." There seemed to be a lunacy in Carmine's smile now. "Who brings a knife to a gunfight?" the man said, muttering to himself. "You'll thank me later, Silvio."

Aaron wondered why Benjamin didn't attack. The odds of getting shot could be greatly reduced if Benjamin jabbed at the man's arm while moving his leg out of the way. Another jab or two, and the man would be on the floor.

Then, it came to Aaron in a wave of understanding.

Benjamin was paralyzed with fear, as irrational as that was, immobilized by it. He'd been shot so many times over the years that he couldn't handle guns anymore. A few years ago, when they did jobs for Sarah, Benjamin almost sounded like he was whining about whether there'd be guns involved. They all brushed it off as comical, but now Aaron was an eyewitness to the fear that had come from the trauma the guns over the years had caused his friend.

Which meant Aaron had to do something.

"Last chance," Carmine shouted. "Take the knife away from Silvio's throat."

"If I do, it'll slice his neck open along the way." Alex was in one of his I'm-not-negotiating-shit-with-you moods.

"Then your friend here will walk with a limp for the rest of his life if he makes it out of here alive."

Aaron stared at the man's trigger finger. It slipped inside the guard and applied pressure to the trigger.

He wasn't bluffing.

On a count of three, Aaron launched out of his seat from four feet away.

The weapon, pressed against Benjamin's thigh, fired at the same moment, the sound shockingly loud in the closed area behind the bar.

And then all hell broke loose as several men screamed at once.

Chapter 18

SARAH AND PARKMAN GOT out of their car, then she turned to Daniel in the driver's seat. "Wait here. Leave it running. I'd like to scout the area first, make sure there's no cameras or security guards."

"What about the gasoline in the trunk?" Daniel asked.

"We'll leave it there for now. Just keep an eye out for security."

"Will do."

They started off to navigate the construction site with a flashlight each.

"Mavros Homes," Sarah said as they passed the sign at the front of the subdivision. "I wonder where he got that name from."

"A lot of these houses are just starting to be built," Parkman said. "There's no plumbing, no electricity in them yet."

"That works. We don't need to burn plastic and metal

anyway."

The gravel road under their feet hadn't been paved yet.

"It's like they just broke ground."

Sarah nodded, aiming her beam at the outside of a couple of houses that already had plywood siding. "Maybe they contract out the framework because some of these houses are further along than others."

"I'm sure they do. I understand a basic frame can be erected in a week nowadays."

Sarah whistled, keeping her volume low. "Wow, that's fast. Those houses sturdy?"

Parkman nodded in the dark. "Oh, yeah. They look great all finished, too."

Ten houses later, they hit a series of dug-out basements, with some cases where the concrete hadn't been poured yet.

"I think we've hit the end of what I'd consider useful for what we need." Sarah clicked off her flashlight and glanced back at the idling car. They had to be five hundred meters from Daniel now. "Thoughts?"

"Yeah, this'll work." Parkman turned and waved at a row of houses that had been framed, their prefab roofs lying on the mud beside the houses. "Let's hit those. They've had the most work done and will cost the most in losses and rebuilding."

"Works for me."

They started back, causally listening to the crickets in the bush surrounding the construction site.

Something moved in the darkness behind their idling car. Sarah slowed her step and placed a cautionary hand on Parkman's arm.

He stopped and faced her, whispering, "What's up?"

She jerked her head toward the car. "Something moved behind the car."

They were still four hundred meters away.

"Flashlights off," she said. "Don't give ourselves away. Keep walking."

Both of them started forward in the dark, their steps lit by the distant glow of streetlights one block over, a section of the construction site that had been mostly completed.

Sarah's eyes remained glued to the area behind the car, but nothing moved again.

"Maybe it was an animal," she whispered. "Investigating the car."

"Could be," Parkman whispered back.

Daniel lowered the window as they approached. "Pop the trunk?"

"Not yet," Sarah said, raising a hand. "We want to check something out first."

They strode by the car and stopped at the edge of the bush. Sarah kicked at the base of the foliage, then listened.

Nothing moved from within.

"Hmmph, maybe I was imagining things."

They turned back to the car, where Sarah slapped the trunk. Daniel popped it from the inside.

A vehicle approached from the main road. Her eyes met Parkman's. She lowered the trunk, and they waited in silence. The vehicle, a dark-colored SUV, raced by the entrance to the construction site, heading south toward Toronto.

Once the sound of the engine retreated, she opened the trunk.

Inside, five large red gas cans were lined up and tied to one another to ensure they didn't topple over on the way there. A couple of small red stick-like things sat off to the side.

Parkman grabbed one of the metal sticks and held it up to the little light they had.

"Ever use one of these before?" he asked.

Sarah shook her head, staring at it.

"Okay, crash course. It's called a lightning strike fire starter." He popped off the black end piece, then pulled out a tiny disk. "This is what they call the tinder. Some people fluff it out like the cotton ball a woman will use to remove makeup, and others leave it compact like it is, which is the shape of a small coin, similar to a quarter. This is what starts the fire."

"How's that?"

"The cylinder here focuses the sparks along its shaft and out the end." He placed the tinder on the gravel at their feet. "Take the tip, the striker, and insert it here." He demonstrated for Sarah to see. "Then strike downward. Sparks come out of the end and ignite the tinder. If there's gasoline in the area or some other accelerant, everything goes up quite fast." He handed it to her. "You try, so when you're alone in the house, you can set the fire yourself."

Sarah lowered to her knees, placed the striker into the shaft of the device as she was shown, aimed the tip at the small coin-like piece of tinder, and then shoved it downward.

Sparks shot out immediately, igniting the tinder on the gravel into a small flame.

"Damn, that works well. Where did you get these?"

"Picked them up online as part of a survival program. I never know when I'm on a case up north and get stuck out in the trees somewhere. Wouldn't mind having a fire." He smiled wide, so proud of himself.

Sarah rose to stand beside him, admiring the small fire starter in her hand. "What have you been up to these few years we've been raising Willow?"

"A number of adventurous things."

"Any female interest?" Sarah asked, reaching inside the trunk to grab two red gas cans.

"Actually, yes."

She paused, holding the cans at the bumper of the car. "How come I haven't heard about this yet?"

Parkman shrugged, pocketed a fire striker, then grabbed two gas cans and lifted them out. Gas sloshed around inside, and the gas smell was strong even though they were sealed.

He shrugged. "No one's asked about her."

"She got a name? How long have you been seeing her? Where's she from? How old is she? How long have you been seeing her?" Sarah stomped the ground once. "I'm asking now."

Another vehicle approached along the main road. It sounded more like two.

They exchanged a glance, then placed the gas cans back inside the trunk, lowering it until it was almost latched.

Then, they waited for the vehicles to pass.

It was more than two cars, and they were coming fast.

Sarah searched for Vivian, but she was nowhere to be found. On the surface, it was frustrating, but it also meant everything would work out. Vivian showed up to steer them in the right direction when things were going wrong. So she had faith that this was the right path, the righteous one.

The engines slowed as they approached.

"Who would be coming to the construction site at this hour?" she mumbled, her stomach turning at the thought of being caught.

Parkman touched her arm.

When she turned toward him, she followed his gaze.

A man stood twenty feet away, a cell phone in hand.

The man was dressed in a security uniform.

"Fuck, how did we miss him?" she mumbled.

The man spoke in whispers on the phone, nodding frequently.

Sarah slammed the trunk closed. "We're out of here."

She moved to the side door as Parkman did the same.

Then, car after car turned onto the construction site's property. Police cars, one after another, pulled up to them until four cruisers blocked them in.

There was no way they were leaving now.

"You may want to turn off the car, Daniel," Parkman said. "It looks like we have some explaining to do."

Officers were launching out of their vehicles, a couple of them with weapons drawn, hiding behind their car doors.

"Out of the car," one of them shouted. "Hands where we can see them."

"No one opens that trunk," Sarah said. "No one."

Then she moved away from the car slowly, hands raised.

Chapter 19

He decided he would kill the man.

He'd killed before.

This time, killing Silvio "the butcher" Mancuso would be doing the world a favor.

How was it possible for a man like that to exist in the modern world? Salvatore didn't understand it, couldn't reconcile it in his head. Mancuso was insane and enjoyed hurting—torturing—people too much. Maybe he would've found a home in a prison camp during the war, but in today's world, he had to go.

Sal's left hand was wrapped in an abundance of bandages. He tried to eat several candy bars from the hospital vending machine in an effort to keep something down to gain some strength back. After being stabbed, he'd gone into a mild shock, his face turning a greenish-white. The paramedics had staunched the blood flow and got him to the hospital, where they did a thorough exam and stitched him up.

The wary eye of the doctor told Sal that he didn't believe the story that Sal had stabbed himself by accident. How could he ever speak the truth, though? Anyone who ratted out Mancuso ended up in a ditch somewhere, never to speak the man's name again. That's how a bully elevated himself to be a bully his entire life—get involved in a criminal organization to be protected so he could bully people for years to come.

Even if Mancuso got arrested, Lorenzo would have him out the same day, and by the time charges were brought against Mancuso. A trial set, everything would be worked out with a kickback, a donation to the mayor's office, or some other bullshit Lorenzo would come up with. All this is because Silvio Mancuso was protected inside the Lorenzo organization. He was his security advisor and trusted lieutenant.

To hurt the Lorenzo Bartleson Group, Salvatore had to kill Mancuso.

Sal's life was hanging by a thread as it was, which meant he'd probably be dead by the end of the week.

He hadn't done much good with his life, and his mother was dying, so what was there left to live for anyway?

And since he was going to die, why not do something for the sake of humanity? Why not kill Silvio Mancuso?

He'd need Diego's gun back from Johnny's Bar and Grill to do that.

Sal laughed to himself. Wasn't that ironic, Silvio being murdered by his own man's weapon, the same man Sal killed last night?

Maybe if Sal lived long enough to kill Mancuso, Lorenzo would hire him back. A new position would open, and Sal would've proved himself worthy by taking out two accomplished men in Lorenzo's organization.

He stumbled out into the dark of night and checked his phone. The battery was about to die, and his charger was in the car back on Queen Street, a block from Johnny's Bar and Grill.

He checked his wallet. Ten bucks.

He tried to estimate the time it would take to walk downtown to the restaurant and figured it would be a couple of hours at least. Once he got there, he'd find a way to break in, grab the gun from under the sink before the security company or police investigated the alarm he would set off, and then leave in his car.

Later, after some sleep, he'd contact Silvio and tell him he wanted to meet as he had new information about Bianca and Frankie.

Then he'd kill him.

A bullet to the face or the throat. He wasn't good with guns, but he'd figure it out somehow.

He had to because knowing who Mancuso was and what he was capable of, Sal couldn't leave the man alive.

Besides, he was filled with a burning vengeance for what the man had done to his hand. Sal had done nothing wrong. Sal hadn't stolen any money, and they wanted to kill him. Sal hadn't taken Lorenzo's daughter, and they wanted to kill him. All he'd done was defend himself from being killed, and now they wanted to kill him.

So, Sal would take out Lorenzo's number-one hitman.

He smiled to himself as he left the Trillium Health Hospital and started walking behind the Sherway Gardens Mall toward The Queensway, which would take him on a direct route to downtown.

In two hours or so, he'd have Diego's gun back.

By sunrise, he'd be sleeping in a secure location.

By the end of the day, Silvio, "the butcher," Mancuso would be dead, Lorenzo's organization hurt, and Sal would be on the run as far as his five hundred dollars in the bank would take him.

"There's no stopping me now."

He picked up his pace.

Chapter 20

AARON SMASHED INTO CARMINE, his right shoulder connecting with the man's hip bone, shoving him sideways into the bar's counter. Glass shattered and broke around them as Aaron grabbed for the man's throat, twisting him toward the floor.

Someone was screaming behind him, but he kept his focus on Carmine.

They hit the floor in a heap, Carmine's hands coming up to ward off the attack, which told Aaron that the man had dropped the gun.

Aaron delivered several quick jabs, aiming for the man's nose and teeth. Carmine bucked under Aaron, trying to shove him off, but all that did was knock Aaron forward, his arm slamming into the man's throat.

Carmine's eyes widened, and his tongue popped out of his mouth when Aaron's forearm jammed down on his throat, pressing his head into the ground.

The weapon came into view on his left side.

Aaron jumped back, sitting upward and leaning out of the way.

Benjamin had crawled over to get it and was lying on his belly now, gun extended in his right arm, aimed at Carmine's head.

"Benjamin," Aaron shouted. "Don't."

The weapon fired.

Carmine's head snapped to the side so violently that his body jerked under Aaron.

A darkness shot across the floor, forming a small, scattered mass behind Carmine's ear. Aaron stared at the brain matter as blood pooled like sludge under the man's head, his body convulsing in the throes of death.

The convulsions were enough to get Aaron up and off the man in repulsion. He turned his attention to Benjamin, who had dropped the weapon and was pressing both hands on his leg wound as blood seeped through his jeans.

"It hurts, man, it fuckin' hurts," Benjamin squealed.

"We'll get you out of here and to the hospital. Just keep pressure on it."

He glanced around for a towel, then found a small pile of folded-up white ones by the dishwasher, exactly the cliché sort of white towel every bartender had draped over their shoulders in the movies.

After snatching several of them off the counter, he tied two together, then wrapped Benjamin's leg above the wound and tightened them.

When he glanced up to the entrance to the bar area, Alex was standing there, a knife in his hand.

"We have to get him out of here," Aaron said. "We have

to get him to a hospital."

Alex nodded. "Can you carry him? Drag him? I'll bring the car to the back door."

Aaron nodded, slipped a hand into his pocket, withdrew the keys, and tossed them to Alex, who caught them without looking away from Benjamin.

"Where's the other guy?" Aaron asked.

"He's dead." Alex pointed, then turned to where they'd been standing. "I sliced his throat open right there—"

Alex stopped talking. He just stared over the countertop, his mouth open.

"What?" Aaron asked. He couldn't see over the top of the bar from where he knelt on the floor beside Benjamin.

Alex lowered his arm. "He's gone."

"What do you mean, *gone*?" Benjamin moaned. "How could he be *gone* if you cut him open?"

Alex glanced back at them, then moved his gaze to the main area of the strip club. When he turned to face them again, he seemed lost.

"I sliced open his throat. He dropped. I came to help you …" He trailed off, his eyes seeing nothing as he thought about the events that had transpired. "He dropped to the floor. I thought he was dying that he'd be dead."

"Doesn't matter now," Aaron said. "What matters is Benjamin." He wrapped Benjamin's arm and lifted upward. Benjamin helped by putting weight on his good leg.

"Alex," Aaron shouted.

The young man snapped to attention.

"Get the fucking car."

Without another word, Alex bolted through the strip club

toward the door they'd entered through, the keys jangling in his palm.

Aaron and Benjamin hobbled out from behind the bar, then started around the counter toward the back door.

"We really fucked up this time, didn't we?" Benjamin said.

"Yeah, well, it is what it is."

"What kind of answer is that? Sarah said no one gets hurt."

"She did."

He pointed at his leg. "I guess we fucked that up."

"She also said no one dies today."

"Carmine's dead."

"Better him than us, wouldn't you agree?"

Aaron stared at the stage, Benjamin leaning into him with most of his weight, making him bend at the waist.

"What are you looking for?"

"The man Alex was dealing with. If he's not dead, he could pop up at any moment."

Benjamin raised his free hand. The gun was still there.

"If he pops up anywhere, I'll just shoot him."

Aaron nodded and kept moving toward the back door, Benjamin hobbling along on his good leg.

"Sarah's going to be pissed," Benjamin said, grunting several of the words.

"I think it's Lorenzo who'll be pissed. We didn't burn a thing. All we did was break in, kill one of his men, and cut the other."

"Well, whoever's pissed about this, I have a feeling we just started a war with the mafia."

"Me too. And I'm afraid it might be a war we can't win."

Benjamin soldiered on a few more steps, faltered a couple, then dropped to the floor five feet from the exit, almost dragging Aaron with him.

Aaron lowered to the floor and tapped his friend's face.

Benjamin had passed out.

"Hey man, wake up."

There was no response.

A car door shut hard outside the exit. Alex appeared in the doorway a moment later.

"Help me get him in the back seat. He just passed out."

The two of them went to work on Benjamin and got him loaded into the car without another word to each other.

With Alex driving, they headed to the nearest hospital. Aaron thought about calling Sarah but decided to wait until after Benjamin was safe in the hospital.

Then he remembered the weapon Benjamin had held in his hand. He glanced at it, but the weapon wasn't there.

Benjamin must've dropped it when he passed out. Aaron had forgotten all about it, and it had Benjamin's fingerprints on it.

The weapon that killed Carmine.

Maybe they were in more trouble than they could imagine.

Chapter 21

"ON YOUR KNEES," ONE of the officers shouted.

Sarah did as she was told. Parkman and Daniel followed, three of their car doors propped open.

"Hands on your heads, fingers intertwined."

They complied.

"Don't move."

Officers ran toward them, hunched over. The first cop ran behind Sarah, holstering his weapon and placing a hand on hers, pushing down on the top of her head. Cuffs slapped onto her right wrist, then it was yanked from her head, and her left followed, the cuff locking them together behind her back.

She considered complaining, protesting how rough he was being, but knew it would fall on deaf ears. This was their choice, to be out here, on Lorenzo's property, so they'd deal with it however it all played out.

"On your feet," the cop ordered.

Other officers had cuffed Daniel and Parkman.

"Are you carrying any weapons? Anything sharp in your pockets?"

"You want to tell us what this is all about?" Sarah asked.

"Answer the question."

Sarah held her breath a moment, then said, "No weapons."

"How about you two?"

Parkman and Daniel shook their heads. The cops holding them began to pat them down. A female officer stepped up to Sarah and did the same.

"What's this?" Parkman's cop held up the lightning strike fire starter tube, then read the name off the side of the device.

The female cop checking Sarah pulled Sarah's out of her pocket.

"Looks to me like you guys came here to start a fire," the first cop said.

"Uh, Officers." The security guard called from the other side of their car. "You might want to check the trunk. I overheard them talking about igniters and accelerants. I think they came here to burn something."

"That right?" the cop asked, yanking on her cuffs once for effect. "You came to burn something?"

"We were out driving around. Always thought about buying a Mavros home." She glanced at Parkman. "So, we stopped in and checked the area, map how far it is to the gym my boyfriend owns."

"You own a gym, do you?" the same cop asked. "What's this about accelerants?"

"Private conversation about how fast shit burns. Nothing

to do with anything. If he saw us from the moment we arrived until now, this guard will tell you that all we did was walk the length of this street"—she jerked her head back toward the way they'd walked—"checking out the area."

"Yeah," the guard said. "Sure, that's exactly what you did. Plus, the man taught her how to use those fire starter devices. And four or more red gas cans in the trunk. Just so you know, Officer, I wasn't wasting your time. If you guys didn't show up when you did, they would've burned something down."

"Did you actually see the gas cans, kid?" the cop asked.

Every officer from the four cruisers had gathered closer, forming a semi-circle around the three detainees.

The security guard nodded enthusiastically. "Yes, sir. I called my boss first. He's on his way but said you guys would get here faster."

"How many gas cans?"

"Four at least, one in each of their hands. This guy," he pointed at Daniel, "stayed in the car with it idling like they wanted a getaway vehicle all ready to go."

"How about we take a look in the trunk, then assess the charges you three will be facing? That sounds about right to you?"

"No one opens the trunk," Sarah said. "Not without proper paperwork."

The officer close to her whistled, glancing around at the other cops.

"Strong words for someone facing attempted arson charges, trespassing on private property, and probably a dozen others we can arrange."

"No warrant, no search." Sarah kept her tone firm, non-negotiable.

The officer edged away from her and addressed the security guard. "What's your name, son?"

"Drew Miller."

"Okay, Drew Miller, I need you to tell me once more what you saw in their hands."

"Red gas cans."

"And what did they do with them?"

"Shoved them back in the trunk of their car when they heard you coming."

The officer whistled again and turned to face the other assembled cops. "Sounds like probable cause to me."

"Sounds like it," the male officer holding Parkman said.

"Sounds like bullshit to me," Sarah said.

"Well, whatever *you* think means nothing to us." The cop moved to the driver's side of their car. "What *we* think is most important, and as officers of the law, we think you were about to commit a dangerous crime." He leaned down into the car, and then the trunk popped open. "So, let's take a look in this trunk of yours."

He strode to the back and lifted the trunk lid.

"Ooowheee," he whistled again. "What a smell." He met Sarah's gaze over the trunk lid, shaking his head. "What the hell were you going to burn down with all of this? The neighborhood?"

"Illegal search." Sarah grinned at him. "This gets tossed out of court as fast as you file the charges. You fucked up. And you may intend to commit a crime, but you don't have the act of committing a crime. Private citizens are allowed to drive around with gas cans in their trunks and fire strikers in their pockets. No law against it."

More vehicles approached the remote construction site. Sarah glanced over her shoulder as two SUVs turned onto the gravel road and headed their way, engines revving.

"Tossed out of court, eh?" the cop said, moving closer to Sarah.

She turned her attention back to him.

The cop was shaking his head. "You are one stupid bitch." He looked her up and down as the SUVs slowed to a stop, kicking up dust from their violent entrance. "This'll never see the inside of a courtroom."

Five large men exited the SUVs and strode confidently over to them.

"We got it from here," the lead man said.

"What the hell is this?" Parkman asked, speaking for the first time since the police had arrived.

"Looks like Lorenzo's men have arrived," Sarah said. "And these cops are hired thugs."

The officer moved behind her, pulling on the cuffs.

"What are you doing?" the lead man from the SUVs asked.

"Taking my cuffs back."

"Leave them on her."

"No, that wasn't the deal."

"Fuck it. Take your cuffs and go."

The other officers removed the cuffs from Parkman and Daniel, too. Lorenzo's men moved into position, their hands hidden in their jackets. They were packing, and if any of them tried to run, they'd be shot.

The cops took their cuffs and started for their cruisers, not one of them looking back. Not another word was spoken between them all.

Sarah rubbed her wrists, leaning on the front of their car as all the police cruisers backed up, then disappeared on the road outside the construction site.

"Good thing you showed up," she said.

"Shut the fuck up."

"We were about to kick their asses and make a run for it."

A gun came out and was placed under Sarah's jaw, tilting her head skyward.

"I said shut the fuck up," the man shouted.

"Instead, we'll kick your asses and make a run for it," she added, her voice strained as her neck was arched back.

"You don't listen, do you?"

"Not very well, I will admit."

"Uhm, what's going on here?" the security guard asked, backing up a few steps.

"Nothing," the man holding Sarah said. "You did good, kid. There'll be a bonus for you. Calling us first was the right move. You're free to go now. Take the rest of the night off."

The guard backed up five or six steps, then turned around and stomped quickly in the other direction, his footsteps fading with him.

"You and your crew are dead," the man said. "Whatever drugs you guys are on must make you stupid."

"Stupid drugs?" Sarah's stomach twisted when he said, *crew*. Was he talking about Aaron, Alex, and Benjamin, too?

"Attacking Lorenzo after he offered you a hundred grand

to help him out was the stupidest thing I've ever heard." The man laughed, stepping back off Sarah. "I mean, the man was being generous." He turned to the others standing around. "Wasn't he being generous?"

The others all nodded, a few guffaws added for effect.

"Sure he was," Sarah said. "Generous to a fault with his threat of stealing my daughter. He's an asshole, is what he is —"

The man swung fast, his hand coming quicker than Sarah could anticipate. She barely had time to brace herself, her eyes closing, before the back of the man's hand whipped across her face. The impact made her keel over, stumbling a few steps until she caught herself. The taste of blood filled her mouth where her teeth cut the inside of her cheek.

"Don't disrespect the boss. Your whore mouth doesn't say a word against him. Not after he showed you such kindness."

Sarah stood back up to her full height, a hand over her cheek. After a moment, she lowered the hand. This wasn't going so well at all, and Vivian was still gone.

How is this all working out, Vivian? Is there any chance you want to pop in and help us out a bit?

The men surrounding Daniel and Parkman had weapons in their hands now, lazily pointed at them.

"We doing it here, boss?" one of them asked.

The man in front of Sarah shook his head. "No, I don't want to carry the bodies. More work than necessary."

"Then where are we doing them?"

"In the basement of the house numbered thirty-eight. That basement hasn't been poured yet. We bury them under one foot of dirt, and the concrete truck will do the rest later today."

"Sounds great, boss."

"That won't happen," Sarah said, having no idea why she said it but wanting to instill some form of hope in Parkman and Daniel as if Vivian had told her something important.

"And why won't that happen? You so fucking dumb and blind you don't see who is in charge here?"

There was no way they could be led to house thirty-eight, walking on their own accord to be slaughtered in some basement.

"Because I know where Bianca is," she said, trying anything to stop their senseless murders. Under the circumstances, it was all she could come up with.

"I don't care if you know where the Queen of England is. You die in the time it takes to walk you to that house." He pointed over Sarah's shoulder. "Finding Bianca isn't something Bartleson needs you for now."

She was lost for words momentarily.

"Start walking." He shoved her so hard that she stumbled, caught herself, and then got to her feet.

"Hey, take it easy," Parkman shouted.

"You're worried she might fall, scuff a knee?" The man laughed. "That should be the least of your worries."

The men following Parkman and Daniel pushed them toward the same house.

"I mean, what were you thinking sending those assholes to burn the strip club?"

Sarah gasped before she could catch herself. So they knew about that, too. Holy fuck—she had underestimated

Lorenzo's people far too much.

"That's right. Gasp again because they're dead. All three of your crew or whatever the fuck you call yourselves."

Sarah stopped walking. That wasn't possible. They couldn't be dead. She searched for Vivian, but her sister had betrayed her—she was nowhere.

Sarah turned around to face the man, a hardness on her face.

"How is that possible?"

This time, the man didn't push her to continue walking. He enjoyed toying with her, tormenting her.

"Mancuso and Carmine were doing the collections tonight because our regular bagman was busy. Seems he might have found Bianca. Anyway, that doesn't matter. They were at the Peaches 'N Cream when your three idiots arrived and broke in with gas cans. Silvio called us to be on full alert and have teams ready to go at a moment's notice. So, when our security guard called this in, we knew what you were up to and ensured our people in uniform were here first."

She fought the tears that came to her eyes. Alex, Aaron, Benjamin—all dead because of her. Willow's father? No, she couldn't believe it—wouldn't.

"And you know for a fact that they were killed?"

The man nodded. "I spoke with Mancuso myself. He was about to jump Alex in the changing rooms area, and Carmine already had Benjamin with a gun on him. When he hung up the phone, they were waiting for Aaron to come and help Benjamin. They're all dead by now, sliced and diced and shot or whatever. And now you're all dead."

So, he didn't have confirmation.

Silvio Mancuso about to jump Alex? Not possible. Alex was human and could be sloppy but with someone like Mancuso? Had they been off too long, away from the action that they got careless?

"Now, keep moving."

Cars approached again in the distance.

Sarah stopped walking, wondering if the cops were returning. Maybe one of them had a conscience and couldn't let them be slaughtered in such a way.

Three four-door sedans pulled into the construction area and parked beside the SUVs.

"Now, who the fuck is this?" the man holding the gun on Sarah said.

Then, as if practiced a hundred times, Lorenzo's men hid their weapons inside their jackets.

Seven men and one woman started toward them. Lorenzo's men stood still, waiting.

"Can we help you?" the boss asked.

None of the newcomers responded.

The boss took a couple of steps toward them. "This is private property. Gonna have to ask you to kindly head back to your vehicles and leave the area."

When the group of eight were less than ten feet away, Sarah recognized who they were.

Badges flipped out, as well as weapons.

"FBI, Special Agent Tracie DeOcampo. You Lorenzo men seem to be in the wrong place at the wrong time. We heard everything."

The FBI moved quickly, surrounding Lorenzo's men.

"Drop your weapons and get those hands up. You're all

under arrest for attempted murder."

At that moment, Sarah wanted to kiss DeOcampo as Lorenzo's men dropped to their knees, hands raised high.

They were secured and placed inside two of the FBI vehicles without a fight. Then Sarah pulled DeOcampo aside.

"How did you know we'd be here?"

"Aaron told us."

Sarah frowned. "Why would he do that?"

"Not sure, but Benjamin's been shot, and Aaron had specific information that the Lorenzo Bartleson Group had placed a hit on all your heads."

"All of us," Sarah whispered as if speaking to herself. She paused, "Wait, what? Benjamin's been shot?"

DeOcampo nodded. "You can thank me later."

"I'll thank you now, but for what?"

"Agent Hartman is on his way to meet with Aaron at the hospital."

"Take us there."

"No chance, Sarah." She sized her up. "You're my prisoner now."

Chapter 22

Aaron paced in the hospital's waiting room, hoping to hear from someone soon. Once Benjamin was taken in through the emergency doors, Alex told him what he'd seen on Silvio's phone.

The man had texted someone about their arrival at the strip club and how Silvio and Carmine would ambush them, then execute all three. He texted to watch out for Sarah as she was probably attempting to hit them somewhere else and that this was a planned attack.

Silvio knew about the gas cans as he'd seen them approaching the strip club, cans in hand.

The text Silvio received back was *Take them all out ... and their dojo business*. He received another text instructing Silvio to finish their arrangement with Sarah and her *daughter*.

That meant they were all dead, and Silvio was supposed to pick up Willow, but they'd never find her.

That prompted Aaron to call her in with the FBI detective's business card. Alex had left the hospital twenty minutes after dropping off Benjamin, bound for the dojo to fortify the doors and hunker down to wait for whoever may come.

Aaron told Agent DeOcampo the construction site Sarah, Parkman, and Daniel were headed to and explained that they were in trouble.

DeOcampo said she'd get there as soon as she could.

Since then, Aaron had called Sarah's phone—Parkman's phone, too—no less than a dozen times without any answer. Worried sick as his cell phone battery percentage lowered with call after call, he had to stop.

Alone, waiting for news on Benjamin, cell battery at ten percent, Aaron paced the floor, wondering how it could all go so wrong so fast.

They'd done this sort of thing before. They'd dealt with worse issues and walked away unscathed—well, not always completely unscathed. Sometimes, there was a stab wound, a gunshot wound (mostly Benjamin), or even a broken bone. Sarah had her ankle broken once by some cannibal woman who had murdered and eaten her husband.

But they all survived with a limited amount of time in jail and with injuries they could sustain and walk away from— eventually.

This felt entirely different. Something about this Lorenzo Bartleson situation wore on him, making him feel they'd taken on more than they could deal with.

Or maybe they'd approached the entire thing from the wrong angle.

There was a lesson in there somewhere.

Wasn't attacking Bartleson an act of vengeance? Going after him and trying to hurt his businesses was revenge for his threat to the welfare of their family and the threat to their daughter. That couldn't go unanswered, but were they responding properly? Had they forgotten who they were at their core? Sarah and her people, her family, weren't like the mafia. They weren't organized crime.

Aaron dropped into a seat and hung his head in his hands, allowing doubt to cloud his thoughts.

What had they done?

Could it be undone?

If Benjamin died, that was on him. Alex and Aaron had taken Benjamin with them to protect him and keep him out of harm's way. Sad as it was, the unspoken truth was Benjamin was the weakest link, and Aaron took on the responsibility of making sure he was still involved in some capacity without much effort. Also, conversely, to be involved without holding them back.

And now he lay dying in a hospital bed, and due to their lack of diligence, Silvio and Carmine put the word out to watch for Sarah.

The order had come down from Lorenzo that Sarah and her people were to be executed. This meant that as soon as they knew where Benjamin was, one of Lorenzo's men would show up at the hospital, probably dressed as a doctor —or even an actual doctor—and he'd inject something into Benjamin that would stop his heart.

How would this end? How could they all survive it?

Perhaps the only way was with Bartleson's murder.

Aaron ran a hand through his hair as he sat back and studied the area, taking in everyone, searching for a suspicious nature, an odd glance his way.

Maybe Sarah had been right. Violence was Bartleson's business language, something he used to communicate his needs and wants. Sure, responding to the ultimatum violently had backfired, but maybe that was the route to stopping this. Perhaps they had to attack again, but better this time, with more effective results.

Carmine was dead, and Silvio was injured.

Sitting around and waiting for Lorenzo's people to show up with intent to kill wouldn't go well in Sarah's playbook.

But how would they hit him now? They were divided and weaker.

He pulled out his phone and checked the screen. No one had tried to call. After all his attempts, Sarah and Parkman weren't calling him back.

Nothing had better have happened to Sarah. If so, Aaron would have no recourse but to go after Bartleson himself and murder anyone who tried to stop him along the way. It was a dead-end road, but he'd travel it in Sarah's honor.

Willow came to mind, and he second-guessed that way of thinking.

He lowered his head, chin touching his chest.

Both Willow's parents killed? How could he knowingly go after Bartleson—

"Aaron?" A man shook his shoulder.

Aaron grabbed the guy's arm, twisted it off him, his other hand grabbing the back of the man's elbow in an attempt to snap it upward, then realized where he was—the hospital waiting room.

Benjamin's doctor stared at him, his arm hostage to Aaron's whim.

He let go, holding his open hands in the air. Then he brushed at the doctor's white lab coat.

"I'm so sorry," he muttered. "I think I was dozing off a bit. Didn't know it was you."

The doctor took an extra step back, regarding Aaron with a suspicious look in his eye, rubbing his arm near the elbow.

"Do you always attack people and try to break their arms when they're simply trying to get your attention?"

"I'm sorry," he said again, jabbing a finger toward the double doors where Benjamin had been taken earlier. "With my friend in there, my nerves are shot, and I haven't slept." He clasped his hands behind his back to be less threatening. "I'm truly sorry. That's no excuse."

After a moment, the doctor nodded. "Benjamin is sleeping now. I've sedated him for the pain." His tone was deeper, more professional.

"Is he going to be okay?" Tears leaped from Aaron's eyes.

"Well, I was a little worried at first."

"How so?"

The doctor stared at him a moment as if deciding to continue or not. "Please, sit." He gestured at the row of chairs.

Aaron dropped into the one he had occupied moments before.

The doctor sat beside him.

"The femoral artery runs the length of the thigh, using

the femur as a backstop."

Aaron nodded, wiping at a tear.

"The bullet shattered Benjamin's femur, and I was worried the femoral artery had been damaged, as is often likely in cases such as this."

"Was it?"

The doctor shook his head. "Luckily, it wasn't. We checked for arterial damage. We cleaned the area and removed the bullet. He will wear a cast to minimize movement until the femur heals in six to eight weeks, but that looks about it."

The doctor offered a placating smile. Something else was on his mind.

"What is it, Doc? What aren't you telling me?"

The man clasped his hands over his knees and stared down at them momentarily, then fixed his attention on a couple of noisy children walking by with their crying mother.

"I once heard a doctor give a speech on bullet wounds."

Aaron nodded, but the doctor was still looking away.

"And?" Aaron asked to prompt more.

The doctor faced him. "He said that bullets are magic."

"Magic? How so?"

"A man can be killed with one bullet or survive six bullets to the chest. It's all luck, or as he said, magic. All you need is one bullet to penetrate the heart and sever an artery. People die in minutes or hours, but they die." He took a moment to lean back, then crossed his arms over his chest. "Or you can take half a dozen bullets into the meat of muscle, shatter bones, and even get shot in the head and survive. I once worked on a man who had a bullet shatter his femoral artery. His heart was so strong, his athletic body so firm, that his muscles tightened and restricted blood flow, or should I say, blood loss. He ended up losing his leg below the knee, but he survived the gunshot."

"Why are you telling me this? Is there something I need to know about Benjamin's condition?"

The doctor got up from the chair and stared down at Aaron. "I'm telling you this because your friend has so many scars from bullet wounds, I lost count. Whatever you guys are involved in, you should consider a career move. I'm not sure Benjamin can handle another gunshot. Like I said, a bullet is magic, and he's been given multiple chances to survive. But any one bullet will kill him. Stop whatever you're doing. Find a way to stop this man from being target practice."

"I assure you, Doctor, Benjamin hasn't been used as target practice—"

The doctor raised a hand. "I don't need to know anything."

Feet shuffled on their left as four police officers turned a corner and started toward them.

"Tell them all about it. Gunshot wounds are reported to the authorities. I understand they sent extra officers as soon as they learned your names. Whoever you are, Aaron Stevens, they're quite interested."

The doctor stepped away. Aaron got up and faced the men walking toward him as the double doors leading to surgery waved and closed like the doors of a saloon.

"Aaron Stevens?" the first officer said as he approached.

Aaron nodded. There was no way to avoid this. If it

saved Benjamin's life, he'd endure whatever they wanted to put him through.

"Please, have a seat." The cop gestured behind Aaron.

Aaron lowered to the chair, his stomach a wave of nausea. How the hell was this going to play out?

The other officers fanned out in a semi-circle around him, two of them in plain clothes.

Detectives were already involved?

"What can you tell us about the gunshot wound to the man you brought in?"

Aaron decided on the truth. It would be too hard to develop a story that made sense, not to mention working the story with Benjamin. They would likely ask him a battery of questions upon his waking up.

And in the end, it was a good story. A big mobster abducts Sarah and Willow and then threatens their daughter. So, they decided to hurt him but didn't get to do any damage as they were attacked and Benjamin was shot.

They were able to wrestle the gun from Carmine and shoot him.

"So this Carmine is dead?" the cop asked, making notes as he spoke.

Aaron nodded. "Yes."

"And whose prints will we find on the gun?"

"In other words, who shot Carmine?" Aaron asked, wondering if he should admit that Benjamin had done it. In his weariness and moment of grief, he hadn't stopped to consider the legal ramifications of some of the things he had said. What if he was setting them all up for heavy criminal charges? Should he have broached a lot of this with a lawyer?

He shook his head to clear the doubt. Sure, they were there to stir shit up, but at the end of the day, Carmine was dead in a clear case of self-defense. It was Benjamin who shot after being shot by Carmine himself.

"You'll find Carmine's prints on the weapon because he shot Benjamin with it. And you'll find Benjamin's from when he shot Carmine in self-defense."

The cop raised an eyebrow. "That'll help you three."

"How so?"

He stopped writing and then met Aaron's gaze. "Benjamin got shot, then through a series of events, Benjamin shot his attacker in self-defense. At least, I'm hoping that's how this will play out."

Aaron felt a sense of relief. Maybe something will work out for them after all. Wasn't there a saying about the truth, and how valuable it was, how it would set you free?

"Although, we can't rule out charges for you guys. That was some crazy idea you had, to burn down a strip club."

Aaron nodded. "In retrospect, I agree. We were just so angry at the prospect of having my daughter's welfare threatened."

"If Sarah is at some construction site, and you're here, where is your daughter?"

The cop asked this question so casually that it frightened Aaron. Or was he being paranoid now? This time, he decided to give the cop a half-truth.

"I'm not sure. Sarah's handling that in case I got picked up by Bartleson's people."

A look of unease crossed the man's face, or was it irritation?

"How could a father not know where his daughter is?" the cop asked.

Aaron started to wonder if these men were actual cops. Were the two plainclothes detectives actually detectives? Could they all work for Bartleson? This was another lesson on how well-connected the man was and how easy it was to get to them all.

Or was he just being paranoid?

In his weakened state, he thought about fighting them. They had weapons, guns they could draw on him. Shots would be fired, and like that doctor just told him—bullets were magic. He could take six bullets and live to talk about it, or one could end his life. And if he was to be shot, what a wonderful place for it all to go down—right in a hospital, on the emergency surgery level, so close to emergency care.

The elevator dinged down the hallway, which was a rare occurrence at four in the morning. Two of the men standing over Aaron glanced that way.

He knew something was up by the expressions on their faces.

The two plainclothes officers backed away, then moved several feet to the side as at least seven armed men in suits rounded the corner.

Special Agent Max Hartman with the FBI led the way.

Aaron didn't realize he could feel such relief to see a member of law enforcement in all his life.

"Boy, am I glad to see you," Aaron said. "These four just took my statement, and they're—"

"Aaron's coming with us," Hartman said, flipping open his ID. "This is our case, and our task force takes jurisdiction."

"How does the FBI have jurisdiction north of the border?" the cop who took Aaron's statement asked.

Hartman explained something about special clearance and how it was granted. He even produced a document for the officers to see.

"We'll take Aaron with us and leave two men to watch over Benjamin." Hartman turned to his men, pointing two out. "No one talks to Benjamin." They nodded and disappeared through the saloon doors the doctor had used minutes before.

After a brief conversation, the four Toronto cops sauntered away. There was nothing else for them here.

Hartman sat beside Aaron and listened to the entire story as Aaron told it again, leaving nothing out. When Aaron was finished, Hartman dialed out on his phone, then held it to his ear.

"We had good timing, DeOcampo. Aaron had given a statement to local cops, but they're gone now." Hartman nodded once, then looked at Aaron. He continued, telling DeOcampo a tighter version of Aaron's story, one where he mentioned Silvio being on the loose and Carmine dead, with Benjamin pulling the trigger. "Yes, he's right here. Other than bloodshot eyes, he looks fine." Hartman studied him a moment longer. "Absolutely." Then he hung up.

"This all ends today, Aaron." Hartman stared at him. "Sarah's going to wear a wire."

Aaron gasped, then dropped back to his seat so hard the impact rattled his teeth.

Sarah, undercover, wearing a wire, to catch Lorenzo.

The mother of their child was used as bait to reel in a mobster.

How the hell did she agree to do that?

Chapter 23

"WE HAVE TO GO," Sarah said.

DeOcampo shook her head. "No, it's okay. We don't have to go anywhere. We talk first."

"That guy you just arrested told us Aaron and the others were dead. He said they were all killed." The full realization of what the man had said hit her hard. She stumbled, trying to catch her breath, leaning into the side of her car. Parkman was there to lean on. He held her up and told her to breathe.

The full impact of how close they came to being shot was setting in on her system. By her recklessness, she almost left Willow without her parents.

DeOcampo moved into her field of vision. "Sarah, they're not dead."

Sarah gasped, a hand on her chest, the other clinging to DeOcampo's sleeve. "How do you know?"

"Because Aaron was the one who called me. That's why we're here. I left my card at the dojo, remember? He picked it up."

She wiped her face and stood straighter, slightly bent at the waist. What had come over her? Wouldn't Vivian have stepped in and said something? Wasn't that what they were doing for a decade? In the end, this was all Vivian's doing. Sarah's name got to Bartleson because of her past, a past fueled by her sister's words in her ear, and now her sister was dead silent.

Come back to me, Vivian. Haven't got much more patience for this shit.

"What did Aaron tell you?" she asked DeOcampo.

"It's not good."

"Tell us." She had calmed down, the mild panic attack already over. She wasn't usually susceptible to such attacks, but when it hit her that Aaron was gone, Alex and Benjamin, too, she had to fight to keep it together.

"One of Bartleson's lieutenants, Silvio Mancuso, and Silvio's next in line, a man named Carmine, were inside the strip club your boys went to burn to the ground. They got jumped."

"That explains what that guy said." She gestured at the SUV that held the FBI's prisoners. "What happened? Did Aaron tell you more?"

She nodded. "They got the upper hand. Silvio is cut bad but on the loose, and Carmine is dead."

Sarah suppressed a smile. "Even when they got jumped, it didn't go Bartleson's way."

"I don't see it like that, Sarah."

"How do you see it?"

"Benjamin was shot."

She stared at DeOcampo, not blinking.

"You don't seem surprised."

"I'm not. Sad for Benjamin, but not surprised."

"Why not?"

"Long story. How is he?"

"Aaron said Benjamin was headed into surgery at the time. He passed out on the way to the hospital."

Sarah and Parkman exchanged a worried glance.

"He'll pull through. I'd know if he was in mortal danger." Her confidence restored, she leaned back and rested on the car.

"I sent Agent Hartman to the hospital to ensure agents watch over Benjamin, and Hartman will pick up Aaron."

"Where's Alex?"

"He apparently went to the dojo to keep it safe. After what you guys did tonight, Bartleson will throw everything he's got at you, your friends, your family, and your business."

"Then I need to leave. This needs to end today."

"Sarah." DeOcampo stepped in front of her. "You need to wear a wire. Set up a meeting with Bartleson and go in strapped. Actually, I've already told Hartman and Aaron that you'll wear a wire."

Sarah shook her head. "No way, it's not going to happen. You can call Hartman back and tell him you lied. I'm going after Bartleson my way. He made this personal."

"Sarah, you don't understand. This is the only way."

Sarah leaned on her car again, arms crossed. She quickly told the agent what had happened when Bartleson picked her up and what had happened at the construction site.

Daniel wandered off to collect himself after their close

call with death while Parkman browsed something on his phone, only half listening. Once she'd given her statement, it was close to four in the morning.

"Sarah, think about how many police officers are involved," DeOcampo said. "Think about how deep this goes."

"I know, and the only way to deal with a man like Lorenzo is to kill him. Otherwise, the threat against my daughter does not go away."

"What I'm proposing puts him in jail for twenty years, easy—perhaps longer. What you're proposing puts you in jail for the same amount of time."

Sarah glared at her a moment, then looked away. "Even if he goes to prison, men like Bartleson can reach us from the inside."

DeOcampo shook her head, then glanced away, following Daniel's progress a hundred yards away. Most of her colleagues were tired and getting fidgety. They had to be bored, standing around while Sarah and DeOcampo negotiated their terms.

"Look, we saved your lives tonight, not to mention stopped you from breaking the law." DeOcampo moved closer. "Meet me halfway. Wear a wire and go about your business. Beat the guy up, attack him, I don't care. But don't kill him, or I'd have to arrest you, and where would that put you with Willow?"

Sarah tightened her jaw at the sound of her daughter's name. She almost shot out some half-witted remark but knew it would serve no purpose.

"Look, I don't know everything, and sometimes I'm not

all that smart—"

"I'd go with stupid," DeOcampo cut in. "What you guys did tonight was stupid."

"Fine, call it stupid then. We make mistakes. I was coming from an emotional place, a mother lashing out at the people who threatened the welfare of her daughter."

"Smartest thing you've said all night."

Sarah raised one finger. "Easy on the sarcasm. I don't want to get pissed off."

"Fine, but you're wearing a wire for me."

"You know, DeOcampo, I admire that fire in you, the level of confidence you bring to the table."

"Great, you respect me. I'm hearing you, but we got a bad guy to catch. A bad guy who deals in drugs and launders a lot of his proceeds right here in Toronto. We followed the money for months, and it led us here. You are our biggest break in quite some time, and I need your help. If you don't do it willingly, I'll force you."

Sarah pushed off the car. "We're done here."

"Sarah," DeOcampo shouted.

Sarah stopped moving.

"We saved your life tonight. You owe me."

She turned back to face her. "You may have saved my life tonight, but you'll kill me by making me wear a wire to a meeting with Lorenzo. The questions you'll want me to ask in that meeting will raise suspicion." She shook her head. "No, I can't allow you to send me to Lorenzo's lair wired up. He'll knife me or shoot me before you could ever send in help." Sarah inhaled, then sighed. "You saved our lives tonight, only to kill me with this wire shit."

"Then you'll leave me no choice."

"No choice? What's that supposed to mean?"

"Wear a wire, or get arrested."

Parkman, who had remained mostly silent, made a sound of derision.

"Come on, DeOcampo," he said. "Find another way. Hasn't she had enough ultimatums for one twenty-four-hour period?"

The agent shook her head. "I'm desperate. Help us get this done, or I'll have to arrest you. Besides, with you inside, it serves two purposes."

Sarah placed her hands on her hips. "Oh yeah, what two purposes?"

"One, you're safe. I can keep an eye on you. And two, you're not out here going after Lorenzo on your own. I don't want to have to keep cleaning up your messes."

"What charges are you proposing?"

"All kinds of charges, starting with Carmine's murder. Until it's all figured out, which could take months, Carmine was shot, and I'm sure one of your guys' fingerprints will be on the weapon as Carmine wouldn't shoot himself. You arranged to have your boys show up in the middle of the night with gas cans to burn the place down, and they used some fancy martial arts to disarm them, shoot one guy, and cut the other. You're complicit no matter how you look at it."

Sarah whistled and spun around on her heels. "Listen to this shit."

"And," DeOcampo sounded proud of herself. "What were you doing here, in the middle of the night, on a Bartleson property with gas cans in your trunk?"

"We willingly told you what we were doing—"

"Willingly or not, charges are now pending." DeOcampo moved closer and lowered her voice. "Look, Sarah, I don't want to have to go that route, but you're forcing my hand—"

Her phone cut her off. She slipped it out of her pocket and stepped away to speak in private. Sarah caught a few sentences, but one in particular where DeOcampo said matter-of-factly that Sarah would wear a wire.

Without notice or warning whatsoever, Vivian popped into her head, rambled a few wild sentences, and then disappeared.

Blindsided by the violence of her sister's visit, Sarah clutched at Parkman as she gasped and turned away.

"What?" Parkman asked. "What is it?"

"Vivian …"

"Sarah?" DeOcampo said. "Everything okay?"

She inhaled a few times, patted Parkman's arm, then faced DeOcampo.

"Everything's fine. I now know who will help us. He will wear your wire."

DeOcampo glanced from Parkman to Sarah, then back to Parkman.

"Who?" she asked.

"We need to leave. What time is it?"

DeOcampo checked her watch. "Slightly after four."

"We need to leave," she said again. "The man we need to speak with will be on Front Street within the hour."

"Who is this man?"

"Go," Sarah said. "Get in your vehicle and follow us."

"Sarah," DeOcampo said, drawing out her name. "I'm

not buying this shit. I'll have you arrested."

Sarah rushed her, grabbing DeOcampo's sleeves. Two other agents moved in quickly, but DeOcampo shook her head. They stopped a foot from grabbing Sarah, Parkman shoulder to shoulder with her.

"Do you know who I am, what I can do?"

DeOcampo nodded.

"My sister just explained a few things to me. I think I see how this ends." She released the agent's arms and then patted down each sleeve. "Two phone calls end this somehow."

"What do you mean, *how this ends*? What two phone calls?"

"My sister showed me the image of a house in the bush."

"A house in the bush?" DeOcampo's sarcastic tone revealed a lack of belief.

Sarah nodded. "An A-frame house."

"And where is this house?"

"Look, DeOcampo, we're almost out of time. We have to go meet Sal."

"Who's Sal?" She blinked like she just realized something. "Do you mean Salvatore Prezzie?"

Sarah nodded. "He'll wear your wire."

DeOcampo shook her head in a short burst. "No fucking way. Bartleson's own bagman? And why would he do that?"

"DeOcampo, you'll just have to trust me on this. Now, give me your cell number in case we get separated."

DeOcampo recited it, and Sarah memorized it by saying it to herself several times. Then she stepped around the hood of her car. "Daniel," she called. "We're leaving."

She stopped at the door. "I'm going to get in this car and

drive away. You're either going to follow me and see this through, or you're going to arrest me. But know that arresting me means you'll never get Bartleson, ever." She waited a moment, offering DeOcampo her own brand of ultimatums. "The choice is yours."

Daniel ran up behind her. "You driving?" he asked.

Sarah nodded, her eyes locked on the FBI agent.

Daniel jumped in the back, and Parkman dropped in the passenger seat.

A moment later, Sarah slipped into the driver's seat, heard DeOcampo curse several times, and then ran for her SUV.

When Sarah hit the road, DeOcampo's SUVs were right on her tail.

"What did Vivian tell you?" Parkman asked.

"To ditch the FBI and meet with Sal at a restaurant on Queen Street."

"I thought you told them Front Street."

"I did."

Parkman nodded his understanding. "That's the part about losing them."

Sarah slapped the steering wheel. "This is fucked and just got worse."

"How?"

Then Sarah told them what Vivian shared with her and the reasons Bartleson's daughter took off.

That was the worst part—the most shocking.

And she told them about the darkness Vivian warned was coming.

One of their team wouldn't make it.

A funeral was coming.

Chapter 24

SAL WAS LOSING STRENGTH fast. He was so close now. The night sky hadn't lightened yet, but the sun was less than an hour away from rising.

The throbbing in his hand told him two things. One, he needed more painkillers, and two, there was no second-guessing his decision about killing Silvio Mancuso. Once he got Diego's gun back, he'd take his car and sleep in the back seat somewhere by the lake. Then call Mancuso with the lie that he found Frankie.

They'd meet, and he'd shoot the asshole point-blank.

Of course, it would be the end of his life, but if that's what suicide looked like, then he'd take it because he was dead anyway. There was no way Bartleson would let him live after killing Diego. Sal thought he was dead earlier during their meeting at the back of Johnny's Bar and Grill. It was Bartleson's whisper to Silvio that called it off—temporarily.

Sal's steps faltered as a thought came to him.

How did they know he'd be there? Or was Bartleson already there when Sal walked in, and he hadn't noticed the man and his entire fucking entourage of security at the back of the restaurant?

A dizzy spell made him lurch into the brick wall beside him. Some fashion design store with pretty mannequins in the window already had their open sign-on. He leaned against the brick and peered inside the dimly lit store while collecting his breath. It was still closed, the lights low, with no one inside. Maybe they just forgot to click off the neon sign the previous evening.

Something in the window's reflection caught his eye when he pushed off the wall.

Sal spun around so fast he almost lost his balance, but the man was gone when he locked eyes on the spot he'd seen in the reflection.

He blinked several times to ward off the dizziness, then peered up and down the street on the other side. No one was around.

After a moment, he focused on the window pane again, staring at the area where he thought he'd seen a man standing, watching him, but it now looked like a shadow.

"Fuck, I'm paranoid."

Sal started up the street again, lumbering along, his head a jumble of thoughts about his mother, never seeing her again, and what the hell had Frankie been thinking. It seemed like a half hour had zipped by, and he was now walking along the block where Johnny's Bar and Grill was located.

After several backward glances and no one watching or following him, Sal logged the sighting as his overactive imagination. Who could know where he was, what he was doing?

"Oh, wait," he whispered to himself. "They know I went to the hospital, and they would know where my car is parked."

So, this sojourn made sense.

And if they were watching him—in case he met up with or made contact with Frankie and Bianca—they'd be sorely disappointed. What a waste of manpower.

Sal strode slowly past the restaurant, glancing awkwardly at the door and the windows. How the hell would he gain access at this hour without tools and a bum hand?

The back of the building.

Wouldn't their alarm go off?

Sure, it would, but he'd be in the bathroom, grabbing the gun, and back out to his car before cops could arrive.

At the back of the building, the sky lightening as the sun made its way into southern Ontario, he scanned the ground for tools.

The sound of an engine slowed, then stopped out front. After a few moments, it pulled away.

Could the cook be coming in early? At this hour? Or was it just bakeries that opened this early?

Didn't matter in the end. Sal needed that gun, and there was no way around it. He had to break in and retrieve it.

The back alley only contained two large dumpsters. No tools to break in, no chunks of metal, and certainly no screwdrivers.

But there was a rock—a large rock.

Sal grabbed the rock with his good hand, took a couple

of breaths to steady his rapid pulse, then leaned back with the rock easing over his right shoulder and threw it at the glass in the back door.

The pane shattered near the thumb latch, the alarm sounded, and Salvatore reached inside to unlock the door, mindful not to cut himself.

The door popped open.

Salvatore Prezzie ran inside, headed straight for the men's bathroom; only two things on his mind now.

Get that gun and revenge.

Chapter 25

SARAH WAS TOO LATE.

She'd missed him.

Vivian had said a man named Sal would walk by this restaurant, and then he'd disappear inside.

Sarah was supposed to stop him from going inside.

She checked the time on her phone—missed him by several minutes.

She'd stopped the car, hopped out, and given instructions for Parkman to wait a block away and for Daniel to drive up to Front Street to delay DeOcampo and the other FBI agents.

She told Parkman not to intervene with her no matter what he saw. His only task was to stop the FBI or local authorities from stepping in.

Luckily, she'd been able to lose DeOcampo's SUVs when she'd taken the Yonge Street exit and drove up to Bloor. She took the Bloor viaduct and dropped south to Queen Street via Jones Avenue, which was off of Pape. She'd gone this route because she remembered Drake Bellamy's parents had lived on Hunter Street, which was just off of Jones.

But that little side trip had cost her precious time.

And now she'd missed out on meeting the man who would—

The alarm inside the restaurant blared beside her, making her jump and almost drop her cell phone.

"What the fuck is he doing?" she muttered to herself. Then to Vivian, "What's the play here?"

Sarah took in the street, glancing up and down it, but only saw a large milk delivery truck easing along, moving away from her.

Without thinking of what she had to do other than make contact with this man named Sal, she ran to the end of the block, rounded the corner at full speed, and hit the alleyway, pumping her arms hard.

Strong security lights lit the back area as she guessed how many stores she had to pass until she reached the back of the restaurant.

However, counting wasn't necessary as a small sign saying *Johnny's Bar and Grill* had been tacked above a door with broken glass that sat slightly ajar.

Approaching a burglar in the middle of a break-in while unarmed was quite stupid as she had no idea if he was armed, and no idea what his intentions were, or why he would break into a restaurant at five in the morning.

All she understood from Vivian was that the man inside the restaurant was her key to getting to Bartleson, and she had to utilize him—at all costs.

At the back door, she stepped inside quietly, but that wasn't necessary as the blaring alarm would've covered any sounds she might have made.

There was enough light from the emergency lighting fixtures to see the tables and chairs and to move around without stumbling.

The man she needed to find was nowhere in sight.

He wasn't at the bar stashing bottles into a garbage bag or at the cash register pilfering cash.

"Then what the hell did you break in here for?" she asked aloud, the sound not traveling farther than her nose as the alarm had to be well over one hundred decibels.

The only area she couldn't see was the short hallway to the bathrooms.

The second she started that way, the wailing siren of the alarm silenced.

It was so sudden that she stumbled into a table, bumped a chair, and knocked it over. The siren left a ringing in her ear in its wake.

The back door hadn't moved. The flashing alarm panel near the front door still had lights blinking, but no one stood by it.

The siren must have timed out. Within several moments, the siren would start up again.

And when the police got there, she couldn't be inside the building. Getting arrested for a break-in, she didn't do would fuck everything up.

She started for the men's room, hoping that this criminal broke in, and got so nervous about what he was doing that he had to detour to the bathroom first.

If he wasn't there, she'd missed him completely, and Bartleson would never be taken down.

She wanted to curse Vivian's name as she grabbed the men's room doorknob and pushed it open.

Chapter 26

DeOcampo punched the dash of the SUV above the glovebox.

"Where the fuck is she?"

Her driver shook his head.

DeOcampo twisted around in her seat. "Mark, bring up all of Bartleson's businesses in the downtown area. I want to know if Bartleson has a financial finger in anything down here."

The driver glanced at her a couple of times. "Where do you want me to go?"

"Just keep driving along Front Street until we see her, Parkman, or their car. She said Front Street, so she has to be here."

They rode in silence for several blocks.

"Mark? Anything?"

"I've got two restaurants, one pizzeria, and two coffee shops."

"Okay, which ones are closest to us right now?"

"One sec."

"Pull over," DeOcampo ordered.

The driver eased to the side of the road.

"We wait here until Mark gives us a location."

"I'm getting nothing on Front Street, though," Mark said.

She hadn't been deceived like this in such a long time. If it weren't for her, there was a solid chance Sarah, Parkman, and Daniel would be dead. And then Sarah pulls this stunt. A ruse to get them off her ass. Sarah's level of deceit showed no limits, no bounds.

DeOcampo shouldered into the door, opened it, and jumped down to the sidewalk. She wanted to scream and shout Sarah's name in anger, but all she could do was clench her fists and pace back and forth, two steps, then two the other way, seething with fury.

"Anything?" she asked from outside. There was no doubt Mark heard her because half the block would've heard her.

"The closest business Bartleson has in this area is a place called Johnny's Bar and Grill. It's a five-minute ride from here."

DeOcampo hopped back in the passenger seat. "Then what are we waiting for?"

The driver put the SUV in park and released the brake.

DeOcampo gawked at him. "What the fuck are you doing?"

The driver nodded forward. "Look."

Daniel, Sarah's martial arts man, was walking toward them.

"Well, I'll be ..." DeOcampo didn't finish the sentence.

She jumped back out of the SUV and started toward Daniel.

"Where is she?"

"Who?"

Her hand twitched as she reached for her weapon. Someone would give her answers today if she had to shoot it out of them. Her hand on the butt of her gun, willing herself not to draw it on Daniel, equally afraid she might just pull the trigger out of a rage-filled madness, she asked him again from five feet away.

"Where's Sarah?"

"Oh, she had to meet someone."

DeOcampo could barely contain herself. It was Mark who showed up beside her, tugging on her arm.

"It's cool," he said. "Daniel, you're under arrest. We'll start with aiding and abetting and go from there."

DeOcampo found her voice. "Unless you want to tell us where Sarah is."

With an innocent look, he glanced over his shoulder, then spun back to look over DeOcampo's shoulder. After a moment, he shrugged. "Your guess is as good as mine."

"Arrest him."

Mark slipped behind Daniel and cuffed him. Lucky for Daniel, he didn't protest.

"You know," Daniel said as they escorted him to the back of the SUV. "The way to Sarah is through her heart."

DeOcampo spun him around at the side door of her SUV. "What the fuck does that mean?" Her voice was louder than intended, but the fury pulsing in her veins at being hoodwinked seemed uncontrollable. "We saved your life. This is the thanks I get?"

Daniel shrugged. "To you, it may look like you saved our lives."

"What the hell does it look like to you?"

He shrugged again. "On the surface, the same. But Vivian knew you were coming. Otherwise, she would've warned Sarah to stop what she was doing and leave way before Bartleson's men showed up."

"Oh, I see. So this is all a game only Sarah can play? Are we just props on her stage of life, like fucking marionette dolls, letting her pull the strings?"

"Something like that."

"Get in the fucking car before I shoot you."

"As I said," Daniel muttered as he climbed in, his hands cuffed. "The way to her is through her heart."

"And how do I do that?"

"Stop threatening her. Talk to her head, and you lose. Talk to her heart; you win."

"Okay, tell me what to say, what to do." DeOcampo couldn't believe she was still listening to Daniel's bullshit. "I'm all ears."

"Take me to Benjamin."

"What?"

"Take me to see Benjamin in the hospital. Your people are watching him. At least let me stay with him while he recovers with your people watching over us. Sarah will see that as kindness. She'll be more inclined when the time comes to get her to listen to you."

"Who the fuck are you people? You're unbelievable."

Daniel didn't answer. He just rested his head back and closed his eyes while sitting at an odd angle to account for the cuffs on his wrists.

"This situation is out of fucking control," DeOcampo screamed, then got back in the SUV, slamming her door.

235

Chapter 27

Sal had removed the tape and easily retrieved Diego's gun. Once he checked that it was loaded and ready, he got to his feet, and the siren stopped.

He froze on the spot, listening for whoever turned it off.

A chair had moved or been bumped over.

He listened for more indications that someone was there by placing his ear to the door, but nothing else came from inside the restaurant.

Siren or no siren, he needed to leave as soon as possible. That alarm would draw the authorities.

Wasn't he the one with the gun? Why was he cowering behind the men's room door?

Maybe his hand injury was messing with his head. If so, was he thinking straight? Should he be trying to kill Silvio in the first place?

Sleep would help. Once he got several hours' sleep in his car, he'd decide what to do next.

When he reached for the door, the knob was already twisting.

Someone was opening the door from the other side.

Sal lifted the weapon with his good hand while stepping back.

He would shoot first and ask questions later. Because whoever was coming through that door was the person who had been following him all morning.

It had to be.

The ghost in the window pane was one of Bartleson's people. Who else would know the code to silence the alarm?

His back bumped the wall, and his finger tightened.

The door opened all the way.

A blonde woman stepped inside, glanced around, and met his eyes.

"Don't shoot." The woman paused, raising her hands. "Salvatore Prezzie? Put the gun down. I'm unarmed."

Chapter 28

SARAH TURNED THE KNOB and slowly opened the men's bathroom door. The light was on in there, so Sal had to be inside the men's washroom.

If given the choice, she'd rather let him do his business and wait outside the door, but that would startle him too much when he stepped out, and they were running out of time. That alarm would summon cops, along with Bartleson's people. They needed to leave, and they needed to do it immediately.

She pushed the door all the way open.

A man stood against the back wall, a gun extended from his hand, pointed at her.

She fought the instinct to jump back and duck down.

"Don't shoot," she said, raising her hands. "Salvatore Prezzie? Put the gun down. I'm unarmed."

"You a waitress or something?" he asked.

"We have to leave."

He pushed off the wall, rushed her, and shoved the gun an inch from her belly button. Sarah raised her hands higher to appear as non-threatening as possible.

"*We* aren't going anywhere together."

"You're looking for Frankie, right?"

Salvatore regarded her warily, studiously eying her face, then her raised hands.

"What is this? Bartleson sent you? Or do you work for Silvio?"

"Neither, I'm involved because Bartleson kidnapped me and threatened to take my daughter if I didn't help him—"

Something banged out in the restaurant.

Salvatore jumped, and for a second, Sarah wondered if he would pull the trigger.

Instead, he pushed past her, gun raised, pointed down the hallway. When no one appeared, he turned back and whispered, "Who's with you?"

"No one. I'm alone. But we have to leave. That alarm means people are coming, and you don't want to be here when people arrive."

He grabbed her hair and tilted her head back with a hand that was wrapped in a bandage, making him wince.

What was it with men and pulling hair to show strength and dominance? It was great in the bedroom, but she was getting sick of it on the street. If she wanted her hair pulled, she'd do it herself like she used to as a teenager.

At least the gun wasn't pointed at her anymore. And if things turned sour fast, he had a weakness—that bandaged hand that held her hair.

"Okay," he said close to her ear. "We'll leave together

because you're my hostage now. I'm so done. You have no idea. I will kill you and everyone else who tries to stop me."

"That's why I'm here. To help."

"Bullshit, you couldn't know I would be here."

"We need to leave," she said, her tone firm.

They could argue outside, far from the building.

Sarah started toward the main seating area. He let her go, her head only tilting back slightly until he released her hair.

Gingerly, she stepped around the corner and glanced at the back door. It sat open farther than how she had left it.

"Someone else might be here," she whispered over her shoulder.

"If they try to stop us, I'll kill them and you, too."

His voice came out ragged like he was vibrating with rage.

How is this a good idea, Vivian?

Was she supposed to stop him from breaking into the restaurant and setting off that alarm? Now they had to not just leave the building, they had to leave the area undetected, and at five in the morning, they'd likely be one of a few people out walking the streets.

She led the way to the back without being interrupted, Salvatore holding her shoulder. At least it wasn't her hair anymore.

No one lingered in the shadows or behind pillars. No one jumped out at them or tried to stop them.

A red light blinked in the back corner, up near the ceiling.

A camera.

It moved ever so slowly with their progress toward the

back door.

"Shit," she mumbled. "They're watching."

"Who?"

She pointed at the camera, and the alarm sounded again, making them both jump.

At the back door, she didn't waste any time getting outside. Luckily, the back alley was clear.

What had banged inside the restaurant then?

Salvatore pushed her. "Keep walking."

"We have to get hidden. I know a place."

"Yeah, my car. It's parked a block up."

"Lead the way."

Salvatore pushed her again, which was trying her patience, but she let it happen. He had the gun, after all, and she needed him to trust her.

"So, what do you do for Bartleson?" he asked as they crossed Queen Street, which was mostly empty.

Where were the cops? Or what about a security company? Why was there no response to the alarm that had to be going for five minutes at least?

Could Bartleson's people be monitoring it themselves? The way that camera tracked them—it had to be Bartleson.

"I don't work for that man," she said. "I already told you he kidnapped me and threatened to take my daughter."

"Why?"

"He wants me to find Bianca, and I refused."

"Bad choice. Life expectancy decreases quickly with decisions like that."

"As I've discovered."

"How did you know I'd be here?" He slowed by a car

and pulled out his keys, allowing her to walk around to the passenger side.

It would take too long to explain who she was and how Vivian told her he was the connection to a man named Frankie and ending Bartleson.

"I staked out your car." She shrugged.

The door locks popped. She tore open the passenger side and got in before he could stop her.

"Wait a second," he said, dropping into the driver's side.

"No time. Just drive."

"I'm not going anywhere with you."

She faced him. "I thought I was your hostage."

"Yeah, to get me clear of that place." He jerked his head back toward the restaurant. "I have something else to do now, someone I must meet. So, get out."

"No, we go together. This is the only way."

He placed the gun at her side, shoving it painfully into her lower ribs.

"I said, get out."

"You're not a murderer, Salvatore."

"I won't traipse around Toronto doing what I have to do today with one of Bartleson's bitches in my car."

Sarah shoved her left elbow backward, pushing the gun into the seat, and leaned forward in the same motion in case it went off. Twisting her body around to face him, she grabbed at the bandaged hand, gripping it tight.

Gun hand secure, wounded hand in her grip, she leaned in close to him.

"Stop fighting me. I'm the only friend you got. It may not look like it right now, but I am. And I don't work for

Bartleson—in fact, I'm working on ruining his life. You're just going to have to trust me on this."

Salvatore whimpered in pain. He let go of the captive gun and grabbed at her hand that held the bandage, trying to dislodge it.

Sarah let go without a fight in order to pick up the gun. She aimed it at him and settled back against the passenger door as tears oozed down Salvatore's face.

"Cry later, drive now. We have shit to do."

He stared at her a moment, glanced at the gun aimed at him, then turned on the car.

Sirens wailed from somewhere on the Yonge Street side.

"Now they come," she said. "Stay on Queen Street, but drive away from the sirens. We're heading to a martial arts dojo."

"Why there?"

"I have a friend waiting for us there. Together, we'll set up something to end this shit."

Salvatore performed a U-turn and drove the way she had told him to.

"I already have a plan," he said. "I'm going to kill Silvio Mancuso."

"That asshole with the knife."

Salvatore nodded.

"Good plan." After a moment, she lowered the weapon to her thigh. "Also, don't ever pull my hair again. Don't ever pull a woman's hair again without permission."

"What woman would give permission for that?"

"You'll know it when you have it. Just shut up and drive."

Sarah watched the mirrors as several police cars stopped in front of the restaurant about two blocks back.

Something about the delayed response bothered her.

And what caused that bang? Had someone else been inside the restaurant with them?

Just like the construction site, when the guard called it in, Bartleson's own people responded, or the people he owned responded. Either way, it was always Bartleson's people which convinced her that Bartleson knew they were together now.

"Why did you break into a restaurant at five in the morning? To use the toilet?"

"That was Bartleson's place."

"Thought so. What were you doing in there?"

He nodded at the gun on her thigh. "I stashed that in the bathroom yesterday. Needed it back."

"For what?"

"To kill Mancuso. Already told you that."

"Oh, right."

They rode in silence a moment longer.

"Well, if my calculations are correct, you're going to receive a phone call this morning, and that will set into place a series of events that'll take down the entire Bartleson Group."

"How could you know that? Who's going to call me?"

She yawned, staring out the window. She really needed sleep soon.

"I just know shit sometimes."

Chapter 29

PARKMAN STOOD A BLOCK away, listening to the alarm's siren wail from the restaurant, not moving any closer to intervene as Sarah had asked him to. This far down, the noise wouldn't be the caterwaul she'd endure inside the restaurant. Instead, it resembled the sound of a distant fire alarm.

It had stopped for some time, but he hadn't seen Sarah surface. Then, the alarm started up again.

He hopped on the spot from foot to foot, watching the street in front of the restaurant for any sign of movement, but Sarah didn't emerge.

About a minute later, he finally saw her hustling across the street with a man, making their way to a car. They paused by the doors, speaking to each other over the roof, then dropped inside.

Sirens came from the downtown area as the car Sarah had gotten into made a U-turn and headed his way. As planned, she would take this guy to the dojo to meet Alex and wait for Parkman to show.

The gun in the man's hand had concerned Parkman, though. Even from this distance, he was sure of what he saw. The man also carried something large and white in his other hand.

Either way, he had to assume Sarah was safe and headed to the dojo. As far as they knew, Alex was holed up there.

He leaned back into a recessed doorway as the car passed his location. Inside, Sarah was speaking, the man driving. From this close, because the man was driving with both hands raised on the steering wheel, Parkman could determine the white thing he thought the guy was carrying was a large bandage. His other hand was on the wheel and empty.

At least the gun was out of play now, but the guy was an idiot. If he wanted to keep a weapon on his victim, he should have made her drive.

Parkman checked the time. The dojo was a fifteen-minute walk from where he was.

He stepped out of the recessed doorway and turned to the right.

Four men moved into view from around a corner.

"Not so fast."

All four of them eased back their jackets to show semi-automatic handguns. The guy on the far right had a semi-automatic Ruger AR clipped to the inside of his trench coat-like jacket.

Two Suburbans pulled up to the curb, and a man jumped out of the passenger side of the closest one.

At first glance, Parkman despised the man. The evil glint in his eye, the malicious sneer on his mouth. Below his pale face was a huge wad of white padding and bandages that stretched from one collarbone to the other. It looked like he'd returned from a war zone with battle wounds and escaped the Doctors Without Borders tent with the field dressing still intact.

"You must be Silvio Mancuso," Parkman said, still staring at the huge bandage stained red at the center.

"Get him in the back," the man said, his gravelly voice no doubt affected by the injury to his throat.

One of the men shoved him so hard that he stumbled into the side of the SUV, bumping it hard with his shoulder.

Rough hands felt him up, checking for weapons. When they found his cell phone, the man with the Ruger AR threw it on the concrete and stomped on it.

"Hey, man," Parkman protested. "You're going to have to replace that."

They glared at him a moment, stunned by such a ridiculous comment.

"You won't need it where you're going," Mancuso said. "You'll never need a cell phone again."

They opened the back door and gestured for him to enter.

This was a one-way trip. He knew who they were and what their intentions were. Having arrested several members of organized crime in the past when he was a cop and having dealt with assholes like this for years with Sarah, Parkman was well aware of what getting into that Suburban meant.

But what choice did he have? The amount of men and weapons outnumbered him by ratios he didn't even attempt to consider.

With one last look down Queen Street at Sarah's

retreating vehicle, he stepped up and into the back of the Suburban.

The interior had been modified so the back seats faced another set of seats, similar to several limousine styles.

A thug sat on either side of him, with two facing him. Their knees were no more than an inch apart. None of the men held a gun on him. What would be the point? He was unarmed and surrounded by four heavily armed, able men. Holding the gun on him was redundant.

The Suburban pulled away from the curb.

"So," he said. "This some sort of fancy Uber? You driving me home now?"

"You're going home all right."

"You got the address?"

Mancuso turned in his seat. "Sure do. We're delivering you to Hell."

"Ahh, a place you know well."

Mancuso's lips turned down at the edges. "That mouth will only make the end more painful."

"Actually, I was thinking it would work the other way."

"How's that?"

"When the end came, I was hoping to piss you off so much that you do it quickly." He snapped his fingers in the confined space, making two of the men closest to him jump in their seats. "Guess that's not working."

"How could you think you could come after us? Why not just try to help find Bartleson's daughter?"

"Because Sarah doesn't work that way."

"So, Sarah, you, her boyfriend, her daughter, all of you, and all of her friends will die because Sarah doesn't *work* that way?" Mancuso shook his head. "Those are some high standards to adhere to."

"Carmine's dead. We got him. That's just a tease of what's coming."

"Big talk for a man who will be dead before the sun sets." Silvio adjusted himself, lifting an elbow on the back of the seat. "We're called organized crime for a reason. You don't think we're organized?"

Parkman nodded. "Of course, you're organized. But just because—"

"We're so organized. We knew about all of the attacks as they were happening. You three showing up at the construction site. The other three are at the strip club. Even now, when Sal broke into the restaurant, we watched him on camera. I sent one of my men here"—he nodded at the man to Parkman's left—"in through the back door to execute the fucker, but then I saw Sarah enter the back. Luckily for me, I was able to call him off. Figured Sarah and Sal would team up and eventually lead me to the asshole who did this." Silvio pointed at the bandage below his chin.

Parkman glanced through the windshield. The car Sarah and Sal were in was out of sight.

"You've lost them. How could they possibly lead you anywhere?"

Silvio raised a handheld device. What looked like Google Maps was on the screen; a flashing red dot indicated a car moving along a street. He moved the device close enough for Parkman to read the street names. The car they were tracking was ahead of them on Queen Street.

"We've been tracking Salvatore since he got hired. Every

employee gets a tracker built into their phones, and as head of Bartleson Security, I monitor everyone. One can never know what an employee might do. You know, talk to the authorities, the feds." Mancuso shook his head. "Can't have that."

"But yet, you don't know where Bartleson's daughter is?"

"Some people are above my pay grade. Bianca never had a tracker, but the man she was with did. She must've told him about it because the night Frankie disappeared, so did his phone."

They'd been tracking Salvatore, and now that he was with Sarah, they were tracking her, too, and she was heading straight to Alex. How was this supposed to help anything? Why would Vivian send her to meet with Salvatore if this was the result? Could it be because she was late getting to him? Seemed a minor detail since they were still tracking Salvatore regardless of Sarah's timing.

Maybe Mancuso wanted Alex more than Sarah or Salvatore.

There had to be a way to get them off the trail and away from the dojo, which was minutes away.

"You want Alex? I can take you to him."

Silvio turned back in his seat. "That's not necessary. Sarah's already doing that." After a moment, he added, "I get the feeling you'll all be dead before I enjoy my morning coffee."

"Funny, I was just about to say the same thing about you guys."

The man to his left jammed an elbow into his side,

knocking the wind out of him.

He was still breathing raggedly when they pulled to a stop half a block from the dojo and began discussing their assault plan.

Chapter 30

Sarah knocked on the front window, wanting to ensure Alex saw it was her right away. After the second knock, with Sal beside her asking why they were stopping at a closed martial arts gym at such an early hour, Alex somehow popped up from the side wall.

Sarah frowned. Where the hell had he been?

He strode up to the front window and shouted through the glass for her to meet him at the back door, but don't touch it.

"Don't touch it?" she shouted back.

He placed his hands together, then separated them fast in the dramatization of an explosion.

"Ahhh," she said, nodding at Alex. She turned to Salvatore. "C'mon." She grabbed his arm and dragged him up the street with her.

"What's going on?" he asked.

"We're getting you safe until that phone rings."

"Who's going to call me?"

"Salvation."

"What?"

"Just come with me."

She still had the gun, but it was hidden from public view in her pants. With Sal's wounded hand, she wasn't worried he'd try to fight her. Overpowering him wouldn't prove difficult.

At the back of the dojo, they waited. After half a minute, she thought about banging on the door, but Alex knew they were coming, so she waited.

Then, the back door to the convenience store popped open, and Alex stepped out.

"This way," he said.

Sarah pushed Salvatore toward Alex.

"How are you inside the convenience store? They don't open until eight or nine, do they?"

"I've followed old Bob inside when he opens in the morning several times and studied the alarm code he types in."

Sarah stopped to stare at him. "You know their alarm code?"

"How else am I supposed to gain access without it?"

She smiled. "Of course. How come I didn't think of that?"

Moving inside the back of the store, they skirted around boxes of supplies, shelving leaned up against the wall, and a large Coke display.

"Why are we in here and not in the dojo?" she asked.

"The only thing that separates our businesses is flimsy

drywall. I cut out a man-sized hole in the drywall quite some time ago in case we ever needed out in a hurry. You know, with all the shit we've dealt with in the past."

"Right. Makes sense." She smiled. Alex was always working his angles.

He led them to the side display, between one shelf that held canned goods and the other that held small bags of pasta. The wall looked perfectly normal to Sarah, but a large rectangular hole opened when Alex touched it. She couldn't see the seams because they had been concealed behind the lip of the metal wracking on the shelving unit to the right of the hole. On the left, Alex had affixed two small hinges on the dojo side.

"Does Aaron know about this?"

"Probably, but we haven't discussed it in a long time."

All three of them moved onto the dojo side, and Alex closed the door in the wall behind them.

"What about Bob? He knows?"

Alex shook his head. "Probably better he doesn't."

Sarah nodded. "Imagine so." She looked up at the front windows where she'd knocked. "This is where you came from when we knocked."

Alex nodded.

"What are we doing here?" Salvatore asked, taking in the gym, staring at the mats scattered around them, some tied to the walls.

"Keeping you safe," Sarah said. "I've mentioned that."

"I don't want safe. I want Silvio. He did this." Salvatore held up his bandaged hand.

"You'll get your chance. Probably sooner than you

think." She held out her hand and waved her fingers in a give-it-to-me gesture. "Let me see your phone?"

"Why do you want my phone?"

"Because when the call comes, I'm answering it." Her hand stayed where it was, flat with the palm facing the ceiling.

"Fuck that. Someone calls, I'll take it."

Alex moved.

Sarah jammed a hand into his shoulder. "Alex, wait. Let me try once more."

Tensed, Alex inhaled and eased back.

"What the hell is this?" Salvatore asked, staring at Alex with concern. "You're going to beat me up?"

Sarah cleared her throat. "It seems you may not understand the gravity of the situation."

He turned to Sarah. "Then explain it to me."

"There's no time. You're just going to have to trust us."

"And why should I do that?"

"Because I've got a weapon more powerful than a gun, and I've got your gun."

He frowned. "What's more powerful than a gun?"

She nodded at Alex. "Him."

Salvatore moved his gaze to Alex, then back to Sarah. "This is fucking out of control. For the record, it sucks, too." He pulled out his cell phone and handed it to Sarah, muttering something under his breath.

She turned away and dialed DeOcampo's number from memory. After a moment, the FBI agent answered.

"Who's this?"

"Sarah."

"Oh, yeah? Wow, calling me, eh?" Then her voice turned serious. "Where are you?"

"I've got Salvatore Prezzie with me."

"Fabulous, but that doesn't answer my question."

An announcement came over a speaker system in the background on DeOcampo's phone.

"Where are you?" Sarah asked.

"We're all at the hospital, visiting Benjamin with Daniel."

"You picked up Daniel?"

"Yeah, he was on Front Street, but you and Parkman were already gone. So, I brought him here to be with Benjamin—"

"And to keep an eye on him."

"That, too."

"Look, I'm going to talk with Prezzie about the wire, and we'll wait for our phone call. In the meantime, you're going to receive a call within the hour."

"From who?"

"Officer Ron Smith, Campbell's old partner."

"And why would Smith call me?"

"He's decided, after a sleepless night, that he'll take the heat for being paid off by Bartleson to pick me up in exchange for being an eyewitness to the murder of his partner, Officer Jack Campbell."

"Who killed Campbell?"

"Silvio Mancuso. Right in front of Smith and me, on Bartleson's property—the front lawn, actually. He was acting on orders from Bartleson."

"And you didn't want to tell me all about this until

now?"

"That officer's life meant something, and I knew we'd get to it, but the previous twelve hours have held other priorities for me."

"Every bit helps, but that doesn't get me Bartleson."

"That's why I'm here. Salvatore will wear a wire, Mancuso goes down for murder, and Bartleson goes down for so many other atrocities."

"And you're sure he'll wear a wire—"

Something smashed into Sarah so hard that she was shoved sideways and landed on the floor near the wall. Her landing was softer than she expected.

She opened her eyes to see Alex under her as something like an angry hornet buzzed by her head, followed by a massive amount of glass shattering.

Then, a man shouted from their kitchen area.

It all happened so fast that she barely had time to register the two men she now saw standing at the broken front windows of the dojo, both of them holding weapons.

Alex rolled her away toward the opening in the wall. A moment later, he opened the rectangular drywall and was shoving her through it into the convenience store.

Then, something exploded at the back of the building, sending a mild shock wave throughout the dojo.

She lay on her side, open-mouthed momentarily, trying to gather her wits as so much had happened in only seconds.

The phone—it was gone. They were both inside the convenience store now, with Salvatore stuck in the kitchen of the dojo.

"Wait," she screamed as Alex was about to shove a steel

rack in front of the hole. "We need the phone I was using. This doesn't end without that phone."

Alex snapped his head around to stare at her. "Give me that gun in your pants."

Sarah yanked it out and tossed it at him all in one movement. Alex caught it easily, flicked off the safety, then dropped to the hole, leaned in, and fired twice.

After a quick glance inside, he lowered onto his belly and crawled back into the dojo.

The explosion at the back had to be Bartleson's men coming in that way. The only reason the men at the front didn't set off any explosives was that Alex had rigged them to the door. These guys shot out the glass and entered through the broken floor-to-ceiling window panes. Typical mafia, hitman, shootout shit. Make a spectacle of the kill. Show the others in the war that you didn't have a care in the world. It made Sarah think it was one level away from what cartels did in Mexico when they hung bodies from bridges.

Alex reappeared at the hole, miraculously unscathed, Salvatore's phone in his hand. She released the breath she'd been holding. If something had happened to Alex, she would lose her mind.

He tossed the phone to Sarah, and she caught it, then placed it at her ear.

DeOcampo was still there.

"What the hell's happening? Sarah!" The agent was screaming.

"I'm here. Bartleson's men attacked us. We're under fire."

"Where are you?" DeOcampo shouted.

"Leaving the dojo on Queen Street now. They've fucking destroyed it."

"Fuck, I'm too far away to help. This is why you have to tell me where you are and what you're doing at all times, Sarah, or I can't help you, and—"

"Gotta go," she cut in.

"Tell me you still have Salvatore—"

Sarah clicked the off button and slipped the phone away. Alex was still at the hole, staring into the dojo.

"What's going on?" Sarah asked in a muttered whisper.

He turned back to face her. "When I shot at the two guys, I hit one. The other ran back outside. I'm waiting for them to reappear."

"Where's Sal?"

"He's still in the kitchen."

"Then he's stuck in there without a weapon."

"I know."

She waited a moment, thinking about what to do.

"I've got an idea. Why don't we—"

Something loud, like some heavy military machine gun, blasted the interior of the dojo, holes punching into the walls all around the convenience store's side, candy wrappers and gum packs flying off the shelves.

Sarah shouted in the wake of such violence while covering her ears as she dropped to the floor to flatten herself out.

Alex had dropped, too—quieter than her, though—choosing to remain in the rectangular hole.

"We need Salvatore," she shouted at him.

Alex glanced up into the hole, examining the interior of

the store.

Salvatore shouted something about a gun from inside the kitchen, but Sarah's hearing had been affected by that monster of a weapon.

Did they bring a tank with them?

Alex twisted on the spot, moving onto his feet to lean half in and half out of the hole. His body jerked once, but Sarah couldn't see what he was doing. Then he retreated from the dojo, closing the hole behind him.

"Wait," she shouted in a panic. "We can't leave him behind."

Alex was already shoving the steel rack in front of the hole.

"I tossed him the gun. He said he'd run out the back now that the explosion blew out the back door."

Alex grabbed Sarah's wrist, half lifting her off the ground, half dragging her, and ran for the back of the convenience store as the thunder of that monster weapon roared throughout the building again, punctuated by heavy thuds as bullets embedded themselves everywhere.

They hit the back door running bent over, Sarah fearing some huge bullet would smack into an ass cheek.

Outside, two men dressed in long coats lay on their backs on the concrete, their faces mangled by chunks of steel, blood making a grotesque mask of what was left of their noses and cheeks.

Alex glanced at her. "Small IEDs loaded with scrap metal." He shrugged. "Not big enough to blow people apart. It's the dispelled shrapnel that does the killing."

He led her behind a dumpster, where they huddled down

to wait, staring at the ruined back door of the dojo.

Sarah breathed deeply, trying to calm her nerves, waiting for her hearing to return to normal.

"What the fuck?" she muttered. "That weapon sounded like it came from a tank."

Alex placed a comforting arm on her shoulders.

Even his hand was shaking.

Chapter 31

Salvatore had to credit the saving of his life to the man Sarah called Alex. The guy was remarkable.

He'd seen Bartleson's men first.

Without screaming or shouting a warning, Alex had shoved Salvatore toward the kitchen so hard he landed just inside the door.

The way he landed afforded him a clear view of what Alex did next.

The man ran at Sarah, tackling her in a precise manner that not only had him landing under her to cushion the blow but also had them landing at the base of the rectangular hole in the wall.

Salvatore had watched as Alex dove, twisting and spinning in the air. He hit Sarah hard but kept twisting until he was under her before they impacted the floor.

Then they were up and through the hole to safety. Even through the noise of the explosion at the back, he was yelling at them. It wasn't a plea for help or a cry of *don't leave me.* All he wanted was his gun.

If Silvio Mancuso walked through those broken windows, Salvatore wanted to take the shot.

Through several of the large holes in the kitchen's wall, Sal had peered through to the front windows and caught a glimpse of Silvio "the butcher" Mancuso. This was his chance, perhaps his only chance.

The man beside Silvio had some sort of large Uzi—Salvatore wasn't a gun expert, but the sound and power of that weapon only meant one thing: death to those who didn't have one.

So, he dropped to the kitchen floor and stared across at the hole in the wall where Alex had popped his head through.

"I need my gun," he shouted. "It's the only way."

Their eyes met.

"I'll go through the back door."

The understanding in Alex's eyes was intense. Even from where Sal was sprawled out on the kitchen floor, he could easily see the intelligence in the man's eyes.

With the machine gun man taking a break—reloading?—Alex leaned through the hole and tossed Diego's gun toward the open kitchen door.

His right hand extended, Salvatore missed it. The gun smacked the floor and rolled deeper until it was under the table that had a dozen chairs arranged around it.

Then, the gun from hell was firing again.

Salvatore curled into a ball and screamed until the thunder of that fucking weapon stopped.

Without thinking or uttering another sound, Sal crawled

under the table, retrieved Diego's weapon, and checked that it was still loaded.

Three bullets left.

He only needed one.

"Sarah?" Mancuso shouted, his voice sounding shittier than ever, like he was caught with a mouthful of gravel. "Come on out. We won't shoot now. We want to talk."

Sal got to his feet and moved to lean on the kitchen's doorframe, the gun held tight in his right hand. Miraculously, not a single bullet had hit him yet. Perhaps the machine gun man was shooting warning shots and not intending to hit anyone because if he was aiming, he could've torn half the kitchen apart with that thing.

"Sarah?" Mancuso called again. "This was a retaliation for your attack on the strip club, the construction site. Now we talk peace."

The man's voice was closer but not close enough.

"We have Parkman. Let's talk about a trade."

Closer still. Salvatore decided on a plan.

He slipped the weapon into the back of his jeans.

"Mancuso?" he called in a weak, fragile voice.

"That you, Sal?"

"She kidnapped me. Brought me here."

"Come on out."

"I'm unarmed."

"I imagine you are. Wouldn't be good for Sarah to have armed Bartleson men hanging around her gym."

"You won't shoot me?" Sal asked, using a scared little boy's voice. It even cracked in fear like he wanted it to.

"Why would I shoot you? My boss actively employs you.

Last time we spoke, he tasked you with finding Frankie and Bianca. Have you done that yet?"

Mancuso was moving closer as he spoke, step by agonizing step.

Salvatore's heart was in his throat, affecting his breathing and weak stomach.

He whispered his goodbyes to his mother, then stepped out from around the doorframe to face Mancuso, his hands slightly out at the side to indicate they were empty.

Mancuso held his trusty knife.

The man beside him carried the large weapon that had made so much noise.

"Where did they go?" Mancuso asked.

"I need assurances—"

The weapon swung his way, the barrel aimed at his midsection.

"I'll allow you to live. How's that for assurances?"

Sal stepped closer. "I can tell you where they are." He moved closer still. "I can even tell you their plans."

"I'm listening."

The man with the gun lowered his aim, then let it swing off his shoulder on a long, thick strap, where it dangled by his right leg.

Salvatore moved within four feet of Mancuso.

"But, I'll need you to call Bartleson and make him understand that I never was a part of any of this."

Mancuso rushed him, bringing the knife up under his chin. Salvatore felt the knife's tip prick him, entering his skin.

"I will not call anyone at this hour." The knife moved.

Sal felt his skin opening, but no pain had come with it yet. "You will tell me what I want to know, and you will tell me now."

Salvatore reached back and wrapped his fingers on the butt of Diego's gun.

"Okay, okay, you got it. I'll tell you everything. Just don't hurt me."

Salvatore brought the gun around and placed it dead center against Mancuso's stomach. The man was so close that Salvatore could smell his breath.

He watched as Mancuso's eyes widened in surprise.

Then he pulled the trigger, hoping the first bullet would sever the man's spine.

The knife moved quickly, but Salvatore didn't care. He was already lifting the weapon to place it under Mancuso's chin.

He fired again and closed his eyes as blood and brain matter splatted onto his face.

Then, for some reason, he was falling, the floor coming up fast and knocking the wind out of him.

Mancuso's body beside him was convulsing.

The man with the huge weapon stood over him, looking down. Breathing was becoming difficult for some reason. And warm liquid seemed to be covering him, dripping off his neck.

"You killed my boss," the man said.

Salvatore smiled wide. He'd done it. Silvio "the butcher" Mancuso was dead, and he felt so much better for it.

Thunder came then. Roaring and loud.

And it offered him freedom from the pain, freedom.

Then Salvatore Prezzie knew no more.

Chapter 32

ALEX TIGHTENED HIS GRIP on Sarah's hand. "There's a lull in gunfire. Wait here."

She tugged him back. "Where are you going?"

He met her gaze and stared into her eyes. "To see if Salvatore needs any help."

"But you're unarmed. You could get yourself killed." For the first time in a long time, she sounded hysterical. Alex hadn't heard that tone in her voice for years, if ever. "I can't lose you," she added.

"I'll be fine, Sarah. If I'm not back in a few minutes, and that insane gun goes off again run for it. I'll meet up with you later."

"I'm not leaving without you."

He patted her shoulder, then crawled to the blown-out back door of the dojo. A moment later, he slipped inside.

Two men were talking just around the back corner. Alex waited behind the wall, listening.

The one man's gravelly voice was unmistakable. He'd cut him at the strip club. He was a wiry bastard and slipped out of his arms as if he'd died from shock. When Alex glanced down at the floor, he was gone.

"I need assurances—" Salvatore's voice.

Alex frowned. Was he going to give them up?

Alex slid along the back wall until he was at the opening that led to the main area and the kitchen, but still remained hidden.

"I'll allow you to live. How's that for assurances?"

"I can tell you where they are. I can even tell you their plans."

"I'm listening."

Alex peered around the edge. The man with the gun lowered it, slinging it onto his shoulder. It dangled on his right side.

Salvatore moved within four feet of Mancuso.

"But, I'll need you to call Bartleson and make him understand that I never was a part of any of this."

Mancuso moved fast, bringing the knife up under Salvatore's chin.

Alex watched as Salvatore wrapped his fingers on the handle of the gun.

"Okay, okay, you got it. I'll tell you everything. Just don't hurt me."

Alex was less than seven feet from them. Blood already coated the knife's blade.

"I will not call anyone at this hour." The knife moved. "You will tell me what I want to know, and you will tell me now."

Salvatore had planned this from the beginning.

It was a suicide mission.

And if Alex ran out now, he'd die, too, because the man with the large machine gun was still glancing around, his finger on the trigger of the weapon slung over his shoulder. Even though it hung by his leg, Alex was sure the man could right it faster than he could reach him.

"Okay, okay, you got it. I'll tell you everything."

Salvatore brought the gun around and placed it at Mancuso's stomach.

Then he pulled the trigger.

Alex watched the knife move across Salvatore's throat, opening it wide as Mancuso faltered, his stomach bleeding now.

Salvatore moved the weapon up under Mancuso's chin and fired again. The man's head exploded, a portion of the wet mass landing on Salvatore's face. Then he dropped to the floor, Salvatore falling a moment later to lie beside him.

Mancuso's body convulsed as the man died, his life source leaking out of the crater of a hole in his skull.

The man with the machine gun aimed it at Salvatore.

"You killed my boss," the man said.

Alex stepped out of hiding and ran at the man with the machine gun, his hands ready for the killing blows that would be required of them.

But the thunder came, the weapon tearing Salvatore literally in half on the floor before Alex could reach the shooter.

He landed on the man, wrapped his arms around his head, and jammed them into the base of his throat with so much force he wondered if he'd be able to decapitate the guy.

They hit the floor hard, but Alex clung to him for the full minute it took until the man stopped moving. Alex's forearms had taken a beating as the man clawed at them, but all it did was spur Alex on to grip tighter, to end it sooner.

When he released the man and checked for a pulse, he didn't find one.

A quick glance over at Salvatore confirmed he was dead, too.

It was in the glazed-over eyes, the smile on his face he died with.

"You okay?" a man said behind him.

Alex jumped forward in a somersault, landed on the dead guy, his hands on the machine gun, and spun to face the voice.

"Hey," Parkman said, his hands raised. "Take it easy. It's just me."

Alex relaxed, dropping his forehead to the floor. "Sarah is out back, behind the dumpster. She's safe, not hurt."

"She armed?"

"No."

Parkman walked by him. A moment later, Sarah and Parkman stepped back inside, and Alex rolled onto his back to look up at them, the panic and exhaustion oozing off him.

"This is so fucked," Sarah whispered.

Alex nodded.

"How did you get here?" she asked Parkman. "And how did you cut your neck and hands?"

"Mancuso gave me a ride."

"You mean he kidnapped you?"

"That's another way of saying it." He held up his hands to examine the cuts and the small amount of blood. "It wasn't looking good for me there for a while. But when things went south here, Mancuso and this guy"—he pointed at the man Alex had just killed—"left the SUV and locked it, saying they'd be back soon."

Police sirens could be heard in the distance. Fire trucks, too.

Parkman and Sarah turned to stare at the street. Alex twisted around to see two people looking inside the dojo through the broken front windows. Dead bodies littered the place. Explosives had detonated, and bullets had been embedded everywhere.

They had to vacate the premises or spend a day or two answering questions, which was a day or two they didn't have.

"Anyway," Parkman continued. "As I was saying, they locked me in the SUV. The doors wouldn't open from the inside, and I couldn't crawl into the front, so I kicked out a window. Got cut climbing out."

Alex pushed up off the floor to stand beside them.

"I got here in time to see Alex lunge at that guy as he shot the guy on the floor." Parkman pointed at Salvatore.

"We need to leave," Alex said.

"Right." Parkman nodded. "Out the back."

They started for the blown-out back doors, getting outside and past the dumpsters before hearing tires screech to a stop out front on Queen Street.

The phone Sarah was carrying rang as they were already a block away.

"DeOcampo," she said. "Yes, we made it out." A pause, then, "I've got good news and bad news." She glanced back at Alex as they turned down another street. "Silvio Mancuso is dead."

Sarah pulled the phone away from her ear and then put it back. "Hey, hold on," she shouted. "Salvatore shot him. Mancuso's entire team is dead. And, they had just kidnapped Parkman, but we got him back safe."

She stopped walking and stared at Parkman. Alex surveyed the area and saw no immediate threats.

"It'll take too long to explain how we all survived, and Mancuso's team is dead. Police are on site now—" she stopped, staring down at the sidewalk. "*You* sent the cops?" Sarah nodded. "Well, I know that when Officer Smith contacts you, it won't matter as much because Silvio is dead now, but remember who ordered Silvio to do what he did."

They started walking again.

"Look, DeOcampo, I'm hanging up. When I know more, I'll call you. Besides, I'm waiting on a call with this phone, and the battery is really low."

Sarah squinted as DeOcampo ranted on about something else, her tinny voice barely audible from where Alex was.

"Gotta go, Special Agent. Will be in touch soon. Oh, and thanks for taking Daniel to be with Benjamin and Aaron at the hospital. That was sweet of you."

Sarah clicked off and slipped the phone away.

"Holy fuck is she pissed."

"I'd be, too," Parkman said.

"Well, it'll all go away when I deliver Bartleson to her."

Parkman popped a toothpick in his mouth. "How are you

going to do that?"

"I'll tell you all about it. But I need a coffee first. Fuck, what a morning."

"Insane," Alex whispered and followed them to the Starbucks on the corner.

Chapter 33

"I think I need rest," Sarah said, holding her coffee with both hands. "Either that or the shock of what just happened is hitting me."

Parkman momentarily rested a hand on her wrist, squeezed, and then let go.

"It's almost over," he whispered.

She nodded, staring down at the lid of her coffee. "Alex, you doing okay?"

When he didn't answer right away, she glanced up and squinted at him. The morning sun was bright, rays of light bouncing off a windshield in the parking lot directly into her face.

Alex was nodding, staring at his hands. "I don't think I will ever get used to what I can do, how efficiently I do it." He took a deep breath, his chest expanding, held it, then exhaled. "Sometimes I scare myself."

That was the first time he'd ever spoken about the

emotional toll this life was taking on him. They'd followed Sarah's lead in the past as she went after whatever criminal she was hunting, but this time, it was totally unprovoked. This time, the trouble found them.

"Nothing's your fault," she said. "Sometimes we're just trying to stay alive. That's it. And I'm so grateful you are who you are. You saved my life today."

He faced the street, not meeting her gaze. "As much as I know that, and I feel confident with what I do, I never thought all those years of training would lead me here."

"I'm sorry …"

Parkman stared at him, concern written all over his scrunched brows and tight cheeks. "You know, this doesn't have to be your life. You could move on and do other things. Compete internationally, travel. Imagine the competitions you'd win on a global scale."

A part of Sarah regretted hearing Parkman give Alex an out. She couldn't imagine a life without Alex. Although she didn't interrupt or say anything to the contrary because Alex needed to know his future, his freedom was always his choice.

They stared at him for half a minute before he turned back and sipped his coffee. After setting down the cup, he glanced at Parkman.

"Thanks for saying that, but I'd never leave. This is my home, my family." He shrugged, then averted his gaze to watch the coffee shop's door. "Just not sure I'll ever get used to all the hatred. What fuels these people to do what they do, to hurt others, to kill, boggles my mind."

"In part, that's why we do what we do," Sarah said

gently, her mothering side coming out. "We're their counter."

"That I can understand. In martial arts, there's a move, and then there's always a counter move. We're their counter. I like that."

She drank from her cup, her eyelids heavy. When was the last time they'd slept?

"Alex," she said. "I once heard someone say, 'evil may win battles, but never the war,' or something like that."

"But how long before we aren't so lucky?" He turned back to her, then glanced at Parkman. "How long before we take a hit, lose someone we care about? We may be good—in fact, we're fucking amazing—but not impervious to bullets."

Sarah nodded and looked down at her cup again. He was right. It was something that had tormented her for years. And it was something Vivian had told her at the construction site.

A funeral was in their future. But whose?

The fact that Benjamin got shot should mean they dropped everything and ran to visit him and comfort him, but she couldn't. Bianca Bartleson was with a man who was going to call Salvatore—who was now dead—to explain himself. And Sarah needed to take that call to end this.

Then they could visit Benjamin and put all this shit behind them.

At least Benjamin had Daniel and Aaron with him.

"Parkman, I don't want to use Salvatore's phone until we get the call I'm waiting for, but I need to check in with Aaron and see how Benjamin's doing." She held out her hand. "Can I have your cell?"

He shook his head. "When they nabbed me on the corner by the restaurant, they took my cell and smashed it. I don't have one now."

She turned to Alex. "Do you have yours?"

He shook his head.

"Shit, okay, I'll call him and tell him we're safe. I'll keep it short. Then I need sleep."

"Where?" Parkman asked.

"My place."

"Why there? Isn't that dangerous?"

"Almost all of Bartleson's men are dead. He's on the run by now. I don't see him going after me at my place. Actually, I've got the nod from Vivian. All clear there. And I'd like to charge this phone."

Parkman nodded. "That works for me."

Alex offered her a slight nod as well.

She dialed Aaron's number into Salvatore's phone. He answered on the first ring.

"Yeah," he said, his tone curt, short.

"Hey, honey."

"Sarah?" he gasped in her ear, wet-like, as if his lips were on the phone. "Are you okay?" He sounded as if he was about to cry.

"Yes, we're all fine. We got out okay."

"Oh, my, we've been worried sick over here. DeOcampo's been getting updates from the local authorities. The dojo's been shot up pretty badly. There was an explosion."

"That was Alex."

"Alex?" Now Aaron was sounding like he was in hysterics. "Is he okay?"

Maybe the two-year hiatus when Willow was born made

them more sensitive, softer, less hardened.

"Alex wired the doors in case someone broke in, and then Bartleson's people tried to break in. Those little shrapnel-filled devices may have saved our lives."

"Cops found half a dozen bodies on the scene. And whenever we call Parkman's phone, it goes straight to voicemail. Is he with you, too?"

"Parkman is right beside me." She glanced his way. "He entered the gym when it was all over, so he missed the worst of it. Although Bartleson's men picked him up and smashed his phone, that's why you can't reach him."

"And Alex? He's good?"

"Across the table from me." She faced him. "We couldn't have made it without him."

"Then who are all the dead people in my dojo?"

"Five of them are Bartleson's people and a man named Salvatore Prezzie, whose phone I'm calling you on." She paused. When Aaron didn't respond, she asked, "How's Benjamin?"

She listened as he collected himself a moment.

"Sorry," Aaron whispered, his voice cracking once. "I was just so worried about you guys. And when I couldn't reach Parkman ..."

"I understand. I should've called sooner. Benjamin's okay?"

"He's good, actually. The bullet went through the meat of his leg and broke his femur, but he'll be fine. Lost some blood, passed out, but otherwise, all good."

She sighed in relief, clasping a hand to her forehead while resting on her elbows, her vision on the table, several coffee stains drawing her eye.

"Sarah?" Aaron whispered into the phone. It sounded like he was walking as short spurts of air came over the phone's speaker. "What's the plan here? How does this end? I mean, Benjamin is laid up in a hospital bed with FBI agents guarding his room. My dojo is filled with dead mafia men, and the man some international police task force is looking for has threatened our baby. How is this going to end? When does it end?"

"I'm working on it."

"Vivian involved?"

"Yes, she told me a few things." Sarah glanced at Alex, who was back watching the coffee shop's door. "As far as I understand it, this ends today."

"I sure hope so. I want Willow back, and I want our lives back."

"Me too, honey, me too."

"Okay, DeOcampo is eying me suspiciously. If she knows it's you I'm talking to, she'll want to—"

"Is that Sarah?" DeOcampo's voice in the background cut Aaron off. "Give me the phone."

"I gotta go," Aaron said. The line died.

Sarah set the phone on the table and then related what Aaron had told her about Benjamin's condition.

"At least he'll be okay," Parkman said. "Shitty luck, though. He resisted this the most, too. Tried to convince us to back off the attacks on Bartleson's properties."

"He was right. Those didn't work out too well, but it doesn't make me feel better."

"This isn't your fault, Sarah."

"Feels like it is—"

The phone cut her off. She snatched it up, but the caller ID was blank.

"What do you want, Special Agent?"

"Hello?" a man asked. "Salvatore?"

Sarah's eyes widened. Frankie, Salvatore's coworker, and the man with Bartleson's daughter, were on the phone, just like Vivian said.

"Uhm, listen, my name's Sarah. We need to talk."

"Sarah?" the man repeated. Someone in the background grunted something. "I don't know any Sarah."

"I have Salvatore's phone because—"

"Then put Sal on. I only want to speak with him."

"See, that's going to be a problem." Sarah turned in her seat to face the outside and focus on each word. Her sleep-addled mind struggled to concentrate and focus.

"Who is this?" Frankie asked again, his voice rising.

"My name is Sarah Roberts, and I'm here to help."

"Help? I don't need no help."

She was worried he'd just hang up, and that would be the end of it. She'd never hear from him again with no phone number on call display.

She decided on the truth and the power of being forthright.

"I'm working with an FBI task force to bring down Lorenzo Bartleson for his dealings in organized crime, as well as what he has done to Bianca. He has been hunting for you both since you and Bianca left the area and absconded with Bartleson's money. People have died. I need you to come in and tell us what you know. Special Agent Tracie

DeOcampo will offer you immunity, and they won't press any charges. But Frankie, we need you to come in."

"What the fuck are you talking about? What does that mean, 'what he's done to Bianca?'"

"Just as I said, Frankie, the man thinks he's untouchable, above the law. But that isn't the case. With your help—with Bianca's help—Lorenzo Bartleson can be—"

"Fuck you, Sarah, whoever you are. I won't be calling again. We're leaving the country today. This was supposed to be a goodbye to my friend Sal, but you people …"

There was a pause where she feared he'd hang up.

"Wait, Frankie." Her calm tone was gone, brain alert at how close she was to losing him. "Please, just listen to me."

The line died.

"Frankie?" She pulled the phone away from her ear, looked at it, and then pressed it back. "Frankie?"

She glanced up to meet Parkman's gaze.

"You tried," he said.

"Shit!" She shook the phone like that would do anything, then set it on the table. "I fucked up. I didn't know what I was saying. Like I was pleading with a witness to testify or something when I only wanted to meet with them, talk to Bianca." She rested her head on her forearms. "I'm so tired, exhausted. I wasn't thinking straight."

Parkman's hand rested on her shoulder. "We're only human, Sarah. We can only do so much."

She closed her eyes and felt sleep coming fast. "We need to catch an Uber and get home."

"How about we call a cab?"

"So much more money. Uber's easier."

"You have a cell phone that's connected to your Uber account? I certainly don't."

"Oh, right. Taxi then."

Parkman and Alex got up, and she followed them outside, her limbs feeling extra heavy. They stepped out into the morning sunlight, where they waited for a taxi. Parkman had called for one using Salvatore's phone.

Dejected, exhausted, and feeling old for thirty-two, Sarah leaned her head back on the bricks of the building and wondered what it was all for anyway.

All those men dead, Benjamin in the hospital, Willow in some bunker with Bruno, and Bartleson not being held accountable for any of it.

With Frankie and Bianca leaving the country—if what Frankie said was true—all hope of stopping Bartleson left with them.

What did that mean for Sarah's family?

Could Willow ever come home? Would they ever be safe?

Chapter 34

Something rang and rang. Then there was a knock.

Her alarm?

The knock came again.

Fire alarm?

Sarah's eyes shot open. She was in her own bed.

"Sarah," Parkman shouted from outside her bedroom door. "The phone is ringing."

Sarah snapped fully awake and jumped sideways as she grabbed the phone. Balance lost, she slipped off the bed and landed on the carpeted floor on her back, her legs still tangled in the sheets on the bed.

She smashed at the answer button, gasping for air at the sudden wakefulness.

"Yeah, yeah," she muttered into the phone.

"Sarah? It's DeOcampo. You okay? You sound out of breath."

"Yeah, just woke up. The phone. It startled me." She

swallowed, still on her back beside the bed, blinking up at the ceiling. "What's up?"

"Looks like I'm getting my warrant."

"Warrant?"

"For Bartleson's arrest."

"On what charges?"

"Too many to mention."

"Will the charges stick?"

"Not sure. Have to let the courts decide." There was a pause. "They may not stick, but it'll tie him up in court for a year or more, and we'll be granted more time to investigate him further. We'll find something, and the scrutiny he'll be under will strangle him. Plus, a huge portion of his personal security team are dead or under arrest already."

Sarah licked her dry lips and waited.

"You don't sound too happy about it," DeOcampo said.

"Oh right, no, I am. Very happy about it."

"This means you can get Willow, go back to your life. It's over."

"Okay." She closed her eyes and tried to see if Vivian was close, but she wasn't. "Sorry, just woke up. I'll call you later?"

"Okay, Sarah, but until we pick him up, just keep your head down. It should be today, though. Also, I'm leaving an agent at the hospital until Benjamin is released, just in case."

"Thanks for that."

"And the local authorities want you and Alex to come in for a statement regarding what transpired at the dojo. I told them you'd come in tomorrow."

"Understandable. Will do. Okay, I can do that." She

paused. "Hey, DeOcampo?"

"Yeah?"

"How long before you think you'll pick up Bartleson?"

"Today, most likely. We have a dozen officers hitting his businesses and two agents at his house in Rosedale staking it out until he returns."

"Officers?" She said the word slowly, emphasizing the question in the word, the subtext.

"I know what you're thinking. These are *our* officers, not his. I'll share something else with you. Officer Ron Smith did call me as you said he would, and he's willing to not only testify about Campbell's murder but also that Bartleson paid hundreds of thousands to over ten different cops on the force. His partner, Officer Campbell, was one of the cops being paid huge amounts. The names Smith gave us match all the officers dispatched to the construction site last night, plus a few others. All of them but one have been rounded up. Charges are pending on each and every one."

"Wow, this is really coming together fast. Which one hasn't been picked up?"

"Why? You think you'd recognize the name?"

"Who knows, it might ring a bell."

"One second, I'll check my notes."

Sarah waited in the pause on the phone, eyes closed, enjoying the calm in her room, on the floor, one leg suspended on the bed. It made her feel all of what had happened was nothing more than a scary dream.

DeOcampo cleared her throat. "An Officer Cade, Mark Cade. We haven't been able to locate him. It's his day off, and we were told he heads north to fish on his days off.

Although he's signed out an unmarked cruiser today, so we'll pick him up soon."

"Yeah, don't know that name."

"Aaron said he's going to call whoever has Willow. Actually, he should be home soon. He's on his way to catch some sleep, and Daniel's staying here with Benjamin. You're all safe now, Sarah. I'll call you back the second Bartleson is in custody."

"I appreciate it, Mrs. Special Agent."

"Still sarcastic till the end, eh Sarah?"

"Who me? Little ole me? Never."

"It's your way of telling me you like me, right?"

"You got me. The FBI always gets their man."

"Isn't that a Canadian thing? The RCMP always get their man?"

"I'm hanging up now," Sarah muttered into the phone. "And thanks for everything."

"I'll be in touch."

The line died, and Sarah let the phone drop to her side. She stared at the ceiling, the smell of coffee filtering its way to her on the floor.

Someone knocked. "Sarah, you okay?" Parkman again.

"Yeah."

"Coffee's on."

"Coming."

She maneuvered herself off the floor and entered the en suite. Her hair was a mess, but it didn't matter. Nothing a long hot shower wouldn't fix.

She used the toilet, brushed her hair to something recognizable, straightened her T-shirt, and moved back into the bedroom.

The phone rang again just as she opened the bedroom door.

"Fuck, what is it now, DeOcampo," she muttered to herself as she picked it up.

"Miss me?" she asked. "What's up?"

"You're on speakerphone," a man said.

She leaned over, listening intently, then plopped down on the corner of the bed, bouncing several times.

"Who is this?"

"You said your name was Sarah."

The man's voice sounded distant, like he sat beside the phone at a kitchen table.

"Yes, you're speaking with Sarah Roberts."

"I called you earlier."

It was Frankie. It had to be.

"You did." She didn't stop her free hand from scrunching up the bedsheet in anticipation.

"And you wanted to enlist Bianca's help in stopping her father."

"That's correct."

Her pulse quickened at where this was going. Could it be true? Could Bianca want to put an end to the hell she had been through?

"Sarah?" A woman's voice, soft and fragile, like a kitten.

"Yes."

"I'm so sorry."

"For what?"

"I'm the reason my father knows your name, what you can do."

"I'm not sure I follow." She spoke the words but was putting it together rather quickly. Just the same, she wanted Bianca to spell it out in plain English.

"I've watched you from afar for years." The woman spoke tentatively like she wasn't sure of each word. "Saw what you did in Mexico with the Enzo Cartel. Some of that hurt my father's business, but he let it go. I applauded you for doing something I could never do."

Parkman stepped into the doorway, a coffee cup in hand. He frowned when he saw Sarah's face. She gestured for him to sit on the bed beside her and wait.

"Anyway," Bianca continued. "When Frankie told me you answered Salvatore's phone, we talked about it this afternoon."

"And?"

"And I want to help. It's time."

"How would you help?"

"I'm willing to testify. You told Frankie that he wouldn't get in trouble, right?"

"That's right."

"Then, as long as Frankie is safe, and I'm safe from the monster I have as a father, I'm willing to testify."

"And what would this testimony cover? His business dealings? The people he works with? I'm only asking because the FBI task force will want to know what they're getting in exchange for promising Frankie immunity from prosecution."

"You ... don't know?" She faltered, her voice hesitating.

"I think I do, but if you can't tell me on the phone privately, how can you speak about it in a court of law with so many people listening?"

"This is Sal's phone, right?"

"Yes, it is."

"Then I won't say anything further on this phone. As far as I know, my dad monitors his employees' phones."

"Okay, then we should meet."

"But where?" Bianca asked. She sounded quite upset at the notion they were probably being listened to. "Anything we say might be recorded, and I can't tell you where I am right now. He'll send people."

"Let me think a moment …"

"Wait, Sarah. I have an idea."

"Go ahead."

"Weren't you involved with some shooting a few years back down by Spadina Avenue? Some Canadian military types."

"Yes, we were attacked by men in Hummers. Good soldiers died that day."

"Well, that involved ex-military types with some revenge plan, right? As far as I remember, much of that came out in the papers afterward."

"That's right."

"And you were last seen in a town up north—don't say the name on the phone—where there was some sort of showdown with bombs exploding like landmines in a field of sand."

"I remember it well. Like it was yesterday."

Parkman sipped his coffee beside her, listening to her side of the conversation, looking thoroughly confused.

"Well, on your way north, there was a woman who got

pulled over. A cop had stopped her. You intervened because there was a gun involved.”

“How do you know about that?” Sarah raised her eyebrows in surprise. The woman was obviously well-informed.

“Let’s just say I know that particular cop. He’s one of the many police officers who have paraded through my dad’s house, day in and day out for years.”

“Okay, what about him?”

“Do you remember that coffee shop you’d stopped in?”

“Absolutely.”

“Meet me there in three hours.”

“I’m on my way.”

“If I see my dad or any of his people, I’ll be out of the country before the sun sets.”

“I totally understand. It’ll be me and two friends, Parkman and Alex.”

“Alex? You’re bringing Alex, too?”

“Yes, is that a problem?”

“I’ve just always wanted to meet him. Over the years, that man is an enigma in the media.”

“Trust me, he’s an enigma in our hearts as well.”

“After all that police chief stupidity he went through a few years back …”

“I know. Look, we have to leave.”

“Oh, and Sarah?”

“Yeah?”

“Leave Salvatore’s phone behind. Destroy it. Throw it away. You don’t want my dad tracking you to where you’re going.”

"Will do."

Bianca hung up, and Sarah took a deep breath. She set the phone on the bed beside her, holding down the button to turn it off.

"You won't believe who that was and what she just told me."

"What?"

"I need that coffee now. Right fucking now." She jumped up from the bed so fast, Parkman grumbled as the mattress shook. When she looked back, he'd spilled coffee on his chest. "Sorry, just so pumped that this is finally coming to an end."

"What's going on?"

"I need coffee and a shower. Then the three of us are heading to the Tim Hortons on the highway in Huntsville, just over two hours from here."

"I know the one, but why?"

"Bianca Bartleson is meeting us there to come in and speak with DeOcampo."

"And why's that?" Parkman asked, a sly smile playing across his lips as he stood from the bed. He already knew why. He just wanted her to tell him.

"Because she's agreed to testify to the sexual assaults he's been subjecting her to since she was a young woman."

Parkman didn't respond as she stomped away to pour her coffee.

Chapter 35

Aaron Stevens let himself in and dropped the keys on the side table.

"Sarah?"

When he received no answer, he wandered through the apartment but couldn't find her.

DeOcampo had said she'd spoken with Sarah an hour before and that she was at home, but she wasn't there.

"Shit," he muttered to himself as he started to pack.

Within twenty minutes, he packed two small suitcases for him, Sarah, and items Willow would want. Then he left a note for Sarah to call him as soon as she got the message. He would explain everything then.

After speaking with DeOcampo, they'd decided until Bartleson was in custody, Sarah's little family would stay at a motel just off the 401 in a small city called Whitby. It was a half-hour drive or so, which was far enough out of Toronto and out of Bartleson's immediate reach that they'd be safe.

Pay in cash and use fake names until DeOcampo called them and told them Bartleson was apprehended. Then they would go home.

Aaron grabbed his phone and called Darwin in Italy.

"Hey, it's Aaron."

"How is everyone?" Darwin always sounded so sincere. The man's heart was huge.

"We're good. We're fine. I mean, Benjamin got shot—"

"Again!"

"Yeah, and it looks like everything's all over now."

Aaron filled him in on the details, from Sarah and Willow's abduction to the destruction of the dojo.

"Holy shit, man, wish I was there. Maybe Rosina and I should live closer."

"As much as I appreciate that, we're all good now and not really doing this shit anymore. Bartleson came to us, disturbed our peace, and now he's lost a shitload of men and will be in FBI custody today or tomorrow."

"What's happening with Willow?" Darwin asked. "Leave her with Bruno?"

"That's why I'm calling."

"Go ahead."

"I want to meet him near Oshawa."

"Oshawa?"

"Yeah, Sarah and I will stay in a motel for a few nights, a week tops, until Bartleson is apprehended. Willow will be fine with us."

"You're staying in Oshawa?"

"No, nearby, but if I meet him in Oshawa, I can take Willow off his hands."

"He's been having a great time with her. I had no idea Bruno was such a kid at heart. Spoke with him a few hours ago, actually. Said he sees more of Sarah in her than you."

"Oh, man, that hurts like a sword in the heart."

They both laughed, some of the tension of the conversation evaporating.

"So, we're good?" Aaron asked. "You can make the arrangements with Bruno?"

"Of course. I'll get in touch with him and tell him to meet you. Where do you want this to take place?"

"When I was a kid, too many years ago to discuss, I golfed at the Oshawa Airport Golf Course on Thornton Road with my dad. I have great memories of that place. It still has my five-iron at the bottom of the pond on the eighteenth hole. Anyway, that section of Thornton is isolated, and there's a large parking area. I'll be there in two hours. Bruno knows my car. Does that give you and Bruno enough time to make this happen?"

"I'll text confirmation, but I don't see an issue with it. You take care of yourself, Aaron. I mean that."

"I will, my friend."

"And that lovely family of yours."

"Always. They're everything in this world to me."

"Okay, go. I'll make some calls."

The line clicked off just as Aaron detected emotion creeping into Darwin's voice. This really bothered him, the danger they all faced.

He stared at his phone a moment longer, lost in thought, then slipped it away, grabbed the bags, and lugged them out of the apartment.

Five minutes later, apartment locked, baggage stowed in the car, he pulled out onto Bloor Street and headed toward the 401, which would take him to Oshawa.

After ten minutes of driving, he spotted the tail and thought about DeOcampo. Of course, she'd send an unmarked cruiser to watch over him until Bartleson was in custody.

How did he not see the tail when he drove from the hospital? Had to be his nerves, the fatigue of the past thirty-six hours.

He leaned back, put on some music, and drove toward his daughter, toward the motel where they'd relax, laugh, play, sip wine, and be a family again.

Another look in the rearview mirror revealed the tail three cars back, staying discreet and professional.

He smiled to himself that he wasn't so tired he missed it. Maybe he would call DeOcampo and thank her.

After a moment, he decided against it. She had enough on her plate to try to locate Bartleson.

Once he had Willow and they were out of the public eye and in their motel room, he'd call then.

The FBI agent in charge of the task force deserved their gratitude, and he'd make sure she felt it.

Chapter 36

Even after their three-hour sleep at the apartment, a coffee in her kitchen, and a large black coffee for the road, Sarah felt the weariness of the past few days hitting her as they neared Huntsville.

"This is such a lovely area," Alex said from the back seat. "All these trees, the peacefulness of it."

"It looks that way," Sarah said. "Although, I can't say I've got great memories of coming north."

"Totally understand," Parkman added. He pointed forward. "There's the exit. We're about fifteen minutes early." He glanced at her, then back at the road. "Just happy we aren't late."

"Yeah," she said. "To come this close and then lose Bianca … that would be a tragedy."

Minutes later, they pulled into Tim Horton's, and Parkman turned off the car.

The engine ticked as it cooled while they surveyed the

parking lot.

"I'll go inside, order a coffee, and look around. She'll know what I look like."

"Want company?" Alex asked.

"No, I'll be fine. Once I have her and Frankie, we'll come out here to meet you two."

"Okay," Parkman said, popping a toothpick in his mouth. "Motion if you need us."

Sarah cracked the door open, then stepped outside and stretched. After the prolonged extension of her tired muscles, she spoke through the open door. "Fuck, when this is over, I'm going to sleep for a week."

"Me, too," Parkman said, leaning down to look up at her.

She shut the door, took in her surroundings, then started toward the coffee shop. This is what Vivian told her would happen. In the brief glimpse at the construction site, Vivian showed Sarah snippets of what was coming, and Bianca's involvement was clearly shown.

There was a darkness in Vivian's tone, though. Something Sarah couldn't put her finger on. Like Vivian knew, Bianca would take some work. Or maybe it was Benjamin's leg injury, or who would be killed?

Whatever was bothering her sister was what fueled her recent absences from Sarah. Like she didn't want Sarah to pick up on what it was.

She reached the door to the coffee shop and stopped. A quick glance back to the car and, she saw Parkman in the front seat watching her.

Vivian, it better not be something horrible like I'm going to lose Aaron, Willow, Parkman, Alex, or any of the others.

She stepped inside and glanced around.

Don't hold out on me when I need you the most—

"Sarah?" a woman said to her left.

Sarah turned and looked into the beautiful eyes of a young woman, a tall man standing behind her.

"I'm Bianca, and this here is Frankie."

She shook hands with Frankie, but Bianca pulled her in for a hug, squeezing her around the back. Sarah allowed it even though she wasn't much of a hugger unless it was her inner circle.

"Please," Bianca said as she pulled away. "We feel vulnerable here. Can we take you to where we're staying?"

Sarah nodded. "Of course. We'll follow you?"

Frankie nodded, his expression dour like he didn't want any part of this but was in for the long haul now. Sometimes love—if that's what they had—came with risks, and in this case, the risk was torture and death. Exposure in a public place like a coffee shop, until the threat was neutralized, had made them both uneasy.

While exiting the building, Sarah wondered if Bartleson would actually kill his own daughter to avoid hearing what she had to say in court.

"Our car is over there," Frankie said, pointing at a shiny BMW.

Nothing like standing out.

Sarah nodded. "We're right there."

Parkman had leaned forward over the steering wheel so his face was easy to see, but Alex was shrouded in shadow.

"Is Alex with you?" Bianca asked, her tone soft and calm. The girl had nerves of steel to remain this relaxed while an angry mobster father was coming after her.

"He's in the back seat."

Bianca turned to Frankie. "Start the car and swing around. I have to meet him."

Frankie nodded and turned to go, but not before Sarah saw that dour look again. This time, she recognized it for what it was: jealousy.

Frankie had given up a lot for Bianca, and it bothered him that she was head over heels for Alex. It was probably nothing more than adoration from afar because, ultimately, what did she really know about him? But still, like a girlfriend in love with Tommy Lee or Post Malone, some guys were easily bothered by that, even though their woman never had a shot.

Sarah and Bianca walked shoulder to shoulder toward the car.

The back door opened before they got there, and Alex stepped out.

At the sight of him, Bianca's step quickened, and she got there before Sarah, a hand out to shake.

Alex's eyes scanned her, studying her for any sort of threat. The man was always in combat mode. He even jerked slightly—so slightly that no one else would probably have seen it but Sarah—when her hand shot out like it did.

"Alex, I'm Bianca. I'm so pleased to meet you."

The BMW came around to park close, and Sarah leaned on the hood of the car, watching the parking lot for anything unusual. There shouldn't be, though, as they'd been careful, watching for a tail the entire time.

"I've read about you several times, and once a newspaper

even published an entire piece on you after that chief of police scandal a few years back."

Alex glanced over Bianca's shoulder at Sarah, pleading for help with his eyes. Men with guns he could handle, but adoring beautiful women was something entirely new for him.

"Anyway, I just had to meet you."

"Well," Sarah said. "We are a bit exposed here. We can talk further at your place."

"Right," Bianca said, turning toward Sarah slightly, adjusting the bottom of her shirt, then refocusing on Alex. "Just wondered if I'd ever get to meet you. People talk, you know. They think you're a young Van Damme, Steven Seagal. Even better, like Jet Li."

Alex glanced at the BMW, then back to Bianca. After a moment, he smiled and slipped back into the back seat, closing the door gently.

Bianca pivoted around to face Sarah. "I love your whole group. And that's why we're in this mess."

"You mentioned something about that on the phone. But we really should take this conversation somewhere private, then call Agent DeOcampo."

"Right, right, of course." Bianca started toward the BMW. "Follow us."

Sarah dropped in the front seat and blew out a long sigh.

"What was that all about?" Parkman asked.

"Alex has a fan."

"Well, I don't blame her, but not only is this not the time, but how's it going to make Frankie feel as if she's gushing over Alex?"

"She wasn't gushing over me," Alex muttered, his tone indignant.

Sarah twisted around in the seat to look at him as Parkman got underway.

"Sorry, but that was gushing." She couldn't contain her smile. "You going to be okay going forward, working with her? I mean, we can't have any sort of conflict of interest."

"Sarah," Alex said, his tone cautionary.

"Yeah?"

"Fuck off for now, please."

She burst out laughing and spun back around in her seat. "Shit," she managed to say. "I didn't get a coffee."

"Yeah," Parkman said. "Hopefully, they have some wherever we're going."

"And ice cream."

Parkman looked over at her. "Ice cream?"

"We need something to cool Bianca off. Otherwise, Alex will be in trouble."

She could only hold it in for a few seconds. Then they laughed while Alex sat in the back, his arms crossed, unimpressed.

Even though he was play-pouting, there was the edge of a smile on his lips. The laughter felt good because it kept her from dwelling on the darkness Vivian had left behind from her last visit.

Whatever was coming wasn't good.

Heartbreak and sadness, for sure, mixed with some misery and sorrow. She wasn't willing to voice her concerns for fear of making them real, breathing them into existence. Until something happened, she could brush it off as a portent, a feeling that never came to be.

All of which weighed too heavily on Sarah to contemplate further at the moment.

Chapter 37

AARON GOT TO THE golf course early on purpose. He wanted to stroll through the clubhouse and see how it had changed over the years. The clubhouse was just a trailer the last time he was here in the eighties. Now, there was a large building on the premises, a pro shop, and a restaurant that looked like it could hold dinners for over a hundred guests at a golf tournament.

He toured it all, spoke with the pro shop clerk, swung a few drivers for the feel, the heft, then wandered back outside to watch a foursome coming in on the eighteenth hole.

It was nearing dinnertime, and dark clouds had rolled in, so the parking lot was half empty as no new golfers arrived to play. Aaron glanced skyward, assessing the wind and the location of the clouds. Rain would come anytime, and if it did, he'd just wait inside his car.

The location was an excellent spot to pick up Willow, although he wished he could call Bruno to check on his timing and see how close he was.

Aaron glanced at his watch again. If Bruno encountered no delays, he would be there within ten minutes, so Aaron wouldn't have to wait too much longer. Perhaps they'd beat the rain.

He pulled out his phone and dialed DeOcampo when he saw the unmarked cruiser that had been following him pull off the road and park in the far corner of the lot.

Her phone rang four times, then went to voicemail.

"DeOcampo, call me when you get this. I'm picking up Willow and heading to a motel. I left Sarah a note back at the apartment. Also, thanks for the security detail that followed me out to pick up Willow. Always appreciated. Chat soon."

He hung up, slipped his phone away, crossed his arms, and nodded at the cop in his car. The man appeared to be on the phone, too. Probably calling DeOcampo to tell her where they were.

He wondered where Sarah and Parkman had gotten to. He could tell she'd been home, but she'd left no note, and he hadn't been able to reach her.

Although, as much as DeOcampo had warned them to keep their heads down, the agent also said Bartleson had no teeth left. Almost all of his muscle—his security detail headed by Silvio Mancuso—were dead or in custody. They had nothing to worry about as Bartleson would be in custody within hours as well, but DeOcampo still advised them to be cautious, which was exactly what Aaron was doing.

A black Chrysler slowed on Thornton, then eased into the parking area where it stopped. The windows were tinted so black that Aaron couldn't see the driver. With the overhead clouds just as black, there was no chance in hell of seeing inside that car.

Was that Bruno?

Or Bartleson?

He pushed off his car and stepped around to the side in case a window lowered, and the tip of a weapon slipped out, aimed in his direction. Who knew how connected Bartleson was and how deep his resources went?

The Chrysler moved again, the crunch of gravel under the tires reaching Aaron's ears in the tranquil quiet of the golf course parking lot, the calm before the rain.

He followed the vehicle with his eyes until it stopped in a parking spot six spaces away from him.

A light rain started, drops of water hitting his cheeks and forehead. He squinted and blinked it away as he stepped back until he was standing beside the door to his car. Just in case, he waited there.

The Chrysler's door opened, and Bruno glanced his way, ending his anticipation.

The man nodded once at Aaron, and Aaron let out the breath he'd been holding.

Everything was fine. Bruno was here, and he had their Willow.

When the large man stepped out of the vehicle, it adjusted slightly from his weight. He had to have three hundred pounds of muscle. Why the hell didn't he drive the Hummer that Disco drove, the other man in Darwin's employ?

Aaron took a few steps toward Bruno as the large man opened the back door and lifted out Willow but stopped when

Willow was screaming about something.

Then his cell phone rang.

He grabbed it and saw DeOcampo's name on call display.

"Daddy," Willow shouted, her voice filled with a fearful, childlike wailing.

Bruno swooped her up in his thick arms and carried her toward him. "She keeps saying she doesn't want me to get hurt. That's why I stopped the car there—"

"One sec," Aaron said over his voice. "I have to take this call." Then he placed the phone at his ear, bending slightly to protect the phone from the rain that was already dropping heavier. "Aaron here."

"If someone's following you," DeOcampo shouted into his ear, "they're not one of mine."

Aaron's eyes widened at her words as he turned to face the unmarked cruiser, his stomach dropping at the idea that Bartleson or one of his men had tracked him here, to his daughter, so easily.

Willow screamed his name, saying something about running.

"Aaron!" DeOcampo shouted. "Say something."

The man was already out of the unmarked cruiser, his hand hidden in his suit jacket.

Time seemed to slow down for Aaron as he saw his baby girl five feet away in Bruno's arms, flailing around, trying to be heard.

Willow knew. And the adults weren't listening.

Aaron was unarmed.

Bruno stared at Aaron, slowing his step, a concerned

expression on his face. Then he slowly turned, glancing over his shoulder to follow Aaron's gaze.

Aaron dropped the phone as the man withdrew his hand from his suit jacket. He carried a large automatic weapon and was bringing it around to bear on them.

Bruno adjusted Willow—who had covered her face with her tiny hands, the tears coming in rivers now—in his arms so she rested at his belly, held in place by his massive left arm, his rounded back facing the shooter.

Bruno's right hand was already yanking out what looked like a Glock. He aimed backward from the hip, the weapon upside down as he kept his back to the approaching gunman and fired over and over again.

Both weapons made such an explosion that Aaron acted on instinct and dropped by the front tire of his car. Fighting the urge to keep his head down, he glanced up to check on Willow, but there was no way the gunman's bullets could touch her as no part of his daughter could be seen through Bruno's massive bulk—unless bullets traveled through Bruno's body.

When the guns stopped as abruptly as they had started, Aaron pushed up off the ground and ran to Willow, who was crying—wailing, actually—about how she could've stopped whatever was happening.

Recklessly, Aaron didn't look at the gunman on the ground. He just snatched Willow from Bruno's arms, hugged her close, and ran for the safety of his vehicle.

Bruno whispered, "Take her," when Aaron pulled on his daughter.

With Willow safe but crying uncontrollably, crouched

behind the back tire of Aaron's car, he spun back to make sure the gunman was dead.

He wasn't.

The man was on his knees, staring at the blood seeping from the bullet he'd taken to the stomach. It had to be hard for Bruno to aim in the position from which he'd fired—a small child in one arm, his weapon upside down, aiming blindly behind him—but at least he'd been able to hit the man.

Without Willow now, Bruno pivoted on the gravel and aimed better, firing his weapon until it clicked empty, which was just one more bullet.

This bullet hit the attacker in the arm, not holding the gun, jerking him bodily to the side.

Then he righted himself and, still on his knees, fired what was left in his weapon at Bruno.

Aaron heard the sick thunks as three or four more bullets entered Bruno's battered body.

But then rational thought left Aaron, and a curtain of blackness, hatred, and evil overcame him. He ran at the man with the gun without regard for the gun's ability to kill him.

From four feet away, Aaron launched himself like he was diving off a board into a pool, arms out, body parallel with the ground, his hands already prepared for what they'd cling to.

The man adjusted his aim for Aaron's face in the final second before impact and pulled the trigger.

The weapon clicked on empty as Aaron's bulk smashed into the wounded man. They dropped in a heap on the gravel, rolling once.

Aaron controlled the roll, landing on top of the man, his fists like the ends of hammers as he pounded down on the man's face. He drove fist after fist into the man's cheeks, caving in the man's facial structure, even as one of his knuckles dislocated. A finger on Aaron's left hand snapped with the onslaught, but all he saw was the bloody pulp of the man under him and the rage and hatred aimed at a piece of shit human who would shoot at a child.

The rain grew heavier, spattering bits of dirt up off the gravel drive as Aaron's hands sent considerable pain messages to his brain, pain he couldn't ignore any longer. So, he used his elbows and his arms and continued his assault—the only sound in his ears was his own scream, his own wail of agony.

Only Willow's screaming his name slowed his assault.

Finally, exhausted, the thought of standing and stomping on the man's face with his boots—the face that had been reduced to nothing but broken bone, blood, and brain matter, squashed behind caved-in orbital bones—Aaron slumped to the ground and rolled onto his back, letting the rain pound his face.

Willow screamed again, forcing him to his elbows, squinting with the pain and the rainwater dripping into his eyes. He thrust a foot under him, got to his feet, wavered once, caught himself, and stood bent over. Blood covered his arms from the elbow down and splattered his shirt and jeans.

Willow was still hiding behind his car, eyes wild, mouth in an open wail at the violence she'd witnessed, staring at Bruno.

Aaron took several steps, then dropped to a knee and

keeled over beside Bruno.

The large man lay on his stomach now, bleeding from at least half a dozen holes in his back. He needed a doctor and fast.

With a great effort, Aaron looked at Bruno and shouted his name.

The large man's eyes opened less than a foot from Aaron's face.

"I'll get a doctor," Aaron shouted, his tears mixing with the rain on his cheeks. "Hang in there."

He leaned on his hand to get up, cried out, and dropped back to the gravel.

"Fuck," he shouted.

"Aaron—" Bruno coughed up blood, then inhaled, his breath raspy. "Tell Darwin I did good, okay?"

"You tell him yourself, big boy."

Aaron tried to get up again but failed miserably.

"Someone!" he shouted. "Fucking call an ambulance."

A man dressed in slacks and a golf shirt, holding an umbrella, stepped into view. "They're on their way. Cops, too."

Aaron turned to Bruno. "Hang in there, buddy. Help is on its way, man, they're coming."

Bruno blinked, his breathing worsening. "Tell Sarah I love her and I'm sorry. I should've listened to Willow. She warned me. She warned …"

"Nothing to be sorry for—just tell her yourself."

"Goodbye, my friend. My time here is done." He coughed, hacking out a splatter of blood on the gravel. "Too hard." He coughed again. "To breathe."

"Come on," Aaron shouted. "Stay with me."

Willow screamed once more. Aaron knew she would be able to see Bruno's death and hated it. He felt her sorrow, misery, and young fury, which drove him mad.

"Just tell Darwin and Sarah for me. My life, for Willow." A breath spilled out, blood pouring from his mouth with it. "Always remember, brother, I did good. My life for Willow …"

Bruno didn't take another breath.

Aaron watched in horror as the man's dead eyes glazed over, seeing nothing, his nose and mouth not working anymore.

Then Aaron curled into a ball and wailed with Willow.

He was still screaming up at the dark clouds as they hung over him, soaking him through with rainwater, his bruised and broken hands held aloft when the police arrived.

Aaron had brought the shooter to them. He had killed Bruno by allowing the tail to follow him here—the man who killed Bruno and almost got to his daughter.

Bartleson wouldn't live to breathe another day.

Aaron would make sure of it.

In Bruno's honor, Lorenzo Bartleson would never see the inside of a courtroom because he had to be murdered now. There was no other way, no other option.

Bartleson made this personal on every fucking level.

If Aaron couldn't do it, Alex would.

Whatever happened going forward, Bartleson was a dead man.

Chapter 38

THEY FOLLOWED THE BMW to a house deep in the bush, almost a full thirty minutes from Huntsville. A small A-frame house came into view, the same one her sister showed her in the vision.

Did that dark, morose feeling have anything to do with this place?

The car stopped and was swarmed with insects.

"Northern Ontario sure gets their fair share of flies and mosquitoes," Parkman said, staring out at the swirling black mass.

Sarah nodded, studying the surrounding yard. Wild grass grew waist-high in some places. It waved in the slight breeze. Several dilapidated wooden fenceposts remained standing at the extent of the yard, offering a memory of a fence that once stood proud, bordering the property.

"You okay?" Parkman asked.

She turned her attention to him. "Yeah, something's just

bothering me."

"What? About the area? Like we're being watched?"

"No, nothing like that." She shook her head. "Like something bad happened or is going to happen. It makes me feel dirty, and I can't seem to shake it." She wanted to tell them everything Vivian showed her but thought it best to wait until they'd met with Bianca.

"Okay," Parkman said, spinning in all directions in search of a threat. "Are we going in or arranging to meet elsewhere?"

Sarah glanced off into the distance, searched for her sister's presence, couldn't find her, and then opened the car door.

"We go in."

"But you're not sure we're safe."

She turned back to Parkman, already standing outside the car. "It's not that we're not safe—I mean, that could be it—but it's more like something's coming, and I'm not going to like it."

"What's Vivian say? Anything?"

"She's the one who told me, but not with words. It was more pictures, feelings."

Parkman frowned. "What? How's that?"

"You guys okay?" Frankie shouted over. They'd already made it to the front door of the small house.

Sarah leaned on the open car door, lifting her head above it. "Yeah, we'll be right there." Then she leaned back down. "When Vivian came to me at the construction site, she left behind a darkness, a foreboding feeling of sadness and sorrow."

"Like one of us dying?" Alex asked. "Just as we discussed at the coffee shop this morning?"

She glanced back at him. "I pray to God that doesn't happen."

"Me too," Parkman said, then exited the car.

A moment later, both men followed her to the front door. Frankie held it open and gestured at the small living room, with the kitchen attached at the back in an open concept. Sarah had to admit it was a cute little place for a couple. To her left, a tiny red spiral staircase led to a loft where the edge of a bed was barely visible from the front door.

"We've got coffee or tea," Bianca said as Frankie shut the door behind them. She was already moving toward the kitchen.

"Coffee," Sarah and Parkman said at the same time. They looked at each other and smiled.

They'd gotten to Bianca. They'd come this far. Bartleson would be in custody soon, and everything was right in her world.

Yet she couldn't shake the feeling something was wrong.

"I think I'll call DeOcampo and tell her where we are and what we're doing here."

"Where we are?" Frankie asked. "You trust this person? I mean, is that wise right now?"

"Well, I kind of meant where we are with you two and that we're bringing you with us. Not literally where we are." Sarah glanced out the front window. "I actually have no idea *where* we are."

"That makes sense," Frankie said. "Just dealing with her dad makes us nervous." He raised a hand to his mouth as his lower chin quivered.

"You okay?" Sarah asked, stepping forward.

"We just thought, you know." He stopped to collect himself.

Bianca clicked the coffeemaker button and entered the living room area. She placed a hand on his back.

"We thought we could be free," she said. "Live our lives without my dad or his business. So, we stole his money—what's he going to do, kill his own daughter?"

Sarah was about to respond that a man like Bartleson would kill a lot of people with his twisted sense of retribution, as had happened in the past thirty-six hours. So many lives were lost, not to mention that Bianca's father threatened to take Willow from her. But she kept her mouth shut. Making this young woman feel like she had to take responsibility for her father's actions would serve no purpose right now, as she was willing to help them.

Frankie nodded, looking at Bianca with love in his eyes. "That's why we gave it all away." He turned to Parkman and Sarah as the coffee maker dripped in the kitchen, the only noise in the small dwelling. "We gave over twenty grand to Sal's mother so she could have that cancer operation Sal kept talking about. We thought, if her father was killing people with his way of life, his business, we could take some of his money and help people live better lives."

"A very noble gesture," Parkman said. "The only issue with that plan was your father's temperament. When you two left, he went nuts trying to find you. A lot of people—"

"—died," Bianca finished for him. "I know, and I don't know how to process that. So, in their name, for the people he's hurt, I want to tell the investigators everything."

"And what's everything?" Sarah asked, fingering her cell phone in her pocket. The urge to call DeOcampo was nagging at her.

Bianca met Sarah's gaze, and her face hardened.

"He did things to me when I was young."

In a low voice, Sarah said, "*Those* kinds of things?" Everyone in the room knew exactly what she was talking about. Sometimes, it didn't have to be spelled out.

Bianca nodded, a tear leaping to her right eye. "I want to see him in prison for the rest of his life and then burn in Hell for what he's done."

Sarah pulled out her phone and turned away. "I think you'll get your chance."

She glanced down and almost dropped the phone.

It wasn't hers.

It wasn't Salvatore's phone, either. She made sure to turn that one off and break it before they left the apartment for Huntsville.

When she grabbed the phone on her nightstand and slipped it in her pocket, she hadn't looked closely enough in her state of fatigue.

Frankie and Parkman were talking as they settled on the couches. Sarah detected Bianca in the kitchen, coffee cups clinking as she pulled them down from the cupboard.

Her fingers numbed, her hands and feet given to pins and needles. This wasn't Vivian coming. This was utter and complete fear for what she had done.

"Sarah?" Alex whispered beside her. "You've gone white. What is it?"

No one else seemed to notice as the conversation continued behind her.

Bianca was asking what everyone took in their coffee.

"We have a problem," Sarah said, her voice low so only Alex would hear her.

"Tell me." He moved closer. "I'll fix it."

She held up the phone. "Bartleson gave me this phone when I met him in Rosedale. It has his direct line."

"And they track all their phones," Alex finished her thought.

"Probably the reason he gave it to me."

"Meaning, they're already here or will be soon."

Sarah nodded. "I thought I grabbed mine. I swear it was mine. But I was so tired this morning, and—"

Alex nudged her arm. "Stop. Maybe this is better. If he comes to us, we can end this."

"How? We aren't armed in any way."

"Call him on that direct line. Tell him we have his daughter and will kill her if anything happens to us."

"You guys okay?" Parkman asked.

Alex waved at him. "One moment. Sarah's going to make a couple of calls."

"I have to call DeOcampo first. She needs to know we have Bianca willing to testify and that we're all in danger. If we come this close, then lose Bianca, everything will be for naught."

"Make the calls." Alex started for the door.

"Wait," she said. "Where are you going?"

"Reconnaissance. Reconnoiter. Whatever you want to call it. I'll be outside watching the house."

"Where's he going?" Parkman asked, already getting to his feet.

Sarah turned around and faced them all, Bianca standing with a coffee cup in each hand.

"Do you have any weapons in the house?"

Bianca glanced down at the phone in Sarah's hand.

Alex shut the front door at the same time the mug dropped from Bianca's left hand, shattering on the floor at her feet.

Chapter 39

"WHERE DID YOU GET that phone?" Bianca asked, not looking at the broken glass at her feet.

"It's a long story," Sarah said. "But first, tell me you have weapons."

Frankie nodded. "I brought my gun with me. A Smith & Wesson."

"Get it, and I'll explain everything. But stay away from the windows at all costs."

Five minutes later, the gun in Frankie's hand, Sarah told them about her abduction, their meeting at Bartleson's, right up until driving to Huntsville, and her cell phone mistake.

"They could be outside right now," Frankie said. He clicked something on the side of the weapon.

Sarah raised a hand for calm. "I have to call the FBI and inform them. They have a task force. They'll advise us and send officers to pick us up. We'll be fine."

"In fact," Parkman added, looking at Bianca. "Your

father has lost a lot of men this week. Who's to say he actually has anyone monitoring his mobster-find-my-phone app?"

"That's something he can do from his own cell phone."

"Oh." Parkman looked off at the front window for a moment, then got up and stood beside it. "Shit," he muttered under his breath.

"Yeah, shit." Sarah quickly dialed out.

DeOcampo answered on the second ring. "Special Agent DeOcampo."

"It's Sarah."

"Sarah!" she shouted. "Where are you?"

"I think we might be in trouble."

"Yeah, a lot is going on you don't know about, but let me start by saying Willow's safe."

"What?" Sarah gasped, wavering on her feet. "Why are you telling me that? She's hidden away, staying with a friend."

"No, she's in protective custody right now. At least until you show up."

Sarah covered her mouth with her hand and dropped into a chair. "What happened?" she asked through the fingers that covered her mouth.

"Over the phone?" DeOcampo asked. "Not good. Come in, we'll talk."

"Why is it not good?" Sarah asked. Then, in a stronger voice, "What happened? Just fucking tell me."

"Sarah, listen, Aaron is safe. From what I understand, he just broke a few fingers and a knuckle. Willow is completely unharmed."

"Where's Bruno?"

"Bruno? I don't know that name. There was another man involved, though. Also, that detective I was looking for, Mark Cade. We found him."

"Where?"

"He's dead."

"How?"

"Aaron killed him with his bare hands. That's why they're broken. He fucking punched the man to death. Oh, and a man named Steven Miller shot Cade a couple of times. But it was a righteous kill, Sarah. Over ten witnesses at the golf course said what Miller did was heroic. He literally shielded Willow with his body, taking Cade's fire in his back to make sure Willow was untouched."

Sarah was only half listening now. Golf course? Steven Miller? She tried to recall where she'd heard the name Steven Miller. So much had happened in such a short time.

"Sarah, even though Aaron destroyed Cade's face, and he was a decorated police officer, an accomplished detective from what I'm hearing, Cade shot first. It was unprovoked. I'll make sure Aaron doesn't face any heat over this."

Then the name Steven Miller hit her like a gut punch, and she gasped so violently she choked on her own saliva. After several coughs to clear her throat, she brought the phone back to her ear.

"Steven Miller," she said. "What happened to him?"

Parkman was staring at her from the wall beside the front window with a look of shock and worry.

"I'm sorry, Sarah, Miller died at the scene. The witnesses said he died a hero, holding your daughter in his massive body, shielding her from Cade's bullets. Then Aaron attacked Cade without a weapon, just his hands, even though Cade fired at his face point blank. Witness accounts are all identical. It was raining, and all the golfers were rushing inside the pro shop when the bullets started, and then …"

Sarah let the phone drop from her hands as they were shaking too much. She slipped off the chair and thumped to the floor, her teeth rattling hard when she hit the carpet. She wrapped her head in her knees and wept.

Bruno was dead.

He saved Willow.

Aaron is in the hospital.

What the fuck was going on?

"Sarah?" Parkman said beside her.

He spoke her name a few more times. Then she heard him talking on the phone to DeOcampo.

"Right, yes … we have Bianca Bartleson with us. Yes, she will testify. I understand. But we have to be alive for that to happen." Parkman paused a moment. "We have one gun." Another pause. "How long? Okay, I think we can hold on until then—"

The high-pitched ping of something smacking glass cut off Parkman's voice.

"Shit," he yelled. "DeOcampo, we're being shot at."

Sarah snapped her head up, wiping her eyes with both hands. She would have to grieve later.

Parkman was kneeling, peeking through the front window, the phone jamming to his ear.

About midway up the window, a small hole showed where a bullet had traveled through the glass. Sarah turned to her right to see what the bullet hit.

Frankie's face was a mask of horror.

A small hole had formed in his shirt, roughly where the appendix would be located, slightly to the left at the belt line area. His blood was already spilling out.

The Smith & Wesson sat useless on the couch beside him.

Another ping as the glass was penetrated again. This time, the bullet puffed up the cushion to Frankie's left.

"Get off the fucking couch," Sarah shouted, her voice coming back to her, fury at Bartleson fueling her now. "Stay the fuck down."

She crawled to the front of the couch and yanked Frankie all the way down. He lay on his back in front of the couch, his hands pushing down on the hole in his abdomen.

Sarah grabbed a pillow and placed it under his hands. "Constant pressure," she shouted. "You understand?"

Frankie's white face jerked twice in rapid nods.

"Where's Bianca?"

"Right here," she cried from behind the couch.

Sarah grabbed Frankie's gun, checked that the safety was on so she didn't kill anyone by accident, and then crawled around to the back of the couch.

"Bianca, I need you to trust me."

She nodded just as fast as Frankie did, abject fear on her face, in her eyes.

"Does your father love you?"

She nodded.

"Would he kill you?"

She frowned, then shook her head.

"Then you'll be my hostage." Sarah motioned for her to stand up. "Let's go. If he doesn't kill his own daughter, then I'll hold this gun to your neck, and we'll walk out of here. Got it?"

"Oh." She shook her head and stared at the floor. "I don't know about that. I can't go out there." On the last word, her voice rose several octaves.

"It's the only way. We're probably outnumbered and definitely outgunned. So, when that happens, you have to outthink them."

Bianca was shaking her head. Of course, she'd be worried about being in the front, the one threatened. But wasn't she the one human being that started all of this? Didn't she take off from her father's home without explanation, leaving behind a trail of bodies, a trail that led to Sarah?

"I refuse to be led out of here like some piece of cattle —"

Sarah glanced down at the weapon in her hand. Frankie was bleeding out, Alex was outside somewhere, alive or dead, and they were under siege. Bruno was dead, and Aaron just killed a decorated police officer with his bare hands.

All of this because Bianca ran away from her narcissistic, sexual predator father, and she wasn't willing to try to end this?

Sure, Sarah was grateful Bianca was willing to testify against her own father, but she needed her to step up and end the constant assault on innocents.

Bianca had to end what she started.

Sarah raised the weapon until it touched Bianca's throat,

then she pushed it slightly farther in for emphasis.

"I'm done playing," Sarah said. "Too many people dead, and I won't be one of them because you and your father are having a family spat." Sarah got her feet under her, readying herself to stand. "Get up."

This time, Bianca didn't protest. Eyes wide, staring at Sarah at an angle because the pressure of the weapon tilted her head back, they both got to their feet from behind the couch.

"Sarah," Parkman said. "What are you doing?"

"She's going to walk us out of here. At the door, get behind me, Parkman."

Someone shouted something from outside. A weapon fired, and they all jerked, but the glass in the front window didn't break.

"Doctor," Frankie muttered. "I need a doctor."

"As soon as we can," Sarah said.

She shoved Bianca to the front door, then leaned in. "You ready?"

She shook her head. "Don't do this."

The pleading in her eyes gave Sarah pause. Was this the right move, the right play? Would Bartleson shoot his own blood? She couldn't for a minute imagine the crime boss would kill his own daughter. But maybe that was the point from the beginning. What if he were worried she'd tell the world what kind of monster he was? Then he'd have no recourse but to kill her.

Yet, Sarah couldn't think of any other way.

"You have the car keys, Parkman?"

"I'll be right behind you."

Sarah ripped open the door and pushed Bianca into the opening.

"Don't shoot," Sarah shouted, holding the weapon high and out at the side of Bianca's neck so whoever was outside would see it. "I've got Bianca, and I'm taking her with me. Shoot at us, and I'll kill her."

"Fuck you," Bartleson shouted from somewhere in the tall, wavy grass. "You aren't taking her anywhere."

Sarah scanned the field-like front yard but couldn't see a thing.

"We're going to walk to our car and leave. Your two choices are to let us go unhindered, and Bianca lives. Or try to stop us in any way, and Bianca dies. I'll kill her right here on this doorstep. You threatened to take my daughter from me. Watch how easily I take yours from you. How's that for an ultimatum?"

Bianca was breathing in short, rapid breaths, like she was having a heart attack. Sarah couldn't be mindful of that at the moment as all of their lives depended on getting out of there.

Even if she had to leave Alex behind, he'd find his way to town.

She pushed Bianca forward, and they moved four more steps until they were at the edge of the wooden deck.

Something rustled about ten feet from them, but no one showed themselves.

It would be so easy to shoot several bullets into that area, but what if it was Alex? And who had yelled and fired their weapon before they came outside a moment ago?

"Stop this," Bianca said over her shoulder. "He'll kill me."

Sarah stopped at those words. If that were true, then they were doomed either way. Bartleson's men would breach the house and kill everyone.

This was their only chance, and they hadn't shot at them yet.

"Move toward the car, or I'll shoot you myself."

Parkman kept a hand on Sarah's shoulder so she'd know he was there without having to think about him.

Two more steps from the edge of the wooden deck, walking on the beat-down grass that led to the cars, Frankie screamed for an ambulance again. His cry for help, the cracking of his high-pitched voice, was enough to break Bianca.

She spun around and out of Sarah's one-handed grip to face her.

"I can't do this. He'll kill me."

They were fifteen feet from the cars, out in the open, completely exposed, and Bianca was blocking her view of the yard.

"That's right, baby girl," Bartleson said from somewhere behind her. "I'll kill you. Step aside."

Sarah dropped to her knees, trying to pull Bianca with her, but the girl was already moving back toward the house.

That simple movement was what saved Sarah's life.

Bartleson stood less than two meters away, both hands extending his gun, aimed at his daughter.

The sound of the weapon was loud, the bucking of it in his hands easily visible from where Sarah crouched, already raising her weapon to fire at him.

Bianca's body jerked as bullets hit her. Then she was

falling, and Sarah was applying pressure to the trigger of Frankie's weapon.

At the last hundredth of a second, she moved her aim to the right in order to miss him because something had risen from the tall grass, fast and swift.

In the deepest recess of her brain, Sarah registered Alex rising, his hands out, his body ready, like an animal in the wild.

He landed on Bartleson, and the man was shoved sideways, his left knee buckling under the weight and pressure.

Even as Sarah's weapon fired, the bullet going wild, both Alex and Bartleson were lost from sight in the tall grass. Then Parkman ran past her and dove into that shallow impression in the grass where the men had disappeared.

When she turned to Bianca, the faint sound of police sirens came to her on the soft wind.

Bianca had been hit twice as far as Sarah could see. Both wounds appeared to be away from any major organs, but that still didn't mean much.

She tore off her shirt and balled it up, pressing it down on the bullet in the side of Bianca's abdomen.

"See?" Bianca spurted. "I told you he'd kill me."

"He hasn't killed you yet."

"He will."

"Not if I have anything to do with it."

"He warned me." She coughed. At least there was no blood in her mouth. "If I left, he'd kill me."

"Why didn't you tell me he'd shoot you?"

"I wanted you to ..." she clenched her teeth and grunted.

"I wanted you, Alex and Parkman to have a chance."

Sarah glanced over her shoulder to see if Bartleson was back on his feet—also to prevent Bianca from seeing her tears.

Parkman was standing up now, followed by Alex.

The police cars were almost visible, the sirens so close.

Sarah glanced back at Bianca, adding pressure to her wounds.

When she turned back to Alex, he made a hand-sweeping gesture near his waist. It was over. All combatants were taken care of.

Sarah hung her head, the stress oozing off her in waves.

Police cars and ambulances pulled in, surrounding their cars.

Then Parkman was beside her, lifting her to her feet.

He held her, walking her back to sit on the porch.

It would be a long day of explanations, statements, and questions as to how a Toronto mob boss came to be up north, trying to kill his daughter.

All she wanted was to go home, hug her little family, and put an end to this nightmare.

And grieve for Bruno.

She lowered her head and wept, curling into Parkman, hiding her face in his chest.

Parkman cried with her.

Chapter 40

HAMMERS, SAWS, SCREWS, AND nails, along with drywall dust, had become their daily life as they rebuilt the dojo.

Sarah watched as they installed the new doors at the back. Double doors with reinforced security. During renovations, they added more cameras—ones they could all access from their cell phones—making the dojo security interactive.

They weren't guarding money, diamonds, or some other commodities. They were guarding their lives as they had no idea when the next threat would appear.

Bartleson had come without warning, and they were woefully unprepared, not to mention rusty after several years off.

The front door opened, and Agent DeOcampo stepped inside.

Sarah smiled at her and nudged Aaron. He looked up from the design plans drawn out for the new dojo.

"Take a break," she said.

He nodded and followed Sarah to the front.

"Agent DeOcampo." Sarah shook her hand. "How's life in your world?"

"Got time for a coffee?"

Sarah looked at Aaron questioningly.

He nodded, then turned away.

"Hey, Alex," Aaron shouted over the din of renovations.

Alex stopped hammering on the new door in the wall. Old Bob at the convenience store said they could install it between their businesses.

"Yeah?"

"We're going for coffee with this nice lady. Want anything when we get back."

Alex nodded. "I'll ask everyone, then text you the orders."

"Deal."

They followed DeOcampo outside, then along the sidewalk.

"You guys doing okay?" DeOcampo asked at the stoplight while they waited.

"It was rough for a few weeks, but once Bruno's funeral was over, we were able to attempt to get back into a regular routine."

The light changed, and they started across the street. "How are those hands, Aaron?"

He held them up. "Only one finger with a splint that'll come off in a few weeks. Healing well."

"Not many people get the pleasure of murdering a cop with their bare hands without any court process at all. I'm so glad you had all those witnesses. You're a lucky man."

"I wouldn't consider myself lucky, considering how it all went down."

DeOcampo swung sideways to look at him. "I didn't mean anything by it."

"I know."

They walked in silence until they got to the Starbucks and ordered their coffee. At the table, DeOcampo glanced at her phone, then set it on the table face down.

"As you both know, Bianca came out of surgery just fine, and doctors say she'll recover fully."

Sarah sipped from her cup. "You brought us here to tell us that?"

"Not just that. I wanted to do a little chit-chat first, then tell you why we're here."

"Just get to the point." Sarah smiled.

"A massive list of charges were drawn up for Bartleson. Luckily, when Alex jumped him, he didn't kill the man. I'll have to ask Alex how he disarmed and knocked out three of Bartleson's armed men in that tall grass as they moved to assault that little house. Not one of them got a shot in at him." She shook her head, and she continued when Sarah and Aaron didn't speak. "Bianca gave us a twenty-page statement for what her father had been doing to her for years."

Sarah nodded.

"You guys knew? She told you?"

"Not in detail, but I understand the gist of it."

Now, DeOcampo glanced down at her untouched coffee cup. "She wanted me to tell you she was so sorry for what happened."

Sarah and Aaron touched their legs under the table. A show of support, an understanding to not think of Bruno and start crying again.

"And Steven Miller had a clean record. But when they examined his dental records and matched them to the man who protected Willow, we discovered it was actually a man named Bruno. So many police agencies wanted him in so many cities—"

"We know."

"And you worked with him?" she asked, an incredulous tone to her voice.

"His loyalty to us, to our family, was unprecedented. Of course, we worked with him."

After a moment, DeOcampo said, "One of the witnesses at the golf course said they witnessed something peculiar. Officer Smith told me about a similar event. That's why I'm here."

Sarah frowned. "Hmm, sounds intriguing. What did they say?"

DeOcampo looked at Aaron. "Witnesses at the golf course said they heard your daughter scream something about running and not wanting Bruno to get hurt. This was all before Cade drew his weapon."

A sinking feeling entered Sarah's stomach. People knew. Outsiders were now aware of Willow's power. All she could hope was to dispel those notions and do her best to keep Willow hidden from the world in the future.

"Officer Smith," DeOcampo continued, "had another story. When he originally came to pick you up, Sarah, they brought that CAS woman, Gwen Pasternack. I think her name was Gwen Pasternack. He said he witnessed Willow's power firsthand."

Afraid to speak, worried her voice would betray her, she bumped Aaron's leg.

"What sort of power might our two-and-a-half-year-old daughter have, Agent?" He smirked as if this was funny, but deep down inside, Sarah knew he was shitting himself, too.

This was their biggest fear.

"Smith said Willow slammed the door with her mind. Broke their handcuffs or made them useless until Sarah told her to stop it. Smith said he saw telekinesis with his own eyes."

"Ridiculous," Sarah muttered. She slipped her hands under the table so DeOcampo wouldn't see them shaking.

"Is it?" DeOcampo stared at them for a long moment. "Look, I'm not into telekinesis or spirit guides and angel guardians or whatever the fuck. That's all new-age bullshit. But I will tell you this." She leaned over the table and lowered her voice. "Keep her close because if she can do what they're saying, the wrong sort of people might catch on."

"Has someone said something in particular about wanting to know more?" Sarah asked, leaning forward.

"No, I wanted you to hear it from me before colleagues of mine came knocking."

"Colleagues?"

DeOcampo regarded them for a full half minute. "Word throughout the department has you labeled a psychic and your daughter as even more powerful. All I'm saying is that it threatens some people. Government agencies that are—"

"I'm sorry, DeOcampo. We're not who those people think we are."

"I had a feeling you'd say that."

DeOcampo got up to leave just as Aaron's phone dinged with a text from Alex. He glanced down at the list of five coffees. Even old Bob put in an order.

"We'll be seeing you," DeOcampo said as she stepped away from the table.

"Wait," Sarah said.

DeOcampo stopped, then turned back.

"Should we be watching our backs, looking for *these* people you mentioned?"

She smiled warmly. "No, Sarah. I told them there was no such activity in all my dealings with you. Even that prediction you gave me about Smith calling to tell me he'd testify against Mancuso for killing his partner. I called it a lucky guess, and even though I saw things I couldn't explain, I told them you aren't who people make you out to be."

Her eyes held truth, her smile warmth.

"Thank you."

"Just wanted you aware so you could, you know, keep a wrap on things."

"Understood."

"Until next time," DeOcampo said, walking backward a few steps.

"I surely hope there won't be a next time."

When the agent left them alone, Aaron glanced her way. "Vivian around lately?"

Sarah nodded.

"Are we in the clear? Nothing doing?"

Sarah waited a moment, then shook her head. "She comes to visit, chats about Willow, then mentions something to me about sick people."

"Sick people? Like pneumonia?"

"No, sick in the head. She called them, *The Depraved*."

"Any idea what it means?"

Sarah shook her head. "Not yet, but I think I will know soon enough."

"That's what I'm worried about."

They got up from their table and made their way to the front counter. They had coffee to order for everyone.

What Sarah didn't tell him was the feeling that The Depraved was coming sooner than she thought. Much sooner, and she wasn't sure how she'd handle it.

Sarah glanced over her shoulder to watch the door. She checked the parking lot, then stared out at the street.

Whatever was coming was coming fast.

And she needed to be prepared.

"You okay?" Aaron asked.

"Yeah, I'm fine. Everything's great. Fucking peachy."

Afterword

Dear Reader,

I struggled with how I'd write Sarah's daughter into a novel, and since this was the first one with Willow Roberts, I chose to limit her exposure on the page. Yet, at the same time, I wanted to reveal some of her talents and then remind you of those talents in the final scene when DeOcampo has coffee with Willow's parents.

A lot of this is setting up future books. As the series moves toward book thirty and beyond, Willow will be even more important to the Sarah Roberts Series.

I want to credit my daughter, Odette, for coming up with the name Willow as I struggled for several books thinking about what name would work for Sarah's daughter. After a conversation with Odette, where I explained several of Willow's talents and how excited I was to bring her into the series, Odette said, "Call her Willow Roberts because of how strong-willed she is."

"Willow" is based on her "will."

I fell in love with the name instantly.

That golf course on Thornton Road called the Oshawa Airport Golf Course is a real place. And yes, my father taught me how to golf there when I was fourteen years old. I have so many fond father/son memories of walking that course. I must admit—it still has my five iron in the pond on the eighteenth hole—long story. Perhaps another time …

Also, Beatrix Potter was mentioned in the Peter Rabbit story Willow was reading because I loved that series when I was a tiny boy. Such great memories there, too.

Now, I'd like to take this opportunity to thank Tracie DeOcampo for the use of her name in this novel. Tracie took the time to write me a pen and paper letter and mail it to me in Greece. Her letter starts with her love for Sarah and explains why and how Tracie can relate so well to Sarah Roberts.

Tracie had a difficult upbringing. She survived years of abuse at the hands of trusted males in her life since the age of four. Those kinds of scars take years to heal—and sometimes never heal—yet she's moved past all of that—she's been happily married for nineteen years and has four kids of her own.

So, to the strong Tracie DeOcampo, the survivor, the woman in New Jersey who possesses her own Sarah Roberts in her heart and soul, I dedicate this novel to you.

Thanks, Tracie, for allowing me to use your name and get you in a position in the novel to help Sarah and, most importantly, get Bianca to testify to bring down her father, a monster of an abuser.

I've created fiction, but in my mind, *you* did that. You helped take one down.

This novel is for you.

I sincerely hope you've all enjoyed this outing, and I hope you look forward to the next installment, *The Depraved*.

All the best to you and yours.

Stay safe and take care of yourself and others.

Jonas Saul

About Jonas Saul

Jonas Saul is the bestselling author of the Sarah Roberts Series—more than two million sold!—and has written and published over sixty thrillers. After acquiring an agent, he signed several deals in Los Angeles, with MadRiver Pictures optioning his Sarah Roberts Series— over forty books!—(currently in development).

Jonas has often outranked Stephen King and Dean

Koontz on Amazon over the past decade. He's regularly invited to be a guest speaker, teacher, or workshop presenter at international writing conferences and film festivals worldwide. He hosts an annual writer's retreat in Greece, where he currently lives. He focuses his teaching on how to get tension and emotion in every scene, on every page, how he made it as a creator/writer, the path to success in this business, and the pitfalls to avoid. He also hosts a reading retreat in Greece with guest authors, yoga retreats, and hiking retreats. Visit the Imagine Greece Retreats website at www.imaginegreeceretreats.com, or email him directly to discuss an opportunity to join one of the retreats at jonas@imaginegreeceretreats.com.

Jonas is also a professional freelance editor. He works for several publishers and does private editing for clients, with many testimonials on his website at www.imaginepress.org, which details each author's response to Jonas's editing skills. Email Jonas directly for an editing quote at editor@imaginepress.org.

To book Jonas for a speaking engagement at a writer's conference/festival, to have him on your jury at a film festival, or even to say hello, email Jonas directly at jonassaul@icloud.com.

For updates on releases, hit the "Follow" button on Amazon or Bookbub, and join Jonas on Facebook, where he's most active.

Contact Jonas Saul

Linktree: Find me here

Email: jonassaul@icloud.com